The Rum Runner

by

Christine Marciniak

The Rum Runner

Cover Art by *Kristian Norris*

The Wild Rose Press, Inc.
PO Box 708
Adams Basin, NY 14410-0708
Visit us at www.thewildrosepress.com

Publishing History
First Vintage Rose Edition, 2019
Print ISBN 978-1-5092-2909-3
Digital ISBN 978-1-5092-2910-9

Published in the United States of America

"Tell me what is really bothering you about Hank."

"I think he's a rum runner." Once she said it out loud, she knew it must be true. Of course, he was a rum runner. Tomas had been, and Hank was involved with all the same people and he didn't want her to investigate. What other answer could there be?

Suddenly Trudy got serious.

"Oh. It would seem you have incompatible careers."

Alice nearly choked on her tea. Trudy handed her a napkin.

"That's one way of putting it," she said when she could breathe again. "So, what do you think I should do?"

"Quit your job, of course," Trudy said and winked at her.

Alice sighed. She supposed that would solve one problem, but it really wasn't an answer and they both knew it.

"Short of that?"

Dedication

To all the people in incompatible careers
who manage to make love work anyway

Chapter One

A pile of manila folders landed with a thud in her inbox, startling Alice Grady out of a daydream. The cloud of dust they raised sparkled in the afternoon light, filtering in through the dirty windows. She sighed and opened the top folder. She was surprised the other officers hadn't asked her to wash the windows too. They seemed to think that any act of cleanliness was the purview of women.

She squinted at the chicken scratch on the page in front of her.

"Hey, Piccolo," she called to the lanky officer just taking his seat across the room. "Where did you learn to write? Mrs. Forest would be very upset if she saw this."

"Mrs. Forest wouldn't be the least bit surprised." Mark Piccolo grinned at her. "She failed me in handwriting if I'm not mistaken."

"And for good cause." She'd known Mark since they were in school, tormenting teachers together with their antics. Now he was married to her best friend. It was nice to work with someone every day that she felt so comfortable with. She only wished they'd let her do more of the dirty work in the police department. She'd never particularly liked typing. She squinted at the writing again. "You should type up your own reports."

"Can't." Mark took a quick swig of his coffee. "Got to go back out on patrol in a minute."

Alice shoved a form into the typewriter. She hit the return bar with perhaps a little too much emphasis as she positioned the paper properly. Another case of shoplifting medicine from the pharmacy. People would do anything to get alcohol now that it couldn't be bought legally. Prohibition had caused more problems than it had ever solved.

She didn't have to be typing up reports. She could catch shoplifters as well as Mark or anyone else. But they kept her here, basically chained to her desk, and constantly told her how important her role was to the running of the department. And while she didn't doubt it was important for paperwork to be filled out and filed properly, she was fairly certain that if everyone did their own, she could get a chance to do real police work.

They thought they were protecting her from the dirty streets. But this was Woodbridge, New Jersey. There was just as good a chance the crime was a runaway cow as it was a petty theft at the pharmacy or Christensen's Department Store. She could handle either of those cases as easily as Mark. Maybe easier; he was afraid of cows.

They wanted to protect her because of her father. Officer Sean Grady had died eight years ago while on duty, shot during an arrest gone wrong.

The department had done what they could to help the family, hiring Alice, a serious nineteen-year-old, earning pennies doing piecework with her mother, to work in the department. And although two years ago they'd finally promoted her to the position of officer, she still mainly did the typing.

The other officers still thought of her as a little girl,

as Grady's baby. And since she was twenty-seven, she was beginning to despair of ever changing that.

The phone bell jangled, and through the door to his office, she could see the chief grab it. He sat straighter, as if sitting at attention, while he listened to what the caller said. His brows came together, and his lips puckered. Whatever this call was, it was more serious than a lost cow. He hung up the phone and grabbed his hat.

"Come on, Piccolo. There are reports of shots fired by the marina." He barely paused as he hurried past Mark's desk.

Alice stood too. Shots fired. That was real police work. Something she could sink her teeth into.

"No, Grady." Chief Murphy shook his head even as he reached the door. "You stay here. There has to be someone available if there is another call."

Of course, there had to be. But what would another call be? A fender bender on Main Street? A bored kid throwing rocks at windows? Routine stuff.

She sat back down. She hadn't really expected to be able to go with them. After all, she was Grady's baby.

She typed up Piccolo's report. She could read his handwriting, despite the ribbing she gave him. She'd been reading his chicken scratch for too many years not to be able to decipher it. She pulled the form out of the typewriter and clipped it to the other papers and replaced it in the manila folder. Then she dropped the folder in the "out" box. One done. She stood and stretched and poured herself a cup of coffee.

The phone rang again and Officer Rawlson, who was working the dispatch desk, picked it up.

"Drunk and disorderly at the train station. You want to go get him and bring him in, or should I?" He asked after he replaced the receiver.

"Anything's better than typing up reports all day." She put her unfinished coffee on the desk and settled her stiff blue cap over her bobbed hair. She stepped out into the bright afternoon sun and glanced toward the train station, a block away.

It wasn't hard to spot the problem. Two men were staggering around, poking and pushing at each other, heading toward Bitting's Coal Depot.

She assessed the situation as she approached the two men. They didn't seem overly aggressive. They might be shoving each other, but they were also reaching out to steady each other. She'd see if she could gentle them right into the holding tank. She'd done it before.

"Gentlemen." She put on what she thought of as her schoolmarm voice. "Is there a problem?"

The taller of the two, his straw-colored hair falling into his eyes, stared at her as if trying to focus, then turned to his companion. "Ooh, Patsy, it's a buttoned skirt. They sent a buttoned skirt for us."

Alice rolled her eyes. She'd been called worse, but she rather wished they would see her as a police officer first, and a woman second.

The other one resembled nothing less than a leprechaun, if the leprechaun was five foot five and smelled like a fisherman. "We must be considered weak sisters, Snake, if they sent a skirt for us."

"Well, we're no goons." The one called Snake made a move as if to put his arms around her, but she sidestepped him. "How about a kiss?"

"I know what you gentlemen would like." She ignored the comment about the kiss. If she didn't, she'd end up thinking half the town was in love with her or get so frustrated she'd never get any work done.

"Do you now?" Patsy wagged his eyebrows at her, and she sighed.

"You'd like a place to sit down. A chance to get off your feet."

"Oh, a place to sit would be nice. We could sit right here." Snake started to sit down on the curb. She grabbed his arm.

"Not here." She kept her voice even and calm. These two were lit brighter than a Christmas tree. "I've a better spot. And coffee as well."

"You know what would be better than a cup of coffee? A spot of gin. You got that for me?" Patsy said with a wistful sigh.

"Afraid not. That's illegal."

"Not if it's medicinal." Patsy gave a small cough. "Got a cold, I have."

His nose was red enough to make it look like he had a cold, but Alice was fairly certain it wasn't illness that caused it.

"Coffee will do nicely, I'm sure." She already had Snake by one arm. Now she took hold of Patsy's upper arm as well. "Come along with me, then. We'll get you all situated. You can put your feet up, have a bit of coffee, and maybe even tell me what you were arguing about just now."

They smelled of fish and saltwater and sweat as well as whatever alcohol was seeping through their pores.

"Coffee would be nice." Snake turned and winked.

"You taking us home with you, sweet cheeks?"

"Not quite. This is closer." Home was only a few blocks away, but they certainly didn't need to know that. When she was little her father would sometimes bring vagrants or drunks to their house to get them sorted out. "It's more comfortable than that cold jail cell," he'd say, "and they're no danger to anyone but themselves. It's our duty to help out our fellow man." All of that still held true, but times were different, and she certainly wasn't running a halfway house for drunks. Sometimes it was all she could do to keep her sister in line.

"And a place to put up my feet. I think I need to sit down." Snake started to sit right there on the sidewalk, but she jerked on his arm.

"Just a little further, there, Snake."

"Do I know you?" he asked, a befuddled look in his eye. "I'd remember a lively skirt like you."

"I'm Officer Grady," Alice said. "Come on, we'll make you comfortable."

"Officer, is it?" Patsy asked. "But you're a girl. I'm not so drunk that I don't know that."

"Yes, Patsy." Alice sighed. Mark never had to have these conversations. "I'm a girl. And you're pretty drunk."

"Aye. That's so." He nodded, and then put his free hand up to his head, as if afraid it would fall off.

They reached the town hall. And she led them around to the police department. Rawlson saw her coming and hurried to open the door for her.

"They give you any trouble?"

"None at all. Is their room ready?" She steered them toward the holding cell.

"Fresh linens and all," Rawlson answered, a hint of a laugh in his voice.

"Not exactly the Ritz." Snake sniffed and looked around the cell.

"Where's our coffee?" Patsy asked as Alice locked the door behind them.

"Coming right up," she promised.

"I like two lumps in mine," Snake called after her.

"I'll give you two lumps," she muttered to herself.

Rawlson laughed out loud. "At least they're congenial drunks."

"Oh, yes, charm school graduates to be sure."

"Fishermen?"

"Smells like it. I'll give them some coffee before getting their particulars."

She poured two cups from the percolator they kept going all day long. "Cream?" she called over her shoulder to the men in the cell.

"Black," Patsy answered.

That was probably best. It would sober him up faster.

"A touch," Snake said, sounding as if he were in a fancy drawing room, and not a man who smelled of fish and spirits and was locked up in a holding cell.

Alice handed the men their porcelain cups. "Now…" She grabbed a clipboard from her desk. "I'm going to need a little information from you fellows."

"Anything for a looker like you." Snake winked at her again.

"Okay, that's enough of that, Snake." She tried to keep her tone light but firm. "I'm not susceptible to flattery, and no one is knocking down my door to put me on the next pin-up poster. So let's cut the crap and get on with it, shall we?"

From his desk, she could hear Rawlson try to stifle another laugh.

She shot him a dirty look. She would tell him he could come book these two, but that would put her back typing reports, and honestly, she'd rather be doing this.

"Now, Snake." She turned to the taller of the two. "That's a fascinating name."

"It's because I'm tall and skinny like a snake," he volunteered.

Yes, she would have guessed that.

"Perfectly logical," she answered. "But I seriously doubt it is what your mother named you."

"Ah, no. And to this day she still calls me Willie. Won't call me Snake. Says it's not a name for a man, that's what Mrs. Olsen says."

"So she calls you by your proper name, William Olsen?"

"Aye. Well, she usually calls me Willie. But that's my true name, that's for sure." He took a gulp of his coffee.

"And where do you live, Snake?" She'd rather call him Mr. Olsen, it seemed more respectful, but she figured he'd give her more information if she used the name he preferred.

"My mother lives in Newark." He sat on the edge of the cot in the cell. "She's a good woman. She says I don't visit enough. I should visit her more." He turned to his friend. "I should visit Mama more, don't you think?"

"Ah, sure, Snake. Everyone should visit their mama." The smaller man wrapped his arm around the other's shoulders, giving him an encouraging squeeze.

The two men seemed close to sentimental tears. If they started singing "Mammy" or some such nonsense she would lose it.

She stepped over to her desk for her now-cold cup of coffee and gulped a mouthful before returning to her drunks.

"And where do *you* live, Snake?"

Snake shrugged off the other man's arm and sat up a bit straighter. "Patsy and I here, we live in Perth Amboy, when we're not out on the boat."

She felt the corners of her mouth twitch up slightly in a smile. Now they were getting somewhere. "Do you have an address?"

"It's Mrs. Malone's boarding house we stay at," Patsy said. "On State Street."

She'd get the street number later. For now, that was enough.

"And Patrick." She turned to Patsy, figuring that was a safe bet. "What's your full name?"

"The name my mama called me when she was angry?"

"Sure." Alice tapped her pencil on the clip board. Whatever worked. These men were so pickled, she doubted they even realized they were in a cell.

"Patrick Xavier Joseph Finley."

Patrick Finley it is. She wrote that on her sheet.

"And you say you spend time on a boat?" She was guessing it wasn't a pleasure boat, but one could never be too sure.

"Our home away from home. Though even those bunks are more comfortable than here. You should do something about the accommodations, miss."

"I'll get right on that. What boat is that?"

"That would be the *Katinka*. Finest scalloping boat there is," Snake said with pride, puffing out his chest.

"So you're fishermen, are you?" she asked, filling in one more line on the form in front of her.

"Indeed, we are. And we've just gotten in from nearly two weeks at sea. We really should get better accommodations than this." Patsy looked around disapprovingly.

"I'll speak to someone about that," she said briskly. "I have a few more questions for you. What were you arguing about?"

Patsy threw his arm around Snake. "Arguing, you say? There was never no argument between me and Snake here. We are tight as brothers. We love each other as if we came from the same mother." He paused and considered what he said. Then a grin split his face. "Did you hear that? I made a rhyme. Pretty good, eh?"

Across the room Rawlson laughed, and Alice shot him a dirty look.

"So you weren't arguing by the train station when I got to you?"

"Oh, that?" Snake pushed Patsy away from him. "Yeah, we were having a knock-down-drag-out."

"Brothers do that, you know," Patsy said and casually took a sip of his coffee. "You have any brothers, miss?"

"No," she answered, "only a sister."

"Then you might not know. Sisters are different."

She'd had plenty of fights with her sister, but none of them resulted in having the police called in.

"So it was just a friendly argument between friends?" she asked to be sure.

"That's all it was, nothing to concern your pretty

little head about," Snake said.

Okay then, that pretty much guaranteed she was going to dig a bit deeper on this one.

"Right, right." She turned her attention to Patsy. "He wasn't going after your girl or something?" Taking a stab in the dark here, but sometimes that led to the true information spilling out.

"He ain't got no girl," Snake answered with a snort. "Who would look twice at this little Irish runt?"

"I think he's quite good looking, in a rugged sort of way." If you liked windburned leprechauns.

"Eh, we weren't fighting about a girl," Patsy admitted. "We was fighting about Jiggy."

Snake punched Patsy in the arm and Alice tried to hide her smile. The truth always comes out.

"And who, or what, is Jiggy?"

"He's a customer." Snake's voice rang of feigned innocence. "That's all."

"What does he buy from you?"

Perhaps they weren't as drunk as they looked, because Snake narrowed his eyes at her.

"Fish. We're fishermen. We sell fish. Scallops particularly."

"Right then." That was a dead end. "And who sold you alcohol?"

"No one sold it to us," Patsy declared.

"Did you make it yourselves?"

"No." Snake put one hand to his heart. "That would be illegal. You do know about prohibition, don't you?"

Oh yes, she knew. It would be so much easier if it were repealed, far from reducing crime, as promised, it had increased it. But as long as it was illegal, she was going to do whatever she could to make sure the rules were followed.

"So where did you get the alcohol?"

"Alcohol? We've had nary a drink since we've stepped ashore."

Her eyebrows shot up. They surely knew how pickled they were. Did they really expect her to believe them? "Nothing at all?"

"Nothing except some apple cider." Patsy held up one hand as if taking a pledge. "It must have turned. That happens sometimes, you know. It's quite a natural process. Can't fault a man for drinking cider, if he doesn't know it's turned."

"No, I suppose not." She clearly wasn't getting more out of these two. She'd just leave them here until they sobered up. Nothing illegal about drinking, after all, only against making, selling or buying the stuff. However, there were ordinances against drunk and disorderly, and they definitely had been both.

She sat at her desk and typed up her report before turning her attention back to Mark's reports.

The sun slipped further through the sky and the two men in the holding cell sobered up enough to let them out. Patsy and Snake were digging in their pockets for the cash to pay their fine when the door opened and the Chief and Mark walked in.

Alice looked up from writing out the receipts to see the somber faces of her fellow officers.

"It was bad, then?"

"There's a man dead." Chief Murphy took off his hat and ran his hand through his thinning hair.

The men in front of her paled visibly and exchanged nervous glances.

"Who?" Snake asked, his voice cracking on the

word.

"Tomas Nagy. Know him?" Murphy looked inquisitively at the two men.

Patsy's face crumpled, and it looked like he was doing all he could to keep from bursting into tears.

"We work for him." Snake's shoulders slumped, and he shook his head slowly back and forth in disbelief. "What happened?"

The chief tossed his hat onto the desk. "He was shot. You say you worked for him?"

"Aye." Patsy got himself together enough to answer. "He's the skipper of the *Katinka*."

"That's right, he is. Or was." Murphy ran his hand over his face, his eyes looked haunted. Murder was not common in their quiet town. He picked his hat back up. "And who are you gentlemen?"

"This is William Olsen and Patrick Finley," Alice answered. "They've been enjoying our hospitality this afternoon."

Murphy nodded with understanding. "When did you last see Nagy?"

Patsy rubbed his ear as he thought. The raw emotion on the man's face was heartbreaking.

"Oh, man. We finished unloading around one or two?" He glanced at his companion for confirmation.

"Something like that," Snake shrugged. "Didn't quite check the time. Past noon for sure, but the sun was still pretty high."

"So you unloaded and then what?" Murphy asked.

"Got our pay and headed into town," Patsy answered. He was starting to get himself together now that the initial shock had passed.

"You didn't stay around the marina?"

"No, sir. No point. We had no more work to do, and we had our pay."

Murphy nodded, acknowledging the logic of that.

Snake cleared his throat. "He's a good man, Tomas. He's got a family. Little kids. Know who shot him?"

"Not yet," Murphy answered. "But we will. We will. I want to ask you both a few more questions though, to try to get an idea where Nagy might have been heading after you left him."

Patsy and Snake nodded and, heads hanging, went through the open door to the chief's office and sat in the wooden visitor chairs there.

Mark sat back at his desk, looking defeated. It was always hard when they had to deal with a death. Most often it was death due to an accident of some sort. Then there was the time that she tried her best to forget, when a man had jumped to his death right in front of her. Luckily things like that weren't commonplace. She reached for the next report to type up.

"Grady." Murphy stood in his office doorway.

"Yes, sir?"

"Go on out to the Nagys', will you? See what help the family is going to need and arrange for it."

"Yes, sir." She stood and put her hat on. This was not exactly crime investigation, but it was helping people, and her father had always said that was the most fulfilling aspect of police work. "Address?"

"Berry Street. Three Twenty-Nine."

Just around the corner.

"And does she know, sir? About her husband?"

"Not yet." Murphy shook his head. "You'll be breaking the news gently, won't you?"

"Yes, sir."

She left the office, trying to think how she was going to break the news to the new widow. She knew from experience there wasn't any good way.

Chapter Two

Water lapped gently against the side of the boat as Hank Chapman stood at the wheel. The afternoon sun was at such an angle that it blinded him as he looked over his shoulder to pilot the *Mary B* into dock.

Overhead seagulls circled, squawking and crying to one another. The birds were his constant companions, scavengers, always hoping to get their greedy little beaks on his fish. They could find their own fish, they weren't getting any of his.

He cut the engines, and the boat glided into its slip. Slim jumped from the side of the boat to the worn dock and coiled the line around a rusted cleat. Once the boat was secure, Hank rubbed a hand across his face. Already he wanted to be back out to the peace of sea. He could hear men yelling across the fishery yard. Trucks backing up, machinery grinding. People. He'd rather not deal with people, other than his crew. They were a good group of guys who knew when to leave him alone.

There were some benefits to being home. After nearly two weeks at sea, he was looking forward to stretching out on a nice soft mattress tonight. However, he already knew he would have trouble sleeping, despite the comfortable mattress, without the gentle swaying provided by the ocean.

He left the sanctuary of the bridge deck with its

sweeping windows and warm wood accents, to help with the unloading. He noted that the two narrow metal flights of stairs needed to be repainted while they were in dock. In the storage hold his crew was already digging the fifty-pound bags of shucked scallops out of the ice that preserved them when they were at sea. The men formed an assembly line to get the three hundred fifty-pound bags up to the working deck where they could then be offloaded. He helped get them started, handing the first few bags to Smitty, his first mate. A quick glance showed that the false floors in the holds were intact. Should someone from the fishery decide, for whatever reason, that they wanted to come aboard he didn't need them questioning the storage capacity of the hold.

"You'll all be sleeping in your own beds tonight," Hank said as he handed the next bag to Smitty and then stepped out of the line. He needed to go find Martin, the dockmaster, and make the sale.

"I ain't seen my wife in two weeks," Curly yelled from somewhere mid-line. "Ain't no sleep happening in our house tonight."

Amid the laughter, Ahab called out. "At least you'll be in your own bed."

"Some of the time," Curly responded with a loud guffaw.

Hank gave Curly a slap on the shoulder as he passed him. He squeezed past his men on the steps. On the working deck Mack was stacking the fifty-pound bags so they could be off-loaded quickly. Hank grabbed the gangway and with a bump and a clank, locked it in place with a few swift moves. Once on the dock he took a second to let his legs get acclimated to solid ground.

He'd prefer to stay out on the boat with only his crew at hand. He could deal with storms and high waves and malfunctioning equipment, he just hated dealing with all the people when he came into port. Jack Martin at least wasn't too bad, he'd been a fisherman before he took over the fishery. He understood what it meant to be at sea. That counted for something.

Martin was already out of the raw-boarded office and heading toward him.

"Good haul?"

Hank wiped his hands on his trousers before shaking hands. "Got seven and a half tons for you."

"Not bad. Could be better. The *Katinka* brought in eight a couple of hours ago."

"Good for them." He was not going to get goaded into false rivalries. They worked night and day out on that ship, for nearly two weeks. They brought in what they brought in. They fished until their hold was full. Granted his hold didn't carry quite as much fish as it used to, but for that matter neither did *Katinka*'s. There were no secrets between friends, and he knew Nagy was in the same business he was in. And he didn't mean scalloping.

"Come into the office, Hank, and we'll settle up."

Hank followed Martin into the dim, crowded office. A wooden desk with a scarred top took up most of the space. A brass spike on the desk held a clutter of receipts. A ripped fishing net occupied the one spare chair in the room. Behind the desk was a large black safe with scratched gold trim. The older man spun the dial with a few quick flicks and opened it. He grabbed a pile of bills and after closing the door again handed the money to Hank, sitting down at his desk to write up the receipt.

Hank took the bills, licked his finger and started thumbing through the pile, counting it.

"Don't trust me?" Martin looked over the top of his half-moon reading spectacles, pausing in the act of writing down the numbers.

"Don't trust anyone." It was truer than he wanted to let on. He trusted his crew with his life when they were all out on the water, but other than that, he watched out for his own back. It was the only way to be certain of anything.

"Good policy," Martin answered. "Though you notice I trusted you on how many tons you had."

"You can check for yourself. It will all be on your dock shortly." He shoved the wad of bills into his pocket. "If you found I shorted you, you can take it out of the next shipment."

"I know you wouldn't short me." Martin stood and handed him one copy of the receipt and stuck the other on the spike on his desk, to flutter with the rest in the breeze coming through the open window. "Because your daddy would have your hide if you did."

Hank smiled benignly at him. His father didn't know half of what he did, but he did own the *Mary B* and several other fishing boats and used to fish with Jack Martin. He shook Martin's hand once more. "Nice doing business with you."

"You keep bringing me scallops, I'll keep buying them."

"That's what I figured."

Back out in the yard all work had stopped. The fishermen had gathered around one man and there was no making sense of the excited babble of voices. Hank found his men in the crowd.

"What's going on?" he asked Smitty.

"Nagy's dead."

He swayed, as his body as well as his mind reeled at the information. How was that possible? He'd only unloaded his fish a few hours ago. What could have gone wrong?

"Tomas?" he asked, hoping it was some other Nagy. It wasn't an uncommon last name, after all.

"Yes." It was one of the workers from the fishery who answered him. "Shot."

Hank's blood ran hot and then cold in his veins.

"Who shot him?" Was it related to the rum running? Was it an accident? A random crime? Did he have to worry about the same thing happening to him, or had Nagy just had incredibly bad luck?

"Don't know," the fishery man answered, sucking on a toothpick. "Butch there told us. Ask him."

Hank pushed his way through the crowd until he was within arm's reach of the burly man they called Butch. He reached out and grabbed his shoulder. "What happened to Nagy?"

"He's dead."

Hank closed his eyes, wishing people would stop saying that. He wanted it to not be true.

"When did it happen? Where? What do you know?"

"All I know is he was shot down by Boynton Beach this afternoon."

Right by the marina. Not good.

"Who did it? Why?"

"I don't know," Butch answered with a shrug. "I

wasn't there. Don't know if anyone knows those answers." His face softened slightly with a touch of compassion. "Friend of yours?"

Hank nodded, trying to keep the tears blurring his vision from spilling over. "Yes." He pushed the word out past the lump in his throat. "Yes, he was."

He grabbed Smitty's arm. "Get the crew back on board. We need to finish unloading." He headed back to the boat, trying to process what he'd learned.

Tomas Nagy dead. He couldn't wrap his head around that. And by whom? Even if he'd been caught by the Feds, it was unlikely they'd just shoot him. Jiggy? But that made no sense, why would he shoot one of his best suppliers? Random crime? Personal grudge? Pirates? At this point it seemed anything was possible. He shook his head to clear it.

The crew, working with incredible speed, had already started off-loading the bags of scallops. He took his place to help finish the job. The work was heavy and mind-numbing, and he went through the motions while his thoughts kept tumbling back to the fact that Nagy was dead.

Nagy was one of the few people outside his crew who he could stand to spend time with. Nagy understood him, having also fought in the Great War, granted on the other side of the conflict, since he'd been fighting for his homeland of Hungary. But now, years later, on this side of the ocean, those distinctions didn't matter. What mattered was that Nagy understood the horror of the trenches. Understood the way that a loud noise could set your nerves jangling. Understood how nothing was permanent, that one moment you could be talking to a buddy and the next moment he was vaporized by a bomb. He would miss Nagy. A lot.

There were dangers inherent in rum running. It was one of the reasons he got involved with it in the first place. The danger made him feel alive. But up until now the danger had primarily been getting nabbed by the G-men, and having your boat confiscated, not death.

Once all the bags were on the dock, he went up to the bridge with Smitty while the rest of the crew untied the lines and got the boat ready to head out. He started the motors again, feeling a certain visceral satisfaction in the way their thrumming echoed throughout the boat.

"Next stop," Hank said with a nod to his first mate. He wanted to just go and drown his sorrows, but they had business to complete first.

"Next stop," Smitty echoed. At a signal from the crew on the working deck he said. "You're clear to go."

Hank guided the scallop boat away from the fishery's dock and down the channel toward the slip where the *Mary B* would undergo maintenance until they were ready to take her out again. Before he got to the Arthur Kill and the marina, he turned down another, smaller channel, the entrance to the Woodbridge River. No, this trip wasn't part of their recorded voyage. But no one was going to complain about the detour. It meant nearly doubling their pay. It was a trip he was fairly certain Nagy had made shortly before his death.

He carefully steered into a hidden cove. A plain wooden dock jutted out into the water. He cut the engines and let the boat float in. When they got close, Curly jumped ashore and tied the lines to the cleats. Hank left the bridge and got to the working deck just as Jiggy Malone, short and scrappy with his ever-present pipe and checked sports coat, clambered aboard, barely waiting for the gangway to be put down.

"Thought I'd heard you were in." He stuck out a beringed hand for Hank to shake. "What you got for me?"

"Forty hams." Hank led him to the hold where the crew had already drained the melted ice and removed the false bottoms of the storage areas, exposing the contraband. Each burlap-covered package contained six bottles tied together.

"Of what?"

"The finest Bordeaux."

Jiggy rubbed his hands together in delight, his eyes gleaming.

"Lovely! Let's get it unloaded."

Hank was more than happy to do that. If the wine was found onboard, he'd lose the boat. And since it was his father's, there would be hell to pay. While he knew that technically rum running was breaking the law, the danger in that was part of the reason he found it exciting, but the law was a bad one, and he saw himself as doing a service to humanity. After all, what good was a civilized society without a glass of wine to enjoy with dinner? Or a shot of whiskey or bourbon or rum?

The crew bent to start the task of unloading, and Hank followed Jiggy into the hut for the cash.

"Did you see Nagy this afternoon?" Hank asked, hands shoved in his pockets. Had Tomas delivered the goods before he was killed, or had they been stolen from him? That was what he wanted to know, and he certainly couldn't ask the authorities.

Jiggy's head, which had been bent over his money box on the spindly little three-legged table, shot up. "What do you know about Nagy?" The words came out almost like a snarl.

Hank took half a step back. "I know he's my friend, and I know he's dead. What I don't know is if he delivered his shipment to you before he died."

"He did not."

"So you know he's dead."

Jiggy glared at him from over the smoke curling up from his pipe.

"I hear things."

"Did you hear who did it?"

"What am I, the damn FBI?" He grabbed a wad of bills from the strongbox and shoved it at Hank. "I'll tell you this, though, buddy-boy, you better watch your back."

"Why?" Hank thumbed through the bills, counting them quickly, and pocketed the wad.

Jiggy touched the side of his nose, indicating he was giving him a big tip. "I don't know who shot Nagy, but I do know he was getting involved with some people he shouldn't be."

"Like who?"

"Ever hear of a guy named Vincent Salerno?"

He'd heard the name bandied about a bit but didn't know much about him.

"Don't know him."

Jiggy made a huffing noise and sucked on his pipe. "Yeah, well. Stay away from him. He's dangerous."

"You think he shot Nagy?"

"Not saying he did, or he didn't, but Nagy got involved with him and now he's dead."

"What does this guy Salerno do?"

"Causes trouble, that's what."

Hank tried not to let his impatience show. He

leaned against the doorjamb. "He your competition?"

Jiggy's face slowly turned red. "I ain't got no competition. And don't you forget it."

He was right about that. No one else dared even try to manage the connections between rum row, the runners and the buyers like the speakeasies. Jiggy had the business in this area all tied up, and everyone knew it.

Jiggy shuffled through some papers on his table, finally pulling one scrap from the pile.

"When you go out again, I need Champagne. They should have it on board the *Fleur de Lys*."

Hank knew the conversation was closed. "Fine."

Half of the hams were already on the working deck when they stepped back into the afternoon sunlight. Hank joined his crew to unload the rest and then to move them into the specially built cellar behind Jiggy's shack.

Once all the Bordeaux was secure under the hut, Hank and his crew climbed back aboard the boat.

"Well, you be careful, you hear?" Jiggy called up to him, the pipe in one hand, the other shielding his eyes from the afternoon sun. "Remember what I told you."

Hank didn't have to be told that twice. He'd been well and truly warned. He just wasn't sure what he was being warned against.

He and Smitty headed up to the bridge as the other crew men pulled in the gangway. Smitty gave him the all clear and Hank silently piloted the boat back to the marina near Boynton Beach.

What could have happened out here that led to Tomas's death? What did Vince Salerno have to do with it? He needed to find answers. And he would. He owed that much to Tomas, and his family.

Once the *Mary B* was securely back in her own slip, he handed his crew their cash.

"Take the weekend off," he told them. "We'll start maintenance on Monday."

The crew nodded, much more somber than they normally would be with their pay packets in hand.

"We were talking." Curly cleared his throat and took a step forward. "We want to help out Nagy's widow. Irene's going to need all the help she can get. She's got those three nippers. Ernst, the oldest, is only eight, too young to bring in much money."

It was true, the jobs a boy that age could get— newsboy, shoeshine boy—would not be enough to sustain the family.

His crew each took one crisp twenty out of their pay packets and handed it to Hank. "You'll bring this to her?"

How could he refuse?

"I'll be sure she gets it." He added several twenties of his own to the pile.

It was the least they could do.

Chapter Three

On the short walk from the police station to the Nagy house on Berry Street, Alice thought about how to break the news to Irene Nagy. She remembered when Chief Murphy came to their house, hat in hand, to tell them about her father. This coming Christmas it would be nine years. Hardly seemed possible so much time had passed, since it felt like time stood still when they got the news.

It had been the week before Christmas and Alice was helping Mama bake gingerbread and also finish up some dresses she was making for one of her customers. They were working in tandem, taking turns in the kitchen and at the sewing machine, laughing and joking and singing Christmas carols.

They were singing "Here We Come a Wassailing" and trying to do it as a round but having difficulty because there were only the two of them, so they kept messing up and laughing, and then just when Mama opened the oven to take out the latest batch of gingerbread there had been a knock at the door. Alice was still laughing when she answered it.

The somber faces of Chief Murphy and Officer Burns stopped her in her tracks. Mama came up behind her almost instantly. "What is it? What's happened? What's happened to Sean?"

Alice didn't know how Mama knew that something

was wrong with Daddy. But really, there wasn't any other explanation for the two officers to be on the doorstep.

"Mrs. Grady," Chief Murphy said, turning his hat over in his hands. "Anna." His voice broke. "I'm sorry."

"Where is he?" Already Mama was taking her apron off and shoving it at Alice. "Where is he? I need to go to him."

"It won't matter to him, I'm afraid," Chief Murphy said. "Please, sit down."

"I don't want to sit down," Mama had insisted. "I need to go to Sean."

But despite her protests, Chief Murphy and Officer Burns got Mama seated and Alice put on the kettle for a pot of tea. She suspected they would need it. She checked the cupboard to make sure the bottle of whiskey was still there. A drop of that in Mama's tea might be just the thing.

She made it back into the living room to hear what had happened. Her father had been shot in an arrest gone wrong. Straight through the heart. He hadn't stood a chance. They were confident they would find and arrest the man who had done it, and that he would face the electric chair.

"This won't go unpunished," Chief Murphy had insisted, as if that was supposed to make them feel better.

The teakettle whistled, and Alice reluctantly left the living room to tend to it. Mechanically she scooped the tea into the white Belleek teapot with its delicate shamrock design. It had been a wedding gift for her parents, and one of Mama's prized possessions. She added the water and then opened the cupboard, deciding whether or not to add the whiskey to the whole pot or just to her mother's cup.

"Don't you be adding no whiskey to my tea, Alice Marie," Mama, who apparently had the ears of a cat and could read minds, called from the other room. "I'll be needing my wits about me today."

Alice closed the cupboard and brought the tea tray into the living room.

When she poured the tea even the officers accepted cups. This was not simply a courtesy call regarding a stranger. Sean was one of their own. Alice wondered if either of the men would have happily accepted some whiskey in their tea. Not that they could say so, being on duty and all. And there was the whole factor of prohibition.

"We've already called Greiner's. They'll take care of everything."

"We need to tell Martha." Mama turned to Alice. "Go with Officer Burns, over to the high school, and I'll go with the Chief so I can see Sean."

Alice hadn't wanted to be the one to break the news to her sister, and it turned out she hadn't had to. She'd stood silently by, while Officer Burns did all the talking, and then she held her sister in her arms while they both cried.

Now she was the one who had to be strong and deliver the bad news. She was not looking forward to it at all.

She paused in front of three twenty-nine Berry Street and looked up at the narrow two-story house. The children were probably home from school at this point. She almost wished they weren't. She did not want to have to be the one to tell them their father was dead. Though maybe it was easier if it were her rather than their mother. She could at least spare the widow that pain. Taking a deep breath, she climbed the five steps to the porch. The front door stood open on this warm afternoon. Not seeing a doorbell in evidence, Alice knocked on the door jamb.

A little girl, her dark hair in two long braids, stopped running through the house, and stuck her fingers in her mouth, as she peered at Alice.

"Is your mama here?" Alice barely got the words out, before the child ran toward the back of the house.

"Mama, Mama. Lady here to see you!"

Irene Nagy, dark hair in a stylish bob, wearing a bright yellow dress cinched at the waist, came into view, a questioning look on her face. Alice's heart sank. She was so clearly dressed up and expecting her husband home after a couple of weeks at sea.

"May I help you?" Her words were accented and awkward, as if she were not accustomed to speaking English. Even before she finished speaking, she seemed to take in the uniform and Alice's somber expression. She paled visibly. "Is something wrong? Has something happened to Tomas?"

How is it that wives know? Alice wondered.

"May I come in, Mrs. Nagy?" Alice asked.

"*Igen*," she answered in Hungarian first and then switched to English. "Yes, of course." Irene waved her into the house, her expression wavering between hospitality and wariness.

"I'm afraid I have some bad news," Alice began.

"Tomas?"

Alice nodded. "Perhaps you would like to sit?" She

didn't like how pale the woman had become, and she hadn't even told her the worst yet. Irene sat in a flowered chair and clutched at the worn upholstered arms, her knuckles white. Alice looked at her with compassion. Was there any easy way to say this? Perhaps the kindest thing was to not keep her waiting for what she was afraid to hear. "Your husband was killed today." It sounded so stark to her ears, but to tell her anything less would only delay the inevitable.

"How?" The woman choked out the word. "Was it accident at sea? He drown? The sea is bad. Dangerous."

"No." Alice felt awkward towering over the woman, so she perched on the edge of the sofa. "Someone shot him."

The woman's startled glance turned to one of resignation and Alice realized that this wasn't a complete shock to her. Did she suspect someone would want to kill her husband?

"Who? Do you know?" Her voice was soft but held a quiet strength.

"Not yet. The police are investigating, and we will find out. Rest assured. The murderer will be caught." Alice didn't know how true that was, but she could hardly say anything else under the circumstances.

She became aware that the three Nagy children were sidling into the room, apparently aware that something was very wrong. She looked at the narrow little faces with sharp noses and pointy chins of the two boys and little girl. Life would not be easy for them. She knew. She, at least, had already been an adult when her father died and was able to go to work. What would these children have?

"Tell them," Irene said, clutching the skirt of her

dress between worrying fingers.

"Children, I have some very sad news." They stared at her with wide wary eyes. The girl stealthily moved toward her mother until she was leaning against her knees. The oldest, a boy of eight, stood tall. Bracing himself. "Your father won't be coming home. He has gone to heaven."

"Just say it," the oldest said. "He's dead."

"Yes." Alice swallowed hard. "He's dead."

The middle boy ran up the stairs and shortly a door slammed. Irene looked up toward the ceiling and her shoulders slumped.

"Papa's not coming home?" the little girl asked, looking at her with big dark eyes.

"No."

"Someone shot him?" the oldest boy asked, and Alice realized they'd heard her tell their mother the news.

The girl's eyes filled with tears.

"Yes." Alice addressed the child. "The police are investigating." She turned back to Irene. "Do you have any idea who might want your husband dead?"

The woman looked at her, uncomprehending, for a moment. The boy said something to her in Hungarian, and she shook her head. "I don't know. Everyone like Tomas. No one want to hurt him. He a fisherman. Who has something against a fisherman?"

Who indeed? Alice wished she knew more of what had happened this afternoon, so she could give more information to the family, but that would have to wait. In the meantime, she had to make sure the family was provided for. First things first.

"Do you want Greiner's to handle the

arrangements? I can take you there if you'd like."

Irene nodded numbly. "Yes. That is fine. We go tomorrow?"

"Yes," Alice said. That would be soon enough. "And which church?" There were a couple of Hungarian churches in the area; she didn't want to make any assumptions.

"Mount Carmel," Irene said, and Alice made a note.

"I can take you there as well."

Irene shook her head. "No. I do it. It's fine."

"We want to help." What would really help this woman? For her husband to not be dead. Barring that, to bring the killer to justice. Whether she was put on the case or not, she would do everything she could to get answers for this family.

The front steps creaked as someone climbed them. The children's head turned expectantly toward the front door, as if still hoping their father would appear. The boy's eyes widened, and he rushed toward the door. Alice almost expected there had been some mistake and Tomas was here. She turned to see the boy throw himself into the arms of a tall, rugged-looking fisherman.

"Uncle Hank, Uncle Hank! She says Papa is dead!"

Alice stood to greet the newcomer. He held the boy in his arms. "I know," he said softly. "It's a horrible thing. Your papa was a good man. No one should have wanted to hurt him."

He unwrapped the boy's arms from around himself and walked straight to Irene, who had stood when he came in, ignoring Alice completely.

"Hank," Irene said, faintly. "Is it true?"

"I'm afraid so." He took the widow's hands in his.

Alice wrinkled her forehead in irritation. She wasn't believed? In her uniform as an official representative of the police department? Why would she lie?

"We got in after him. I didn't see him, but I was told what happened. The crew and I, we've put together a little something for you and the children." The man handed a wad of money to the widow, and she looked up at him with dark, grateful eyes.

Money. Of course, money was what the young widow needed. She could take up a collection at the station. She was sure her fellow officers would be willing to contribute. But there was another factor to consider, this person might know something that could help in the investigation. She had to find out what she could. It was her duty as a police officer.

"You knew Tomas Nagy?" she addressed the stranger.

He turned and seemed to notice her for the first time, studying her with his clear blue eyes.

"He was like a brother to me." He looked her up and down, taking in the uniform. He didn't look impressed.

"I suppose you are here as the official detachment to give Mrs. Nagy the bad news."

"Yes, and to see what help we can give the family." She didn't back down, despite his dismissive glare.

"The family will be looked after. We take care of our own." There was an iciness in his tone that made Alice stand taller.

"So do we," she said, just as coldly. "In town. We

look out for each other. It's not just a code among fishermen."

"Why don't you official people just try to find out who did this to Tomas? We'll look out for the family."

Alice refused to be cowed. She had every right to be here. She didn't need to apologize for doing her job.

"Is there anyone you can think of who would want to do this? Anyone with a grievance against Mr. Nagy? Perhaps a rival fisherman?"

The man looked at her as if she didn't deserve to be alive. "Fishermen do not have that kind of rivalries. It is a big ocean. There is enough for everyone willing to work for it."

"Perhaps a crewman who thought he had been treated unfairly?" They wanted the killer found, they'd have to tell what they knew.

"Tomas was all too fair. There is no one among his crew who would have anything but wonderful things to say about him."

Alice thought of the two men who left the ship and immediately got drunk. They had expressed dismay and horror at Nagy's murder, yet they hadn't seemed completely shocked. She didn't have the whole story here, and she aimed to get it. But maybe not right now, when the wounds were fresh, and the grieving widow had barely gotten her breath. She was a professional, not a ghoul.

"I'll contact Greiners and set up an appointment," she said.

"We'll take care of it," the man answered, his voice a low growl.

She took a deep breath and counted to three. She was not the enemy here. And that this man seemed to think so made her wonder. What did he have against police? What was he trying to hide?

"Mrs. Nagy had agreed I should take her to the funeral home tomorrow to make arrangements." She turned her gaze to the widow, who looked back and forth from her to the fisherman.

"Hank will take me," she said finally. "I thank you, officer. For coming. And giving me the news."

Alice could hardly say it was her pleasure. She inclined her head. "If there is anything you need, do not be afraid to contact our department." They were paying no more attention to her, so she took her leave and headed back toward the station. At least it was almost quitting time. She was ready for today to be over.

Chapter Four

"Who does this, Hank?" Irene clung to him and looked up at him with those deep dark eyes as if he had the answers. He had no answers. He had some guesses, but no answers. He gently removed her fingers from his lapel and sat her down in the chair. Two of the children were standing there, staring at him, wanting him to make it better. He couldn't make it better. He didn't want people relying on him, especially kids. He didn't want to be the one to ruin their perception of human nature. But then again, with their father murdered, maybe it was too late to worry about that. He also didn't want to be the hero. Right now, he didn't have a lot of choice. He was the only person in this house who was still capable of thinking clearly.

"Ernst," he said to the boy. "Can you make tea? Do you know how?"

"I can do it," he said, with a stoic nod of his head. Tomas would be proud of that boy, Hank thought, swallowing over the lump that had arisen in his throat.

The little girl trailed after him, with offers to help.

"Was it Chiggy?" Irene asked him, in her thick accent. "I no trust him. He no good. I no like Tomas involved with him."

"Jiggy's okay," Hank said, perching on the edge of the davenport. "I don't think it was Jiggy."

"Someone who work for Chiggy?"

Hank wasn't sure how much Irene knew about what Tomas's involvement with Jiggy entailed. He didn't want to tell her things she didn't need to know. The police were going to be asking more questions, and he supposed that was a necessary evil if they were going to catch whoever did this. But he didn't want them nosing around Jiggy's operation. The less Irene knew about it the better.

"I don't think Jiggy had anything to do with it. You didn't tell the cops about Jiggy, did you?" He wasn't even going to mention Vincent Salerno to her. He'd look into that himself, but there was no reason to get Irene involved.

"No. Maybe I should. I could tell that lady cop."

"Don't tell anyone. Tomas never even saw Jiggy today. There's no reason to bring him into it."

Irene didn't look convinced.

"You trust me, don't you, Irene?"

It was a long moment before she answered. "I trust."

Ernst came back into the room carrying the tea tray. Sari had a plate of rye bread. Why not? A little nourishment would be good for all of them.

"Where's Kristof?"

"Upstairs," Ernst answered. "Should I go get him?"

"Does he know?" Hank had visions of having to break the news to a seven-year-old that his father was dead.

"He knows," Ernst said. "That's why he went upstairs."

Hiding in anger. That Hank could understand. "I'll go talk to him."

There were three doors at the top of the stairs and

38

only one was shut. It wasn't hard to figure out that was the door Kristof was hiding behind. Hank took a deep breath and knocked. There was no answer, but he let himself in anyway. There was respecting privacy, and then there was being the adult in the room.

The boy sat on his bed, ramrod straight, his fists on his knees. He jumped up when he saw Hank and ran to him. "Where's Papa?"

Hank frowned. He thought the boy knew. Maybe he just didn't want to accept it?

He lowered himself to one knee, putting his face even with the boy's, and gently put one hand on his shoulder. "Your Papa won't be coming home anymore."

"But I want him."

"I know," Hank said. Damn, he hated this. Why did men have to leave families behind to suffer? He thought of the picture, stuck in the mud of the trenches, of two smiling children. It was all that had been left after their father was blown to bits. Who had to break the news to them? He brought his attention back to the boy in front of him. "You and your brother are going to have to take care of your mama and sister. Can you do that?"

The boy took a big breath. "I can get a job. I'm small, but strong."

"I don't think you'll have to do that just yet," Hank said, touched by the boy's bravery. "Your papa wanted you to get an education."

"I can read. But I can work for you. I can shuck scallops. Papa taught me how."

"I'll keep that in mind." Hank wasn't sure whether to smile or cry at the offer. For now, he did neither. "But you have to stay here for now. Your mama would worry if you were out at sea for weeks at a time."

The boy nodded. "Like she always worried about Papa."

"Yes, like that." Hank tousled the boy's hair. "There is tea and bread downstairs. Come down and eat."

"Is there jam?"

"I'm sure we can find some."

Downstairs members of Tomas's crew, and their families, were filling the living room. Irene was in good hands for now, she didn't need him hanging around. He promised her he'd be back in the morning to take her to the funeral home. He didn't want her spending more time with the police than necessary. She might slip and say something she shouldn't.

Hank looked out across the causeway and back toward Sewaren and the marina, across the swampy edges of the Woodbridge River. He took a deep breath of the sea air and started walking. Tomas Nagy was dead. Who had killed him and why? Jiggy came first to mind. He'd been known to use intimidating tactics quite freely, and everyone knew it was important to stay on his good side. He couldn't imagine Tomas running afoul of him, and besides he didn't think Jiggy had it in him to shoot someone outright. That wasn't his style.

Another runner? Besides him and Nagy, there were plenty of other skippers supplying Jiggy, but they tended to leave each other alone, and it seemed unlikely that Nagy, of all people, would have made one of them mad. He was truly one of the good ones. And that was worrisome, because Hank *did* have a tendency to piss people off. He normally didn't care, but if someone was shooting fishermen, or more specifically fishermen who doubled as smugglers, he didn't like his odds.

His long loping strides took him across the bridge and into Sewaren. Before long he was walking up the path to his parents' large house with its view of the Arthur Kill and Staten Island. From time to time he thought about getting his own place, but he spent so much time out on the *Mary B* that there was no point.

"Is that you, Henry?" his mother called from the sitting room, where she was sitting and embroidering. A perfect model of a last-century woman.

"Yes, Mother." He would have liked to go up to his room without having to make conversation with anyone, but that clearly was not to be. He stepped into the room, feeling immediately oppressed by the abundance of lace and knickknacks.

"I was expecting you much earlier. Didn't the *Mary B* get in several hours ago?" Mother looked up from her embroidery and studied him. She was always studying him, worrying about his state of mind, ever since he'd come back from the war. Ten years was a long time to undergo scrutiny.

"I had some things to take care of before I got home." He wondered if she'd heard about Nagy. For someone who, on the surface, led a very sheltered life, she often got wind of the news before anyone else in the family. The woman would have made a remarkable spy.

"Did you have a good run?"

"Seven and a half tons," he answered.

She nodded appreciatively. "Your father will be pleased."

He started to edge back out of the room, but she wasn't done.

"There was quite a bit of commotion down by the marina earlier. Do you know anything about it?"

"I wasn't there at the time," he hedged.

"I heard a man was killed."

He sighed. He should have known she would have heard.

"Yes, the skipper of the *Katinka*. Tomas Nagy."

She shook her head, mournfully. "A fisherman, of all things. I thought all risk of you being shot was finished when you came home from France."

He forced a smile and bent to give Mother a kiss on the top of her head. "Don't worry about me. Whatever happened to Tomas has nothing to do with me." He wished he could be sure he was telling the truth.

"Be sure it doesn't." She gave him a watery-eyed smile. "Dinner will be soon. Wash up."

Hank took the stairs two at a time and retreated to his boyhood bedroom. It had not changed much since those days. Same red-and-blue coverlet on the same twin bed. Same collection of books and odds and ends on the shelf. The only reason they weren't covered in dust was that Rosie was very thorough in her house cleaning. He picked up a baseball and tossed it from hand to hand. Why the hell had someone killed Tomas Nagy? Would he be next?

The door to his room opened, and he turned to glare at his younger brother. Douglas still lived at home too, but he didn't have the excuse of being at sea half the time, he worked in the office for their father. He liked the easy life that staying at Chateau Chapman afforded him.

"Don't you knock?" Hank growled.

"Figured if I did, you'd ignore me."

"I would have, too." Since Douglas didn't seem to be closing the door and leaving, Hank sighed and put down the baseball. "What do you want?"

"Come out with me tonight to the Land and Water Club. There's a dance."

"No." There wasn't anything to even think about. He hated crowds. They made him nervous. He hated silly chattering females primping and fawning over him. He hated making small talk among rich bastards who just wanted to brag about their latest acquisition. He realized most of them thought of him as a rich bastard too, living here on Cliff Road, the son of a ship owner. But he was just a working stiff, out on his boat half the year.

"Yes."

"What the hell? Get out of here." Hank turned his back on his brother. Douglas knew he hated that kind of stuff, why would he pressure him to go? But he didn't hear the door close. He didn't hear footsteps leading away. "Why?" he finally asked.

"Because people are going to be talking about the Nagy murder, and you might find some clues."

He spun on his heel to face his brother. "What do you know about it?"

"Not enough." Douglas remained annoyingly calm. "I know he's dead. I know he was shot. It happened sometime after he unloaded at Martin's, but I don't know why. And I want to. Don't you?"

"Yes, I want to know," he admitted. "Damn it, I want to know."

"Then get dressed and we'll go down. Besides, being in civilized company occasionally can only be good for you."

Hank could hear the smirk in his brother's voice.

"Civilization is overrated."

"Undoubtedly." Douglas was unruffled. "White tie."

"Damn it," he muttered, but he knew Douglas was right and if he wanted the scuttlebutt on what was going on, the club was the place to get it. They might be a bunch of rich bastards, but they were well-informed rich bastards.

"But why do you want to go?" he asked. "What's the real story?"

"I met a girl." Douglas actually blushed while he said it.

Hank sighed. He should have known. Douglas was constantly falling in love on the slimmest of pretense. A girl smiled at him, talked to him, handed him his change in the store. Sometimes a combination of all three.

"And?"

"She works at Christensen's Department Store."

So it was the handing the change that did it this time.

"She said she'd be at the club tonight. It's my chance to get to know her better. But it would look weird if I showed up on my own, as if I really went there to meet her. It's better if I'm there with you, and just happen to run into her."

"Okay, fine." He didn't like many people, but he did like his little brother. He'd do almost anything for him, including getting dressed up and going out when what he'd really like to do is stretch out and take a nap.

So instead of sitting down with two weeks' worth of back issues of newspapers and a cup of coffee, which was his alternate relaxation plan, he found himself shaving and getting ready to go out.

Mother was not happy that he would not be having dinner home.

"We haven't seen you in two weeks, the least you could do is eat with us."

"Why don't you and Father join us at the club?" Though he would really have rather had dinner at home.

"It would be unfair to Rosie, she's made such a lovely dinner."

"I'm sure she has. Why don't you come down after you eat," Douglas said in his smooth and ingratiating way. "You can still be there for the dancing."

Mother waved the suggestion away. "The dancing is for young folks like you. Last time I tried to do those modern dances I threw my back out."

"They are not all the Charleston, Mother." Douglas kissed her on the cheek. "There are still some relatively tame dances."

She smiled at her boys and patted Hank on his freshly shaved cheek. "Maybe you'll meet someone you want to make a life with."

Hank smiled at her but said nothing. He wouldn't inflict himself on some unsuspecting woman. The night terrors he woke up with were not something he wanted to share with anyone. He would never get married, but he let his mother have her dreams.

"It wouldn't kill you to settle down," Douglas said, as if he had read his mind. There was a pleasant breeze off the water as they walked down Cliff Road toward Holton Street and the club.

"It's just not for me." He had never told Douglas of the things he had seen and done in France. Only five years separated them, but they were five years that made the difference between living through hell and keeping your innocence. He wasn't taking that away from Douglas. And he certainly wasn't inflicting his agony on someone else.

He could enjoy a nice dinner at the club, though, and maybe learn something about what happened to Nagy. He'd leave the romance to Douglas.

Chapter Five

Alice clocked out and headed home, walking with Mark, since they lived around the corner from each other. It really was a beautiful spring evening. Hard to believe a murder had taken place in their quiet town only hours ago.

"I know exactly what I'm going to do when I get home," she said as they turned down Pearl Street.

"Let me guess." Mark grinned and gave her a sideways glance. "A long hot bath and a good book."

"You know me too well." She laughed and stopped to smell some wild roses that bloomed near the road.

"It's what you always say you want at the end of the day," he pointed out.

A train chugged into the station, air brakes squealing as it came to a stop across the street from them, effectively halting conversation for a moment. When it had pulled out again, they were nearly to East Park Avenue, Mark's street. "Do you think we'll catch the murderer?" she asked.

"We'll catch him." Mark turned down his street and looked over his shoulder at her as he continued. "There's only so many places to hide."

There's the whole damn ocean. After all, the murder had taken place near the marina. There was no reason to think the murderer had stayed around. But she preferred Mark's way of thinking. She bid him goodbye and walked the one block further to Green Street and her own house.

She stepped onto the porch and felt her shoulders relax. Her house, where she had grown up. Her sanctuary.

"I'm home!" she called to Mama as she stepped over the threshold.

"Did you have a good day at work, dear?" Mama came from the kitchen to greet her. She asked every day. She really didn't want to know the nitty-gritty of police work, whether it was typing reports or telling a widow her husband had been killed. She just wanted to make sure Alice was satisfied with her life. Alice wasn't particularly satisfied with her life, but she didn't want Mama to worry.

"It was fine," she answered, forcing a smile. "I'm going to go draw a bath."

"Already done." Mama touched her cheek. "I know what my girl likes."

"Thank you, sweetheart." Alice hugged her. "You are a gem."

She went up to her room and stripped out of her uniform skirt and jacket and blouse. She pulled off her stockings and wrapped a dressing gown around herself before slipping down the hall to the bathroom with its clawfoot tub full of steamy water. With a sigh she slipped into the tub and let the cares of the world slip away.

Mama had added a bit of lavender oil to the tub and it was heavenly. She closed her eyes, but instead of blissful scenes, she saw the haunted look in the eyes of the young widow. How unfair life was. That woman with her three children, left to the turns of fate. How would she support herself? How lucky they had been when her father died that the police department was willing to give her a job. Too bad they couldn't do that for Irene Nagy.

She opened her eyes. Why couldn't they? If Irene couldn't type, she would teach her. Then there would be someone else to do the typing up of reports and filing, the work she had been stuck with for years. She wanted more. Maybe this way she could get it, plus they'd be helping the family. A family who desperately needed help. Yes. That's what she'd do. She'd suggest it to the chief on Monday.

That settled, she relaxed back into the tub again, until the water started to cool, and her skin had pruned up and she knew it was time to get out. She was just drying off and slipping back into her dressing gown when the bathroom door flew open.

"Marty, really!" she exclaimed, catching her breath. "You shouldn't burst in on people like that."

"Guess where we're going tonight!" Her little sister grinned broadly, showing slightly crooked teeth and deep dimples.

"*We* are going nowhere." Alice slipped past her into the hall. "I've had a long week and I want to relax. At home."

"That's all you ever do," Marty whined. "But that's not what you are doing tonight. Tonight, we are going to the club."

"No, we're not." She headed to her bedroom, but Marty simply followed her and started going through her closet.

"Yes. Trudy and Mark invited us. They'll pick us up in half an hour. That isn't much time to get ready."

Marty took two dresses out of the closet and studied them, then put them back.

"Mark did not have anything to do with this," Alice said, arms crossed. "He would have mentioned it when we walked home from work."

"Okay, so it was my idea, but Trudy agreed. She says they never get a break from the children and she wants a night out. She convinced Mama to babysit her littles." Marty pulled another dress from the closet, an elegant shift dress of pink silk with delicate bead work all along the skirt. "You don't wear this dress nearly enough. It's gorgeous on you. You must wear it tonight."

"Wait." She took the dress from Marty, but she was still sorting through what she'd told her. "Mama agreed to babysit for the Piccolos' children? That means she knew about this when she drew my bath. You are all so sneaky."

"It will be so fun." Marty flashed her that irrepressible smile. "Besides, there's this man I've been flirting with at Christensen's and I told him I'd be there. I don't want to disappoint him. And I certainly don't want to be the third wheel with Trudy and Mark. You simply have to come."

Alice fingered the dress. It would be nice to get dressed up and go out. Marty was right, she didn't do that very often, and there was no reason she shouldn't have some fun. It might be a nice way to get her mind off what had happened today. Her mother was always saying she was too old too soon, not letting herself enjoy her girlhood. She was twenty-seven, well out of girlhood as far as she was concerned, but perhaps too young to put herself out to pasture yet.

"Half an hour you say?" There was no chance to set her hair; at least the bob held its shape fairly well. She'd have time to get dressed and do up her face; that was about it.

"Yes, and I need to go get dressed." Marty started to leave the room and then came back in and gave her an impulsive hug. "Thank you! We'll have fun!" Then she was gone leaving behind her trademark scent of Chanel.

Alice spread the dress out on her chenille bedspread and pulled on a fresh pair of stockings, making sure the seams up the backs of her legs were straight. Then she put on a slip and sat at the dressing table to apply a bit of rouge. Not too much, wouldn't want people getting the wrong idea. Just enough so it looked like she'd been active and energetic all day, not sitting behind a desk in a gloomy office. A little blue shadow on her eyes to make her appear ever so slightly more exotic than she was, and a touch of red on her lips. Then she used her diffuser to spray on a bit of perfume. Like her sister, when she went out, she favored Chanel.

She slipped on the dress and enjoyed the way the skirt swished against her legs. She studied herself in the mirror. Not bad. She actually cleaned up nicely when she wanted to. And lucky for her, the current styles really favored the tall angular woman. She was made for this era, though Marty was much more a flapper than she'd ever be.

She pulled her black pumps out of her closet. Her dancing shoes. Maybe she'd get a chance to dance tonight. To her surprise she was looking forward to going out.

A commotion of children's voices and running feet from downstairs indicated that the Piccolos had arrived. Alice hurried down the steps to meet her best friend. She and Trudy were almost closer than sisters and had been ever since they both stepped foot in the sturdy brick building in the middle of School Street to start their education all those years ago. Trudy, short and round, couldn't pull off the popular flapper look as well as some other people, but it didn't matter. Her cheerful smile made her look good in whatever she wore.

"You are a vision!" Trudy extended her hands to Alice and they air-kissed.

"Is this the buttoned-up woman I saw at the office all day?" Mark gave her a wink.

He cleaned up nicely too, looking quite dapper in his tuxedo, complete with white tie and tails.

Trudy turned her attention to their three children, who were still dashing about the house like miniature whirlwinds. "Now Paul, Dotty, Jack, I want you to behave yourself for Mama Grady. You understand?"

"Yes, Mama. We'll be good," six-year-old Paul answered.

Alice's heart squeezed a little as she thought of the three little Nagy children, now without a father. Life could be so unfair.

With hugs all around they finally managed to get out the door. Mark's Model T was parked out front on Green Street, and he opened the door and guided the sisters into the back seat. Then he helped Trudy to the front passenger seat before he gave the engine a crank, and they were on their way.

It was not a long trip over the Causeway and into Sewaren where the Land and Water Club was. Alice had walked the mile or so plenty of times, but it was nice to travel in style in Mark's car. Maybe someday she'd get a car of her own. She had some money saved up. She could drive her mother and sister into Perth Amboy for shopping or even into Newark. More convenient than taking the train or bus. She could get Mark to teach her to drive. It would be fun.

They got out of the car at the Land and Water Club. The low rambling building on the water didn't look like much from the outside. It mainly functioned as a club house during yacht races, but their dances were considered local high society.

There was a fresh breeze blowing in off the Arthur Kill and Alice pulled her wrap a little tighter around her shoulders. Spring was such an iffy time for weather. Not that she preferred the cold and snow of winter or the sweltering humidity of summer.

Inside they checked their wraps and were led to a table by the maitre d'. An orchestra was already playing light dinner music.

The special for the evening was fresh scallops, and once again she thought of poor Tomas Nagy unloading his boat at the fishery and then being gunned down for reasons unknown. It almost made her not want the scallops. But what good that would do anyone, she didn't know. Besides it was a Friday, and as a Catholic, steak was not an option. There of course was no wine, but the club did offer a variety of sparkling fruit juices to make up for it.

Marty, sitting next to her at the table, was swiveling her head this way and that, even as their meal was set in front of them.

"Who on earth are you looking for?" Trudy finally

asked, unable to keep a hint of laughter out of her voice.

"She met a man at Christensen's," Alice said with an indulgent smile toward her little sister. "She's hoping he'll be here."

"Oh, he'll be here." Marty picked up her knife and fork. "I'm sure of it."

"Well, eat your food." Alice stepped into big-sister mode. "That way you'll be all ready to dance when he shows up."

A few minutes later, Marty exclaimed, "Oh! There he is! I knew he'd come." And with that she studiously set to work on her food, not paying any attention at all to the man who had just entered the room.

Alice looked up to see who had Marty in such a tizzy. Two men were standing by the door. They were of similar build and coloring, possibly brothers, and they both looked smashing in white tie. She could understand why the man had turned Marty's head. She wouldn't mind spending an evening with either one of them.

"Which one?" Trudy whispered across the table.

Marty gave a quick glance and said, "The one on the right."

He was slim and handsome and had a pleasant open face. The other, a bit older, looked slightly more glowering. Alice stared. She knew him. The one on the left. It was Hank. The man who had come to the Nagys' house while she was there. Well, she really didn't want to get involved in a conversation with him. Especially not here, where she had come to relax and get her mind off her day. She turned her attention back to her food.

"Who is that he's with?" Trudy asked.

"I have no idea," Marty said, still not looking up, as if she didn't want to catch the man's eyes. Alice couldn't figure her out. She spent all that time looking for him, but when he got here, she pretended not to notice.

The dishes were cleared away, and the music jumped up a notch to more danceable tunes. Mark stood up and held his hand out to his wife. "You dragged me out here, so we might as well dance." His words weren't terribly gracious, but there was a glimmer in his eye and Trudy took his hand and they joined other couples on the dance floor.

A waiter came around with coffee and Alice gratefully accepted some. She was eager to dance, and a quick look around the room showed several likely partners. There was Mark, of course, who could always be counted on to give her a turn, and at the next table over, Dexter Smith was deep in conversation with Elliot Walton. Both of them were old classmates, who, once they realized dance music was playing, were sure to ask her. In the meantime, she was content to sit and watch.

Next to her, Marty was tapping her feet in time to the music, her whole body nearly taut with tension as she waited for her man to notice her and ask her to dance. She looked everywhere but in the direction of the table where the two men sat. Alice surreptitiously glanced over from time to time. She saw the man notice them, put down his napkin and stand up.

"I think he's coming," she whispered to Marty.

Marty's eyes flashed, and a grin flitted across her face. "Hush. Don't let them know we were watching."

Marty would make a good spy. Alice would have sworn she'd never glanced in the direction of the two men once.

Would Hank come to the table with his friend? What would she say to him if he did? Should she bring up Nagy first, or wait until he did? She wouldn't mind engaging in simple small talk about the weather, but it would seem odd to ignore the obvious elephant in the room.

But when she looked up, it was only one man standing by their table, Marty's man. Hank was still seated, staring into his cup of coffee. She felt a little jolt of regret but then reminded herself that she didn't particularly want to talk to him anyway.

The man in front of them bowed graciously. "Miss Grady, is it not? Douglas Chapman at your service. I believe we've encountered each other once or twice around town."

Alice wondered how long the two of them had been building up their flirtatious relationship.

Marty for her part, was playing it coy.

"Oh, yes! I do recall. How lovely to see you here tonight. The orchestra is simply divine, don't you agree?"

"Quite." He held one hand out to her. "Would you care to dance?"

Marty didn't even bother to say yes. In a flash she was out of her seat and the two were on the dance floor. They looked good together. Almost like a high society couple. She could picture their likeness in the society pages, that is if anyone from the society pages ever bothered to come to the Land and Water Club to take pictures, which they didn't. You'd have to go to Newark for that.

Alice nursed her cup of coffee, accepting a refill

when the waiter came around, enjoying the music and the atmosphere and not really minding that she wasn't home in her dressing gown, curled up on the sofa, reading.

She glanced back at the table where Marty's Douglas had been eating. The man she knew as Hank still sat there, watching her. Heat flooded to her cheeks, and she concentrated on the dance floor once again, trying to maintain an attitude of complete nonchalance. She was as bad as Marty, playing coy, except she really didn't care if he came over to her table or not.

When, moments later, he was standing beside her, her heart gave a little pitter-pat. Maybe she wasn't quite as nonchalant about this as she wanted to be.

"I'm afraid we've not been introduced," the man said, his manner impeccable. Could he really have been the gruff fisherman she had seen earlier? She was usually pretty good at recognizing people, but she could be wrong. It happened. "I'm Henry Chapman." He bowed formally.

"Alice Grady."

"I believe my brother has absconded with your companion for the evening."

"My sister." She waved to a chair, inviting him to sit. He did.

"I know you." His eyes lit up with confused recognition, and she knew he was unable to place her.

She grinned despite herself. She had been right.

"I believe we met this afternoon at the Nagys' house."

His face cleared as he remembered. "Yes. Of course. You look different, dressed."

He had the decency to blush as he realized what he

had said.

"So do you." She raised her coffee cup in a mock toast.

"Touché." He held up Marty's empty cup to return the salute.

"The children called you Uncle Hank." He'd introduced himself as Henry, and maybe that name fit the tuxedo-wearing man in front of her, but Hank was definitely a more appropriate moniker for the fisherman she saw this afternoon. Who was he really? Society man or fisherman? If she had to guess, based on the way he tugged at his collar, she'd say fisherman.

"An honorary title only." A shadow crossed his face and his eyes glistened. She watched as he squared his jaw and took a steadying breath. "Damn shame about Tomas." The tip of his ears turned pink and he added quickly, "Pardon my language, ma'am."

Her eyebrows shot up. Suddenly even the pink dress felt dowdy. "Ma'am? You make me feel old enough to be your mother."

"My apologies," he muttered, dropping his gaze.

"Besides, I'm a police officer. I've heard far worse."

He looked at her again and she liked the warmth she saw in his eyes.

"I suppose that's true, but I've just spent two weeks on my boat with nothing but men. I may be a little rough around the edges tonight."

"I won't be offended," she promised him. "And it *is* a damn shame about Mr. Nagy. Those poor children. I can't get them out of my mind."

"She might go back to her family in Hungary." Hank tapped his fingers on the white tablecloth. "But I don't know if she could scrape together the fare. She'd be better off staying here, if you ask me."

"I was thinking about seeing if the department would hire her as a typist. Do you know if she types?"

"I have no idea, but I'm sure she could learn." He fiddled with a butter knife on the table, as if not sure what else to do with his hands. "That would be very kind of you."

She didn't say anything; the conversation felt impossibly awkward. Maybe she should excuse herself and get up to go to the powder room, give him an easy out.

He tugged once again at his collar as if it were too tight as one song ended and another, a Charleston, began.

"Would you like to dance?"

Her smile as she answered was completely genuine. "I'd love to."

Chapter Six

He wasn't even sure why he'd asked her to dance. He hadn't been planning on it. He'd been quite content to sit and listen to the music. Let Douglas dance and flirt. But something about that young lady, sitting at the table by herself, kept drawing his eye. She was tall and lean, with glossy hair and a fresh face, and she kept tapping her feet to the music, as if maybe she'd like to dance, if someone would bother to ask her.

And then he found himself walking to the table and introducing himself. He certainly wouldn't have gone up to her if he'd known she was the fuzz. But yet instead of going away he asked her to dance. So here he was, dead tired and unfortunately sober, dancing the Charleston with a lady cop. Who would have thought?

He had been right about her being tall. She could nearly look him in the eye. And she was angular. But it worked for her. He'd always thought he rather preferred curvy girls, but maybe he hadn't really given the matter enough thought. The current fashions certainly worked on her. She had a body made for the straight slim dresses women were wearing these days. And she was a surprisingly good dancer. When he had seen her at Nagy's house, he'd taken her for an uptight, dried-up specimen of a woman. From her stiff attitude in her starched uniform he never would have expected this graceful, fun-loving individual. Maybe he was reading too much into it. One really couldn't do the Charleston properly and not appear to be having fun. But then, someone who was averse to fun would probably not have agreed to dance the Charleston with him.

The dance ended, and the orchestra segued into a foxtrot, and neither of them made any move to return to their seats. They danced the foxtrot and a tango and finally a waltz, never speaking, just enjoying the music and the activity. That's all it was, on his side anyway. He had no intention of getting romantically involved, even short term, with anyone. He was damaged goods. He didn't need to hurt someone else. But a night of dancing, there was no harm in that.

Finally, the orchestra announced they were taking a break and that dessert would be served momentarily. "Shall we?" Hank asked, putting his hand loosely on her elbow to guide her. It was the first thing he'd said to her since asking her to dance.

He had every intention of returning her to her table, but his brother had absconded with her seat, and gave him a glance which Hank interpreted to mean, "Take her someplace else, I'm making progress."

"Perhaps my table, if you don't mind having dessert with me instead of your friends."

"That's fine," Alice answered. "He's your brother you say? I think Marty is rather falling for him."

"Marty?" He held out the chair for her and she seated herself.

"Martha." She glanced over at her former table. "I must say, I'll be glad when she finally settles down. It will be a load off my mind, and my mother's."

"No father?" It was a terribly forward question, and he wasn't even sure why he asked it. Had he been at a speakeasy and drinking smuggled booze then there would have been an excuse. Can you get drunk dancing?

"He passed away a number of years ago. That's why I work for the police department. His fellow officers felt sorry for us and wanted to help us out."

So, that explained a few things. "And that's why you thought of offering Irene Nagy a job there."

"I don't know if they'll agree," she said with a small shrug of her shoulders, "but the least I can do is ask." A waiter came and poured them fresh coffee and she took a sip. "Did you know Tomas Nagy long?"

He picked up his coffee cup as well. "He moved here about three years ago with his family. He had sold everything he had in Hungary and sunk the money into the *Katinka*. Irene wasn't happy. She would have preferred he crewed out for someone else and bought their house outright, instead of renting, and buying the boat."

Alice winced, and he knew she appreciated the problem that Irene now faced. A boat that she couldn't run and no way to pay the rent.

"Anyway, I helped him get set up. Gave him tips on the best places to fish."

Alice held up a hand to stop him, a questioning look in her eyes. "Hungary is a landlocked country, isn't it? How is it he decided to be a fisherman?"

Hank smiled to himself, remembering asking that same question. Of course, it wasn't fish Tomas had been after, but a share in the smuggling trade. He'd engaged in smuggling during and after the war, and knew his best way in to the money being made in smuggling in America was to have a boat, and an acceptable occupation to go along with it. Tomas was not a stupid man. Which, of course, led Hank back to the question foremost in his mind all afternoon. Who had killed Tomas Nagy, and why?

Of course, he couldn't tell Alice Grady that Tomas had been a smuggler. She might dance a mean tango, but she was still a cop, and he wasn't a fool.

"He was a farmer back in Hungary. I told him there was plenty of land to farm here, but he wanted to do something different. I took him out a few times, showed him the ropes. He was a quick learner. The fact that he hadn't done it before certainly didn't mean he couldn't do it going forward. He was successful, too. In fact, just today, he brought in half a ton more scallops than I did."

"So you could say there was some professional jealousy?"

He shot a dagger-sharp glance at her. What was she playing at? He had thought she was off duty, but it sounded like she was trying to get him to incriminate himself in Tomas's death.

The waiter came around with the dessert just then and put a piece of decadent-looking chocolate cake in front of him. The interruption was enough to let him rein in his anger before he answered her.

"No jealousy. There's plenty of fish for everyone. I'm happy to see my friends succeed."

The hardness in his tone must have registered with her.

"I apologize," she said, looking truly embarrassed. "I didn't mean anything by it. I am not interrogating you. Honest. It's not even my case."

"Though it would be a feather in your cap if you

could solve it," Hank said, dipping his fork into his cake.

"It would," she agreed with amazing candor.

At least she was honest.

"Then I wish you luck. Because I want to know who killed my friend."

"I'll do my best."

"And…" He glanced at her over his coffee cup. "How good is your best?"

She bristled, sitting up a bit straighter and frowning at him. "Damn good, if anyone would give me a chance."

"Are they going to give you a chance on this?"

"No," she said abruptly. "It will probably go to the chief and Mark." She nodded her head toward the table she'd been sitting at before. Another couple sat there with Douglas and Marty. He was guessing the man was Mark.

"So cops all hang out together after hours?"

She gave another slight shrug. "Why not? We're friends. But normally, no, I wouldn't hang out with other cops after hours. Mark, on the other hand, I've known all my life, and he married my best friend."

"And you're not married." It wasn't really a question. Clearly, she wouldn't be sitting here with him if she were.

"Neither are you," she responded.

"How do you know?"

She took his question seriously.

"No wedding ring, to start with. Now, that isn't conclusive, because many men don't wear rings. But if you were married, you would have brought your wife with you when you went to see Mrs. Nagy." She held up a hand to forestall interruption. "And if she couldn't come with you, you would have mentioned her. You would have said something like, 'Myrtle sends her best and she'll be by later with pie.'"

Despite himself he laughed. "Myrtle? You think I'm married to someone named Myrtle?"

"No, that's exactly my point. I think you're not married."

He conceded defeat.

"No, I'm not married, and my mother despairs of me ever settling down. And yours?"

"Oh, I think she's given up on me. She's resigned to me being an old maid. She's just hoping that Marty won't meet a similar fate."

"But you can't be that old. What are you? Twenty-three, twenty-four?" He knew he was bad at guessing ages, he also suspected he was low-balling it a little.

"Twenty-seven," she admitted. Maybe that was edging into old maid territory, but she was still younger than him, and an attractive-looking woman.

"You don't want to get married?"

"Let's just say the opportunity hasn't presented itself." She dug into her cake with a vengeance, but he still noticed the heightened color of her cheeks.

"I'm sorry." He played with the cake crumbs on his plate. "I'm not sure what got into me. I'm not usually so rude. I'm usually quite cultured and refined."

She looked up at him, studying him. "Cultured and refined. Not often the words I think of when thinking of fishermen."

"And why not?" He looked into her eyes and she blushed again.

"I suppose I think rugged and hardworking, and

perhaps a bit rough around the edges. You clean up nicely, though." She looked at her cake. "Do you think they spiked this cake with rum or something? I'm really not behaving at all like myself."

"I was wondering the same thing." It was like her very presence was intoxicating. He didn't like it. He liked to maintain a proper distance from anyone but a select few people. He didn't want anyone to get too close to him, but what was he doing here, opening up to her and asking her questions that encouraged her to open up to him? This was not the cold and aloof person he preferred to be.

The orchestra started again, and with relief they took to the dance floor. At least dancing they would not be tempted to delve into personal matters. All he wanted from tonight was a little fun. He didn't want to know anything about her, yet he'd asked her leading questions and she'd answered. Maybe there really was something in that cake.

Later, when he got back to the table, there was a folded note where he'd been sitting. He took it and opened it, all too aware that Alice's eyes were on him. The note was simple and direct. "Meet me. Boynton Beach. Midnight." And it was signed "Sal." He didn't know who Sal was, but if he had to guess, he'd say that was shorthand for Vincent Salerno. He checked his watch. Half-past eleven. He had time to figure out what to do.

He shoved the paper into his pocket.

"What's that?" Alice asked.

"Nothing." Should he say something? Would it help her catch Tomas' killer? He didn't see how. There wasn't much to go on in the note, and he didn't want her finding out some of the things he was involved in. Never good to have the cops looking too closely into his activities.

The night was winding down, and his brother came over and told him he was going to be escorting Marty home. Douglas looked at him, as if expecting him to make the same offer to Alice, but he couldn't do that. He apparently had an appointment with a guy named Sal.

"It was delightful dancing with you, Miss Grady." He made a formal and rather stiff bow, before turning her back over to her friends. Then with a nod to the group he left the club.

Once outside he lit up a cigarette and walked toward the water before his brother and the others came out. He didn't want to talk to them right now. He didn't need any of them hanging around when he met with whoever had left him the note. Douglas had no idea of the side business he was involved in, and he wanted to keep it that way. Alice and that Mark fellow were cops. He certainly didn't need them nosing around.

A pleasant breeze came off the water, bringing with it the scent of salt and seaweed and fish. He inhaled deeply, letting the tobacco scent of his cigarette mix with the intoxicating smell of the sea. He needed to be back out at sea. How quickly could they get the *Mary B* outfitted for another run? The steps needed to be painted. There had been a ping in the engine he wanted to investigate. And then there was the matter of the crew. They deserved a few days at home before going out again. He sighed. As much as he'd like to simply hop in the *Mary B* tonight and head back out, that wasn't happening.

Closer to the water, the former Boynton Beach resort was closed and fenced off. He'd spent many happy hours there as a kid, riding the Ferris wheel and the bamboo slide. The property had been bought by an oil company. Progress, he supposed. He tossed the stub of his cigarette to the dirt and ground it out with the toe of his shoe. He wasn't sure progress was always all it was made out to be.

"What you doing in that frog suit?"

The voice, coming out of the night, startled him, and he jumped, his muscles tense, his nerves taut. But it only took a second to register that it was Smitty, his first mate. He spotted him then, walking toward him, coming from the water.

"Why aren't you at home with the wife?" he asked in turn.

"The kids were screaming. I needed some air."

In the light of the moon, he could see that Smitty looked much as he had when he'd last seen him this afternoon. Rough work pants, grimy shirt, stained boots. With Hank in his tuxedo, the two made quite the odd couple as they stood side by side, watching the ripples in the water.

"Word on the street is that Nagy got involved with some guy named Salerno," Smitty said, keeping his voice low.

His gut twisted at the name. That was what Jiggy had said. Was that the person who was going to be meeting him in a few minutes? What did he want with him? What had his connection to Tomas been?

"What's his deal? Any idea?"

"They say he's a pirate."

Pirates were a common enough threat for

smugglers. The *Mary B* had outrun them any number of times. The smugglers took the risk, offloaded the liquor out on rum row, and then had it stolen before they could make the sale to their distributor. But it was always at sea, never on land. If this guy, Salerno, was tracking down smugglers on land, then the game had changed. He didn't like it one bit.

At sea you could at least tell who was around, who was approaching you. How could you protect yourself in town, when anyone could be the enemy?

He stuck his hand in his pocket for his cigarettes and felt the note.

He supposed he was about to find out what direction this danger was coming from. He pulled the note out and showed it to Smitty.

"You think it is Salerno?" he asked after reading it.

"Don't you?"

"Probably." He handed the note back and scuffed his boot in the gravel. "Want me to hang around?"

It was tempting. He'd have backup if this guy was going to try something. He shook his head.

"Go home to the family. If I don't show up at the *Mary B* tomorrow, go to the cops, tell them to look into this Salerno guy. Chances are he isn't going to do anything tonight."

"If you're sure."

He took a deep breath. Was he sure? Yes. He had nothing to lose. He'd been dead inside since the war.

"Go home. Now, before he gets here."

Smitty left, but reluctantly, constantly looking back to see if he would change his mind. Hank ignored him, and lit another cigarette, pretending he was casually looking out at the water, while all his senses were on high alert, waiting for danger.

It reminded him of being on guard duty in the trenches. Standing for hours with your head exposed, staring into the darkness, not sure if what you saw was the breeze moving a tree branch or someone coming to kill you, not wanting to sound an alarm for a tree but not wanting to let your buddies be ambushed. Every sound had the potential to be an enemy approaching. Every movement could mean you were about to get blown to bits.

At the crunch of footsteps in the gravel behind him, he instinctively reached for the rifle he hadn't carried since he'd left France.

"Chapman?"

His heart beat a tight staccato, and he turned to see a rather ordinary man, in white tie, approaching him in the dark.

He nodded, not trusting his voice.

The man held out his hand. "Vince Salerno."

By instinct Hank took the hand. "Hank Chapman."

"Thank you for meeting me. I realize my method of getting in touch with you was a bit unorthodox, but it was necessary."

"Why?"

"In our business we deal with an unsavory element. Often it's best to keep a low profile."

He didn't know what this man thought he knew, but he planned on revealing nothing.

"You're a scallop fisherman as well, then?" he asked, feigning ignorance.

"Not exactly."

He didn't like the rather oily tone in the man's voice.

"Listen, bud, I'm a fisherman. That's my only business. If that's not what you want to talk about, then I think we're done here." He turned to go.

"I thought you might want to talk about your friend, Nagy," Salerno said behind him.

Hank froze. He couldn't pretend he didn't want details there.

"You know who shot him?" He turned back to face the man, who he realized he'd seen at the club on multiple occasions without ever knowing his name.

"No idea, but I think I know why."

Despite himself, he stepped closer to the man. "Why?"

"Let's just say it wasn't over scallops."

"What kind of business did you have with him?" Hank didn't want to play games, he wanted answers. If this man was a pirate, he wanted to know it. Though he supposed it wasn't the sort of thing someone would come out and admit.

"He had something I wanted."

Salerno was annoyingly circumspect. Hank preferred to deal with straight shooters. He liked when someone laid all their cards on the table, but he could play it close too. He was no fool.

"And it wasn't scallops?" If it wasn't scallops, it was hams. He knew Salerno meant that, but he wouldn't admit it. Not straight out. He didn't know Salerno, and in this business, it wasn't safe to trust people you didn't know. He turned back to face the water, not wanting to give the stranger a chance to read his expression. The water lapped at the shore, speaking to him, enticing him back out to sea.

"You're catching on." The man sounded like an

approving schoolteacher. Hank hated him more with each passing moment.

"Did you get what you wanted?" He spit the words out between gritted teeth.

"I did," the man said with alarming calm.

"And Tomas got shot." He turned again, to face Salerno. Was he looking at the face of the man who shot his friend?

"Apparently I wasn't the only person who wanted what he had."

"Let's cut the games. What do you want with me?" he asked, lighting another cigarette out of habit, and as a way to calm his jangled nerves.

"You also have something I want." Salerno's voice rang out in the clear night air.

"Unless you want scallops, I can't help you." He turned to leave once more. He would have no dealings with pirates.

"I can give you a better deal than Jiggy," the man said to his retreating back. "Think about it."

He didn't answer, just stalked off into the darkness. But he definitely had a lot to think about.

Chapter Seven

Alice replayed the evening at the club in her mind as she got ready for the day. She pulled a light green day dress out of the closet and slipped it on. Dancing with Hank Chapman had been almost like being a princess at a ball. She'd not had that much fun at the club in who knew how long. Years probably. Occasionally she would dance with a man she didn't know, but often it was only for one dance, and there was no chemistry.

This had felt different. Dancing with Hank had been effortless and enchanting. They'd moved well together, as if they'd practiced dancing together for years. Of course, like in all good fairy stories, this one had an end. The clock had struck the proverbial midnight, and he had hightailed it out of the club with the barest of goodbyes.

So there was no future there. That wasn't a problem. She hadn't been looking for one. She'd take what came her way. And in this case, it was a pleasant evening dancing with a handsome man.

She ran the brush through her hair and studied the result in the mirror. Maybe she didn't have to be an old maid. She wasn't that old. She wouldn't mind having someone besides Mama and Marty to come home to. Hank was certainly easy on the eyes. Rugged and handsome yet refined as well. She shook her head. No, there was no future with him, that was certain. But maybe it wouldn't hurt to keep her eyes open to other possibilities.

She put the brush down with resolve.

No. She was too set in her ways. It was no use getting romantic notions in her head. The best she could do was make sure Marty was happily settled. That would put her mother's mind at ease. Besides she was too busy at work to think about romance.

In the back of her mind a thought formed that many of her fellow officers were married, so maybe working and romance didn't need to be mutually exclusive, but she pushed it away. Her life was fine the way it was.

Downstairs, coffee was percolating on the stove and Mama was mixing up some pancake batter. Alice took the bowl from her. "I'll do that, Mama. Put your feet up, have a cup of coffee."

"Don't mind if I do." Mama poured herself a cup from the percolator and poured one for Alice as well, adding a touch of cream and a spoonful of sugar to both. "So tell me about last night. Did Marty meet the man she was so keen to see again?"

"She did. His name is Douglas Chapman. I didn't get a chance to talk to him, but she spent the evening dancing with him. And he escorted her home." Perhaps Marty would prefer to keep that part from their mother, but Alice wasn't going to be a party to deceptions.

"I thought I heard you come home at different times." Her mother slipped her feet out of her shoes and put her feet up on the chair opposite her. "Does he seem like a decent sort?"

"Hard to tell. He certainly looks dapper in white

tie. I can tell you that much."

"A looker, huh?"

"Would you expect Marty to go for anything less?"

"No." Mama sighed. "And that's why I worry. I don't want her head turned by a pretty face. I want her to find happiness with a whole person."

Alice flicked a couple of drops of water in the skillet to see if it was hot. The water sizzled away so she spooned some pancake mix in. "Marty's got a good head on her shoulders."

"That's right, I do." Marty breezed into the kitchen, looking as fresh and bright as the spring morning outside. "Why are we discussing my head? Wait!" She headed straight for the percolator. "Let me guess. You gossiping hens are talking about the man I danced with last night."

There was no censure in her voice. Marty was used to being discussed and never appeared to take any offense at it. She was secure in the position of the well-loved, nearly spoiled, youngest child. Marty dropped two lumps of sugar in her coffee and gave Mama a kiss on the cheek. "You don't need Alice to tell you about Douglas. I can tell you everything you need to know. Of course, then Alice will have to tell you about the handsome man she spent the night dancing with."

Alice's cheeks flushed as she checked the pancakes. The tops were dimpled, and she could see the edges starting to darken.

"You first," she said and flipped the pancakes over.

"I rather want to hear about your evening," Mama said, humor in her tone. "I often hear about Marty's romantic conquests, not so much about yours."

"There was no romantic conquest," Alice insisted.

"I'll tell you everything, after Marty tells us about Douglas. After all, you notice, Douglas brought her home. I came home with Mark and Trudy."

Marty apparently had no problem with that arrangement. She sat at the table, her face aglow. "Well, his name is Douglas Chapman. He's twenty-five and his father owns a fleet of fishing boats. They live on Cliff Road out near Boynton Beach. He went to Rutgers and thought about training as a lawyer, but right now he's running the business for his father, who is semi-retired. Soon his father will retire completely, and he'll be in charge."

"Well, that's his resume laid out quite nicely," Mama said, smiling at her over the top of her coffee cup. "Now tell us about the man."

Alice chuckled to herself as she dished up the first batch of pancakes and put the platter on the table. "Get plates and the syrup, won't you, Marty?"

Marty did as she was told, and Alice poured more batter into the pan.

"He's charming." Marty picked up her narrative. "And dashing and handsome and a fantastic dancer. He walked me home, and the distance has never gone so quickly. I could have walked a million miles with him, just talking, my hand in his."

Alice rolled her eyes. Marty, ever the romantic.

"He's taking me boating this afternoon and then out for dinner tonight."

"He moves fast," Mama commented, and Alice thought she detected a hint of disapproval in her tone.

"Don't worry, Mama. He's a perfect gentleman." Marty poured a generous helping of syrup over her pancakes. "I'll have him come in and meet you before we go out. Don't worry. I'm not trying to slide anything past you." Alice set the next batch of pancakes on the table and poured in more batter.

"Sit and eat," Mama said to her. "And tell us about your dancing partner."

Alice sat and put a couple of pancakes on her plate. "I don't know nearly as much about him as Marty knows about Douglas, and I certainly do not have plans with him for today."

"Don't tell us what you don't know or what you're not doing," Marty scolded. "Tell us about last night."

Alice felt her cheeks flush again at the unexpected attention. She didn't mind at all having a special evening to talk about. "He's actually Douglas's brother. His name is Henry, but he goes by Hank. I don't know how old he is, we didn't get that deep in our conversation." Though, she did remember telling him she was twenty-seven. Why on earth had she volunteered that information? And why hadn't she insisted he share in return? Oh, well, live and learn. "He's a fisherman. I suppose he works for his father." Some of this she knew from the afternoon, not from any conversation they'd had last night. "He's a good dancer."

And that was pretty much all she could say about that. She hopped up to flip the pancakes before they burned.

"That's it?" Marty and Mama asked at the same time.

"That's it," she insisted. No point in telling them about her fairy tale romance fantasies. Especially when they were nothing but fantasies. "He was fun to dance with, but it's not the start of a big romance, it was just a fun evening." She sat back down, and Mama patted her hand.

"Nothing wrong with a fun evening now and then."

Alice thought so too. She picked up her coffee and thought of those clear blue eyes. She wondered if she'd ever have the chance to gaze in them again. Not that it mattered, but she wouldn't mind.

"It's a beautiful day for gardening," Mama said as Alice and Marty cleaned up the kitchen. She was right, the sky was clear and blue, there was a light breeze, the perennials in the garden were bursting into leaf, and the vegetable seedlings on the back porch were big enough to transplant.

"I can't help, Mama," Marty said. "I have to get ready for my date."

"I think you can spend some time helping us. I've been boating in my day, and I found it doesn't take that long to dress for such an activity."

Marty pouted but got over it quickly, and soon the three of them were out back, straw hats shading their faces from the sun, gardening gloves protecting their hands. Alice hoed the weeds out of the vegetable garden, which they had turned over the week before. Marty pulled up the weeds that were making themselves known in the flower bed. Mama supervised and planned where the various vegetables would be planted.

They weren't even half done when the sun shone bright overhead and Mama declared it was time to take a break. "You two go sit on the front porch in the shade and I'll bring you some lemonade. Then we'll worry about lunch."

Alice wasn't about to turn down that offer. She

shucked her gloves and hat and stamped her feet to loosen any dirt clinging to the soles before heading to the front porch. She settled gratefully into the porch swing and let the cool breeze wash over her.

"Hey!" Marty said, sitting beside her. "Isn't that the fellow you were dancing with last night?"

Alice opened her eyes and saw Hank Chapman escorting Irene Nagy up the steps to the funeral home across the street. A strange pang, one she refused to acknowledge as jealousy, stabbed her heart. She had no claim on him. None at all. He'd promised to bring the widow to the funeral home to help her make arrangements. That was exactly what he was doing. So why did she feel bereft as she watched him guide Mrs. Nagy with a gentle touch to the elbow? Maybe it was because she could remember his touch as they danced.

Being jealous of someone who was making arrangements to bury her husband was a ludicrous reaction.

"Is it him?" Marty asked again.

"It is," Alice answered as Mama brought out a tray with three tall glasses of lemonade, their sides already beading with condensation.

"What's he doing going into Greiner's? Who's the lady he's with?" Marty wasn't going to stop asking questions until she got answers.

They each took their lemonade and Mama settled into her rocking chair. "Who is going into Greiner's?"

"The man Alice was dancing with last night," Marty answered. "Is he married? Is that his wife?"

Oh, for goodness' sake.

"It's not his wife. That's Irene Nagy. Her husband was killed yesterday, if you must know, and Hank knew him, so he volunteered to take her to the funeral home this morning. I had offered, but she preferred to go with a friend."

"You seem to know a whole lot more about him than you told us at breakfast," Marty said, sounding distinctly disapproving.

Alice sighed. "I met him at the Nagys' house yesterday, when I went there to tell her that her husband had died."

"Wait," Mama said, suddenly realizing what they were saying. "Tomas Nagy died? What happened?"

"You know him?"

"I made some dresses for his wife a while back. He came by to pay me one afternoon. He was a charming fellow. Very European." Mama set her glass down on a small iron table. "So tell me what happened to him."

"He was shot. It looks like murder. Mark is investigating."

"How horrible!" Mama's reaction was genuine. "That poor woman. And I seem to remember her mentioning children."

"Three small ones, yes."

"We'll have to do something for them. I can bake her a casserole or a cake. Maybe a cake is better. Children like cake, and they need to eat and keep up their energy in the days ahead."

"So your man is gentle and compassionate as well as a looker and a good dancer." Marty gave her a significant look.

"He's helping a friend," Alice said. "And he's not my man. He just didn't have anyone else to dance with last night."

Marty nodded as if she didn't quite believe her. In

the meantime, Mama was lost in thoughts of what foods she could prepare for the poor Nagy family.

They'd cleaned themselves of garden grime and sweat and had a refreshing lunch, when Douglas Chapman came by to pick up Marty for their outing.

He bowed slightly to Mama. "A pleasure to meet you, Mrs. Grady. To let you know our plans, so you don't worry, I have a small runabout that I keep at the marina near Boynton Beach. I plan to take Martha up toward the city, perhaps around the Statue of Liberty. We won't be going out in the open ocean." He seemed to notice Alice, standing in the background, for the first time. "Would you like to come as well?"

Marty shot her a panicked look, and whereas a day out on the water would be lovely, Alice was certainly not going to horn in on her sister's romantic outing.

"I couldn't possibly," she answered. "Though it is very kind of you to ask."

After a few more pleasantries, the young couple were on their way. "I think I'll start on that cake for the Nagys," Mama said. "Why don't you go over and visit with Trudy?"

"Trying to get me out from underfoot?" Alice grinned at her.

"Trying to make sure you enjoy life," Mama answered. Alice wrinkled her nose at her. She enjoyed life. She enjoyed sitting on the swing on the front porch with a glass of lemonade and a good book. She enjoyed relaxing with a piece of needlework or a crossword puzzle. They might not be vigorous enjoyments, but they gave her pleasure.

Still, no one had to tell her twice to take the afternoon off and relax. She walked through her garden gate, into Trudy's backyard. Having them live behind her was a huge convenience when they wanted to spend time together. She opened the back door without bothering to knock.

"Hello," she called out as she entered the kitchen.

Five-year-old Dorothy nearly collided with her as she ran through the kitchen. "Aunt Alice! Aunt Alice! Will you make me more paper dolls?"

"Sure sweetie. Where's Mama?"

"Trying to get John to use the potty. He doesn't like it."

The ongoing battle to get John toilet-trained. Alice knew it was driving Trudy to distraction, especially since her older two seemed to practically train overnight. Dorothy knew how to take advantage of a good thing, though, and brought the Sears catalog over to Alice so she could cut it up to make dolls.

"Oh, I don't know if we should use this one. It just came!" Alice said, taking the glossy magazine from the little girl. She looked wistfully at the cover picture of a mother and daughter admiring a dress as they took it out of a box. Pleasant domestic scenes usually didn't stir a reaction in her. Why today?

"Papa says to. He told me to cut it up so Mama couldn't buy anything from it."

She was definitely not getting in the middle of that.

"I have an idea. Why don't we make our own clothes for some dolls? Get your crayons."

So while she waited for Trudy to come back downstairs, Alice drew outlines of dresses for Dorothy to color in.

"Look, this one is pink, like the dress you wore last night. You were pretty last night." Dorothy said with a happy sigh.

"Thank you. You were looking quite fetching yourself."

Dorothy laughed. "I was wearing play clothes. You can't look pretty in play clothes."

"Who says?"

Little John ran into the kitchen just then, his shirt tails flapping against his bare bottom.

"John!" Trudy called as she clattered down the stairs. "Where did you get to? You forgot your pants!"

"He's in here!" Alice answered.

"Oh, Alice! I didn't know you were here. I was…"

"I know, Dorothy told me."

"Did you go, Johnny?" Dorothy was asking in her big-sister sing-song voice. "Did you go on the potty?"

"Big plop!" he said with satisfaction.

Trudy nabbed him and wrestled him into underwear and pants. "Welcome to my life," she said. "I know what it is, you come over here whenever you start thinking you are missing out on something by not having a family, and a few minutes with us cures you altogether."

"Not at all. I'd be delighted to have a family just like yours, if that was the path my life was taking." She took another glance at the happy mother and daughter on the cover of the catalog. How had she ended up on a path that would keep her from having her own family? Was that the path she really wanted to be on? And what about dancing with Hank last night made these thoughts keep coming into her mind?

Trudy handed her John. "Here, practice on this one."

Alice took him, but he wanted no part of being held

and he squirmed to get down. She obliged him.

"Dorothy, take your brother out back and play with him. Give your poor mama a moment of peace."

"Come on, Johnny," Dorothy said, taking her brother obediently by the hand. "Let's go make mud pies."

Trudy rolled her eyes heavenward. "Lord help us," she muttered. She opened the icebox and took out a pitcher of lemonade and poured some into two tall glasses. Then she gestured to a seat at the kitchen table before handing one of the glasses to Alice. "So tell me about this man you danced with last night." She said as she settled into a seat, stretching her legs out in front of her.

"There's not much to tell. His brother was dancing with Marty."

"Oh, Marty's young man!" Trudy gave an approving nod. "What a handsome and charming fellow he is. She could do a lot worse than him, let me tell you."

"She's out on his boat with him right now, and then he's taking her to dinner."

"Wouldn't it be something if it developed into a real romance? We need a real romance around here."

"What about you and Mark? Aren't you a romance story?"

"With three wildcats running around? It's a wonder we ever have a chance to have a conversation. Sometimes we don't. But everyone tells me the years go by quickly." She sighed. "Anyway. I want to hear about the man you were dancing with."

"His name is Henry, but he goes by Hank. He's a fisherman. He's a good dancer." She shrugged.

Honestly, she didn't know much more than that. "We didn't actually spend a lot of time talking. Mostly just dancing."

"But you'll see him again, get to know him better?" Trudy asked hopefully. Alice was convinced that one of Trudy's life goals was to see her happily married. She wouldn't believe her when she told her she was perfectly happy unmarried. Well, maybe perfectly would be overstating the case a little.

"I doubt it. He hightailed it out of the club pretty quickly last night. It was fun while it lasted, but there's nothing more to it."

Trudy studied her face closely. Alice tried to hide behind her lemonade glass, but it didn't work.

"You liked him," Trudy announced triumphantly.

"Of course I liked him," Alice scoffed. "What's not to like? But that hardly changes the fact that I'm not likely to see him again. He didn't seem terribly interested in continuing our acquaintance."

"But you will see him again," Trudy said.

Alice frowned at her, what did Trudy know that she didn't? "When?"

"I can't say for certain what date," Trudy said. "I'm not a fortune teller. But if Marty and Douglas get married, then you'll have to see him at family gatherings. Or at least at the wedding. You'll probably both be witnesses."

Alice laughed. "You're really putting the cart before the horse now, Trudy. They've just left on their first date and already you're marrying them off. Do you have a dress picked out for her as well?"

"No," Trudy admitted. "But I did see one in the Sears catalog that would be perfect for you."

"Let Dorothy use it for her paper dolls. I won't be needing it," Alice assured her, though in her mind's eye she caught a glimpse of herself in white, walking down the aisle to meet Henry. She shook her head to dispel the image. Trudy had to stop putting these crazy romantic notions in her head.

There was no romance with Hank Chapman, and there was not likely to ever be one.

Chapter Eight

The afternoon sun was strong, and Hank rolled up the blue sleeves on his work shirt. The gentle rocking motion of the deck and the lapping of water against the hull of the boat soothed him. This was home. This was where he belonged. Not at the club, dancing with a tall lady cop as the orchestra played. Not dealing with murdering pirates.

He couldn't get the evening out of his mind, though. And it wasn't the pirate that was the focus of his attention.

He hoped some hard work would settle him. He found the paintbrush and white paint in the storage cupboard. He'd paint those steps today. It needed to be done, and it was easier to do when no one else was around and tempted to go up and down them. He approached the top set of steps, paint pail in hand, and realized that first they needed to be washed. Didn't do any good to paint dirty steps. Back down to the working deck for a bucket and scrub brush.

Why had he let Douglas convince him to go to the club last night? He had only wanted to relax and do crossword puzzles. He'd been promised possible information about what had happened to Tomas. And true, he had gotten that information, but not at the club. Instead he'd danced. Danced with a very attractive woman who he pretty much had to stay clear of if he knew what was good for him. Unless he could be sure she was the kind of cop who would turn a blind eye in exchange for having her palm greased, and he didn't think she was, then there was only trouble if he cultivated a relationship.

He splashed soapy water on the steps and set to scrubbing.

Why couldn't he get her out of his mind? Her eyes were so dark and piercing. Her whole body one of angles instead of curves, yet she had moved so gracefully to the music.

The steps scrubbed, he now had to wait for them to dry before he could paint them. It wouldn't take long in the sun. He scrubbed the second set of steps while he waited. There was always something to do on a boat. He'd known that from the earliest days with his father. He'd given the crew the weekend off, though, and some of the chores would be easier with multiple people, checking and fixing the nets, for one. And Smitty was the most mechanically minded. He'd wait for him to check out the pinging in the engine.

Back to the top stairs. Painting was methodical and rather calming. There was an immediate satisfaction to seeing the newly gleaming stairs take shape. Unfortunately, it was also so soothing that it let his mind wander. How did Vincent Salerno know that he was a rum runner? Had Tomas mentioned him? He couldn't believe he would have sold him out like that, but maybe it was under duress. Tomas, somehow, had gotten involved with Salerno and ended up dead. He did not want the same thing to happen to him. He might not have a lot to lose, but he'd still rather spend his days on the sea as opposed to in a box six feet underground.

He was sure Tomas, if able to give an opinion, would rather be on his boat as well.

The boat. What was Irene going to do with that boat? Maybe he could get his father to buy it, to make it part of their fleet. But he needed to know what had happened to Tomas. Maybe it wouldn't hurt to stay in touch with that lady cop. She'd have access to information he couldn't get otherwise.

It wasn't using her. Was it? Did it matter? She'd probably use him if it meant enhancing her career.

"Uncle Hank?" The little boy voice came from the gangplank below him. "You here?"

"Right here, Ernst." He stood up so the boy could see him. Both brothers were there, looking around them expectantly. "What can I do for you?"

"Can we sweep the deck for a nickel?"

"Sweep the deck you say?" His heart broke for these fatherless boys and yet swelled with pride that they were trying to earn money.

"Yes, please."

"You know you don't sweep a boat's deck. You swab it."

"Swab?" They looked slightly uncertain.

He made his way down to the working deck.

"That's right. You pour water on it and swish it all around with a mop. Can you do that?"

"Yes, sir," Ernst said, clearly the spokesman of the duo.

"Okay. You do a good job and I'll give you a quarter each. How does that sound?"

Their eyes grew wide as the promised quarter. "A whole quarter? For each of us? Why, that's half a dollar!"

Good to know they were still teaching math in the schools.

He got them set up, while trying to think of other simple jobs he could pay them to do on the boat. It wasn't much, but it would do something toward helping Irene out. He finished painting the stairs and was putting the paint away when his brother called, "Ahoy," from the gangway.

"Be right there," Hank called back.

"We're swabbing!" one of the boys said, above the sound of their mop splashing away on the deck. He was fairly certain the deck was getting clean. At the very least the boys were occupied and seemed to be having a good time, and that was worth his fifty cents, if nothing else.

"Got some new deck hands, I see," Douglas said as Hank came out from the storeroom. That's when he saw his brother wasn't alone but had with him the girl he'd been dancing with the night before. Alice Grady's sister.

Hank quickly wiped his hands on his work trousers.

"They came offering their services. They're Nagy's boys." He looked questioningly at his brother. It wasn't unheard of for him to visit the boat. It was odd to bring a girl with him.

"I took Marty out on the runabout," Douglas explained. "We're going out to dinner later, but she wanted to see a fishing boat up close. I hope you don't mind."

Hank wasn't sure that was the most romantic place Douglas could have taken the girl, but what did he know? From all the evidence, Douglas had a much more successful social life than he did.

"That's fine. Only thing, I just painted the stairs, so you can't go far." He stuck out a hand to the girl, since Douglas clearly wasn't going to introduce them. "I'm Hank Chapman, nice to meet you."

She took his hand in a surprisingly firm handshake. "Marty Grady. You danced with my sister yesterday."

"I did," Hank agreed.

"She's a little prickly," Marty said. "But don't let that put you off. She's a real sweetheart inside."

He hadn't thought she was prickly at all. But at the same time, he also hadn't been thinking of digging any deeper. She'd been a pleasant dance partner, that's all. Hank wasn't sure what to respond to that, so he talked about his boat.

"Not sure what you're interested in seeing on the boat, but these are the fishing nets over here." He gestured toward the nets and rigging designed for pulling them through the water and up onto deck again.

"Hank, come with us to dinner tonight," Douglas said.

He actually took a step back in surprise. "Why on earth would you want me on your date?"

"Not just you," Douglas explained. "Ask Alice. Marty thinks Alice doesn't get out enough. It will be fun."

He shook his head. "No. No, sorry. I can't do that. I've got things to do here."

"You can't even go up the steps," Douglas pointed out. "And your deck is spotless." He gestured toward the Nagy boys, who were now splashing each other with the water from the buckets.

Hank hurried over to them. He didn't need them to

show up at home filthy. That would just make more work for Irene. He dug two quarters out of his pocket and handed one to each boy. "Great job, boys," he said. "Come back Monday and I'll see if I have other jobs for you."

"We'll be here bright and early," Ernst promised with a grin.

Hold on. Monday the boys had to be at school. "You'll be here after school," Hank said firmly.

The boys' shoulders slumped slightly. "Are you sure? We could get more work done if we came early. We could earn more money for Mama."

"After school will do just fine."

The boys left, and Hank dumped what was left of the water overboard and put the mops away.

Douglas was still looking at him expectantly. "So, what about it?"

Hadn't he already answered him? Hadn't he been clear enough when he said "no"?

"I'm not good company." He leaned against the wall to the storage room.

"Alice had a good time with you yesterday." Marty gave him a beguiling smile.

Little vixen. He sighed. He didn't want to argue with the girl.

"That's because we were dancing. The music was good."

"Alice is a very nice girl." A slight pout formed on Marty's red lips.

"It's nothing against Alice," Hank insisted. "I agree, she's lovely. But I'm not. She doesn't want to spend time with me. Trust me."

"But she does," Marty contradicted him. "She said

she had a good time last night. Didn't you?"

Hank sighed and stared at the clouds scudding past.

Douglas took him by the arm and led him toward the bow of the ship. "I don't know where you get the idea that you are some sort of social pariah unfit for company, but it's not true."

Oh, wasn't it? Douglas didn't know the nightmares. He didn't know what he'd seen. Hank wouldn't let him know. He would do everything to protect his younger brother from that.

"You're just out of practice," Douglas said, giving his arm an encouraging squeeze. "Come with us. It won't be so bad, and you'll see that you are much more fit for company than you give yourself credit for."

And if he didn't go, what would he be doing? Eating at home with his parents. It would be a perfectly acceptable and largely silent dinner, after which his parents would both go into the study with books and he would either do the same, or maybe go to the speakeasy in Perth Amboy and drink until he was just shy of drunk. Or he could spend the evening with Douglas and the two girls, making small talk, and making sure he never said anything wrong, either about smuggling or about the war. There were so many subjects that were off limits. It was much easier to spend a quiet evening at home.

"I don't know." Was he wavering? Why didn't he say flat out "no" like he'd done before?

"Listen," Douglas lowered his voice. "Marty is worried about her sister. She doesn't think she gets out enough. She thinks she's turning into an old maid before her time. It would be a service to all of us if you'd ask her to dinner."

Oh, for crying out loud.

So both he and Alice were the token projects of their younger siblings. Maybe it would be a favor to take her out, and then she wouldn't have to be a pet project at the hands of someone who wouldn't understand. At least if he went, the two of them would have that much in common.

"Fine. Fine. I'll do it." He sighed heavily. He was a fool, clearly.

Douglas gave him a hearty clap on the shoulder. "You won't regret it!"

"I already do," he mumbled.

"Now, go on home and get cleaned up and go over and ask her."

Seriously? They weren't even going to smooth the way by asking her themselves? Fine. He was thirty years old, he could ask a woman to dinner. Even if he didn't want to. And what was the matter with him, anyway? Was it really so horrible to go out to dinner with a pretty woman? Maybe he shouldn't treat this as a special kind of torture but as something that could actually be pleasant. It had been nice dancing with her yesterday, and the bit of conversation they'd had with each other had also been nice.

If he could just forget that she was a lady cop, it might not be so bad after all.

Douglas and Marty left, and Hank went home and took a long steamy shower and shaved carefully. There was always the chance that Alice could turn him down. Just because Douglas and Marty thought this was a good idea didn't mean that she would. She might have plans. She might not want to be manipulated into a date just because her younger sister thought it was a good idea. It was also possible that she had put her sister up to it, but he rather doubted it. Either way he had to be prepared for any eventuality.

He put on his light gray suit pants. He wouldn't wear the white flannels until after Memorial Day. He wasn't a stickler for things like that, but if his mother saw him in white before the season was right, she'd make him go and change. Better to save the step. He put on a fresh white shirt, and a light green tie with a dark green vest. His light gray jacket completed the ensemble. He went downstairs to find Douglas waiting for him, also nattily turned out.

"My two handsome boys," Mother said, clasping her hands together. He knew she'd like to see him happily settled. She didn't seem to believe that he could be happy in his boyhood room when he wasn't on his boat. "You'll knock those two girls off their feet. Have a wonderful time!"

Hank gave her a kiss on the cheek and followed his brother outside.

"So where do the Grady girls live?"

"Green Street," Douglas answered. "Right across from Barron Avenue. I'll drive you over."

"We're not giving Alice much time to get ready." The misgivings started to come back in full force. This was a really bad idea.

"She can take all the time she needs," Douglas said, adjusting his shirt cuff.

"Where are we going?" Hank thought to ask.

"Mulberry House."

Alarm bells sounded in Hank's head. True, Mulberry House was a real honest-to-goodness restaurant by the water in Perth Amboy, but there was also a secret bar. He knew the password to get in; he wasn't sure if Douglas did. There was a lot he didn't know about Douglas. What he did know was they certainly couldn't take Alice there. She was a cop. You didn't take a cop on a date to a speakeasy.

"Alice is a cop. You do know that, right?"

"We'll stay in the front," Douglas assured him. "Unless she seems cool with the idea."

"No," Hank said, slapping at his brother's head, and missing because Douglas had developed pretty good reflexes in that regard. "We don't try to tempt a cop. Have some sense."

"Live a little!" Douglas said as they climbed into his car.

Hank could easily kill him.

They drove over the causeway into town and parked in front of the modest two-story house with its wraparound front porch. Marty opened the door before they even rang the bell.

"I'll go get Alice." She hurried off into parts unknown, leaving them standing in the living room, hats in hand.

From somewhere upstairs they could hear voices, it sounded like Marty was trying to convince Alice to come downstairs. Maybe she wouldn't even let him ask; then he could go back home, take off the suit, have a quick dinner with his parents, and then go sit on the boat and watch the sky change color as the sun set.

But soon two sets of footsteps approached. Marty came down first, followed by Alice, who looked lovely in a pale green day dress. She smiled politely at the brothers.

"Marty said you wanted to see me?" she addressed

Hank.

Hank stood there, hat in hand, Douglas and Marty grinning at them like proud parents. This was ridiculous. He couldn't play this game. But yet it was unfair to her to not see this through, even if she knew nothing about it.

"My brother and your sister think it would be a good idea if we accompany them on their date tonight." He glanced quickly at his brother, who was frowning at his approach. He grinned. Good, he didn't mind annoying Douglas from time to time. "Apparently," he went on mischievously, "they don't think they can be trusted to keep their hands off each other if they don't have chaperons. Care to help me keep them in line?"

Alice's eyebrows shot up, but there was a glint of humor in her eyes. "And that's the only reason you're asking me?"

"Would you go if it were any other reason?"

"Of course not," she said. "Let me just go change."

She turned and went back upstairs, and Hank felt a certain satisfaction at not letting the younger siblings get their way entirely.

Chapter Nine

Alice called down the stairs to her sister in her best sing-song voice. "Help me pick out a dress, won't you, Marty?" Inside she was seething. How dare they presume to set her up on a date as if she were some lovelorn country cousin? She could hear the excuses they used now. *Alice is too caught up in her work, she doesn't have fun. Alice is becoming an old maid. We only need someone to show Alice a good time and she's sure to turn into a normal girl.*

And to put her on the spot like that! What was she supposed to do, turn down the man she'd been dancing with just yesterday? She'd look like a fool. She wondered how much arm-twisting they'd had to do to get him to come. Just what she wanted, a forced date. Didn't Marty realize that going out with someone who doesn't want to be with you is worse than being alone? A hundred times worse.

Marty hurried into her room and shut the door quickly behind her.

"Before you yell at me," she said, just as Alice opened her mouth to do just that. "Hear me out. Douglas is worried about Hank. He is convinced he's not good company, because of something that happened during the war. He rarely goes anywhere but his boat. He's turning into a hermit. We thought you could help him."

Marty looked up at her with those big blue eyes and Alice melted just a little. "Are you sure you didn't try to convince him to take me out in order to help me?"

Marty shifted her gaze away and hurried to the closet. "Of course not," she said as she rooted through the dresses hanging there.

"Liar," Alice said, but without much oomph. "I'll go out to dinner with all of you, because I would be very rude to say no at this point, since he's all dressed and everything, but I'd thank you not to ambush me in the future. I have a very full life. I don't need your help."

"Nonsense." Marty pulled a dark red dress from the closet. "Your idea of a fun evening is doing the crossword puzzle and listening to the radio."

"My goodness!" Alice threw her hands up in frustration. "You make me sound like an old woman. I'm tired when I get home from work. Is there a crime in that?"

"I'm tired too," Marty pointed out. "And I still go out."

"Because your friends are going out. Mine are married and settled down."

Marty gave her a look which Alice figured meant she had just made her point for her. Maybe she had. Maybe she had settled into too boring a life and wasn't giving herself a chance to have fun. It still didn't mean she wanted her little sister arranging her social life for her.

"Not that dress. It's too forward."

"It is not," Marty insisted. "And you never wear it and it looks great on you. It will knock Hank's eyes right out of his head."

"Just want I want," Alice muttered. "A blind date." She flashed a grin at her play on words.

Marty rolled her eyes at the pun. "It will be fun."

"Wouldn't you have more fun with Douglas by yourself?"

"We're just getting to know each other. Sometimes it's easier if there are others around."

Alice stripped off the day dress she'd been wearing and spritzed some perfume on her wrists before slipping into the red dress. Marty was right, it did look nice on her. And she didn't wear it enough. Largely because she seldom went anywhere it would be appropriate. If she was going to the club, she needed something a little fancier, and if she were going shopping or visiting, she needed something not quite as fancy. It was a perfect dress for going out to dinner.

"A little red on your lips," Marty insisted. "It will make you look less washed out. Trust me." Marty found a lipstick on the dressing table and handing it to her.

Alice glared at her. She knew how to make herself look attractive. She didn't need her little sister giving her beauty pointers. Hadn't she worn lipstick when they went to the club? What did Marty see when she looked at her, anyway? A withered specter of a woman?

"I suppose you think I should wear rouge, too?" Alice said, puckering to apply the lip color.

Marty missed the sarcasm completely. "Just a little. Though your cheeks do have a nice glow from being out in the garden today."

Alice sat in front of the mirror at her dressing table and rubbed a little rouge into each cheek.

"Lovely!" Marty chirped behind her.

"I don't know about this." Yes, she looked good, she had to admit. But going on a forced date? Who wanted to go out with someone who had to be convinced it was a good idea? She saw only disaster ahead.

Marty put her hands on her hips and shook her head. "When was the last time you were on a date?" She held up a hand to keep Alice from answering too quickly. "And not to the club. But an honest-to-goodness date where someone asked you out to dinner. And you went?"

She went on dates. She was not as pathetic as Marty wanted to paint her. "I went out to the theater with Mr. Applewhite? Remember?"

"That was in October, and he's nearly twice your age. That wasn't a date. That was a chance to see a play."

"Okay, then I went to dinner with Mark's cousin."

"Hardly counts. Mark and Trudy were there too, and I bet you only talked to Trudy."

That was fairly accurate.

"Well, then this doesn't count, either," Alice said. "After all. He didn't ask me because he wanted to, and you and Douglas will be there."

"But it might lead to a date!" Marty answered triumphantly. "Come on. You look wonderful. We can't keep the men waiting any longer."

Alice took one last look at herself in the mirror. She didn't look half bad. And if she had to be honest, there was a little part of her that was actually quite excited to be going out with Hank Chapman. He intrigued her. She was just worried that since he had left with nary a backward glance from the club the other night, he didn't really want to be with her, and that would ultimately lead to disappointment. Better to keep her expectations low.

She followed Marty downstairs and was gratified to see a look of approval, maybe even admiration, flit across Hank's face. Of course, if he was as much of a hermit as Marty said he was, then perhaps it didn't take much to awaken that glint in his eye.

Mama had been keeping the men entertained, and she looked now with approval at her girls. "Such beauties!" She clapped her hands together in approval. "The four of you will turn heads wherever you go."

"It will be the girls everyone will be looking at, Mrs. Grady," Douglas said smoothly. "They clearly get their good looks from their mother."

Mama actually blushed. "You are a sweet talker, you are. Must be Irish. Have a bit of the blarney in you."

"I wouldn't doubt it in the least," Douglas answered, and reached to take Marty's arm to lead her to the car. Hank and Alice followed, but Alice noticed Hank didn't reach for her arm, though he did open the back door for her, and climbed in next to her.

"Where are we going?" Marty asked as she settled into the front seat and Douglas climbed in behind the wheel after giving the crank a good turn.

"Mulberry House in Perth Amboy," Douglas answered.

Marty turned around so she could see Alice. "That will be a treat. We don't often get into the city for dinner!"

That was true enough. They did sometimes take the bus over for shopping but didn't usually splurge enough to have dinner there.

"It's on the waterfront," Douglas said. "Great seafood."

"Top notch scallops," Hank agreed.

Alice had just had scallops the day before, but perhaps going out to dinner with a scallop fisherman she should order them again. She'd play it by ear. They made a left on the Amboy road and headed toward the city.

She should say something but wasn't sure how to start a conversation with the man next to her, not made any less awkward by their siblings in the front seat, eager to listen to every word.

"I saw you escort Mrs. Nagy to Greiner's today," she said, finally. "Did she get everything taken care of?"

"She did," Hank answered. "The funeral is going to be Wednesday."

"Is there anything I can do to help?" She was haunted by that stricken face and those little fatherless children.

"We'll take care of her. The fishermen."

This was a really bad idea. She should have stayed home. She looked out the window at the passing scenery. They couldn't even have a conversation in the car on the way to the restaurant. How on earth would they make it through dinner? She hoped Marty would recognize how bad an idea this was and not do this to her in the future.

A tentative hand touched her arm. She turned to see Hank, an apologetic look on his face.

"I didn't mean that the way it sounded. I'm sorry. I remember you said you wanted to see if you could get her a job. That would be great. Really."

She swallowed over the lump in her throat.

"I didn't mean to imply that the fishermen wouldn't take care of her. I just want to help."

"I know," he said softly.

"Play nicely back there, you two," Douglas said, sounding like a parent.

Hank rolled his eyes and Alice stifled a laugh.

"Yes, Pa." Hank affected a subservient drawl.

"Insolent grub," Douglas answered, good humor in his voice.

"That's a new one," Hank said with admiration. "Did it take you long to think of it?"

"Came right off the top of my head." Douglas turned the car onto New Brunswick Avenue.

Maybe spending the evening with the Chapman brothers wouldn't be so bad after all.

They reached the Perth Amboy waterfront and Douglas parked the car in front of Mulberry House, a rather nondescript building that had a line of people waiting outside to get in.

"Don't worry. I made reservations." Douglas led them past the waiting people to the front door, where after a couple of words to the man in charge, which Alice didn't hear, they were ushered inside. The dining room was dark and atmospheric, with several tables for two or four, almost all of which were occupied, which would explain the wait outside. Alice didn't see an open table for four, so she wasn't sure where they were being led.

They followed the man past all the dining couples, to a door at the back of the dining room. Dinner in the kitchen? That would be interesting, and not what she had anticipated. But no, this was a separate dining room. It was not nearly as full as the one out front, and it had something the front one didn't have: a long shiny wooden bar, with colorful bottles on display and gleaming glasses on racks.

Well, this was awkward. The maitre d' held out a chair for her. As she sat, she could see that Hank was seething. As soon as they were all seated and the maitre d' had moved on, he turned on his brother.

"You said the front room!"

"They were full. It doesn't matter."

But Hank knew she was a police officer. Maybe Douglas didn't know that. Alice tried to think of the best way to handle this. She was not on duty. Perth Amboy was not her jurisdiction. She had no authority here, and likewise no official obligation to do anything. The only problem for her would be if they were caught here, and as long they weren't drinking it really shouldn't be an issue.

At the same time, she was rather tempted to have a drink. She wanted to know what all the fuss was about. Would it be such a big deal? It would be if she got caught. Better to be safe than sorry.

The waiter came over with menus and handed them around. "Can I get you something to drink while you look at the menu?"

Hank glanced at Alice, uncertainty in his eyes.

"I'm off duty," she assured him.

"Martini," Hank said.

"Tom Collins," Douglas said. "And get the girls Mary Pickfords." He turned to them. "Trust me, you'll love them."

So much for not ordering a drink.

"Douglas," Hank hissed when the waiter left. "Alice is a cop. What are you doing?"

"She's not going to squeal on us," Douglas answered with annoying assurance. "And even lady cops need to let their hair down and relax now and then."

"Don't worry about it. Douglas is right, I won't squeal." Though she did rather hate it that he made that assumption without consulting her.

The drinks came and Alice looked with a mixture of horror and anticipation at the pink drink in the cone-shaped glass in front of her.

"What's in it?"

"Just try it," Douglas said.

Marty was already putting her glass to her lips and taking a sip. "Ooh, it's delicious," she said. "You have to try it, Alice. It's sweet."

Alice picked the glass up cautiously. If she didn't drink it, she wasn't breaking any laws. She had not ordered it. She would not be paying for it. But if she drank it, she really couldn't plead ignorance. But yet it looked so interesting and it smelled good and everyone was looking at her, eagerly waiting her reaction. She took a cautious sip.

She detected pineapple and cherry and a burnt sugary taste, with a heat that warmed her insides as she swallowed.

"What's in it?" she asked again.

"Pineapple juice, maraschino cherry liquor, grenadine, and white rum. Like it?" Douglas answered, grinning like a child on Christmas.

"It's very good." She took one more sip and put the glass back on the table. "How do you know about these things?"

He winked, raising his glass as in a toast.

"Now, that would be telling. A man has to keep some secrets."

"Especially from the cops," Hank muttered under his breath.

Fair enough. She really couldn't expect Douglas to give her incriminating evidence against himself. She picked up her menu and studied it.

The veal cutlet sounded interesting, but she didn't want to insult Hank by not ordering scallops. Then again, she should order what she wanted. There was no reason to worry about his feelings on this. She was fairly certain he hadn't even wanted to go out to dinner.

So when the waiter came around, she ordered the veal cutlet and was pleasantly surprised when Hank did the same.

"I figured you'd go for the scallops."

"Love scallops," Hank said, giving her a lopsided grin. "And there's a good chance the ones they are serving are ones I caught, but a man cannot live by shellfish alone."

"Can I quote you on that?" Douglas asked.

Alice took another sip of her drink. It was really quite tasty. It was rather a shame it was illegal to go into a bar and order it. She was glad they were in Perth Amboy and not Woodbridge. Otherwise she'd feel it her duty to shut this place down. But it was not her town, not her concern. At least not today. If she had heard what Douglas had said at the door would she feel obligated to report that to her colleagues in Perth Amboy? Probably. Good thing she hadn't heard.

"It's horrible about the man who was murdered,"

Marty said in her wide-eyed innocent way. She looked directly at Hank. "Did you know him well?"

He took a swallow of his drink before answering.

"I did. And I'd rather not talk about it, if it's all the same. It's very upsetting."

"Of course," Marty said, only slightly taken aback. She wasn't easily offended.

There had to be something they could talk about other than dead people and illegal booze.

"Tell me about scallop fishing," Alice said, absently picking up her glass for another sip. "What's it like?"

"Damn hard work," Hank answered. "It's not like sitting on the dock with a line in the water and a picnic basket at your side."

"That's the only kind of fishing I've ever done," she admitted. "Maybe someday I can go out on your boat with you." She'd never been out on a boat, which was ridiculous when she thought about it, since they lived so close to the water. Marty had raved about her outing with Douglas, making Alice sorry she hadn't gone along.

"We go out for up to two weeks at a time. And the crew can get a bit rough. I don't think you'd enjoy it much."

No. She probably wouldn't.

"Perhaps not. I didn't realize you went out for such a long time."

"We need to go quite far out to the scallop beds," he explained. "And as long as we're out there, we might as well get as many as we can."

"You use nets?" That seemed like a fairly safe conclusion. Even she knew it was unlikely you would catch a shellfish with a hook on a line.

"We do. We run them pretty much all the time we are out."

"You wouldn't rather have an office job?" She asked, though she had a feeling she knew the answer. And although technically she had an office job, because she spent most of her work day in the office, what she loved about her job was those times when she wasn't in the office. She could never be strictly a typist who had nothing to look forward to each day but sitting at the same desk from the time she clocked in till the time she clocked out.

"Not in a million years," Hank answered. "It suits Douglas just fine, but not me."

"It's not like I'm chained to my desk," Douglas said a bit defensively. "But I couldn't do what Hank does. I've gone out once or twice. But I prefer a routine that allows me to eat at my own table and sleep in my own bed every night."

"I admit beds are rather nice," Hank said, and Alice laughed, taking another sip of her drink. Hank smiled at her and she felt a warm glow spread throughout her body. "Honestly, though, I'm not suited to a traditional life. I prefer being at sea."

"I'm not much of a traditionalist either," she admitted. "After all, most women my age are married with a couple of children, and I'm quite happy, glad even, to be able to go off to work each day without having to worry about anyone but myself."

Hank raised his glass toward Alice in a toast. "To the non-traditionalists!"

She raised her glass and clinked it with his.

"Well, I hope to have a very traditional life," Marty

said. "I would be very happy married, with a couple of kids and a husband who came home to me every evening."

"And mama there to cook your dinner," Alice said with a wink.

"Goes without saying," Marty answered with a sip of her drink. "This is quite good."

"You can't cook?" Douglas asked, one eyebrow raised.

"I'll learn," Marty assured him.

"Or we could hire a cook."

Were the two of them already planning for the future? Wasn't last night their first date? Did things really happen that quickly in real life? She caught Hank's eye, and he had the same befuddled look.

"Do you already have names for your children, too?" he asked.

Their dinner was brought out to them then, which gave Marty and Douglas a chance to hide their blushes, and the conversation turned to discussing how good the food looked, and then how good it tasted.

The secret back room was filling up, and during a conversational lull a stocky man with an impeccably tailored suit and a carnation in his buttonhole approached them.

"What a pleasant surprise to find you here, Mr. Chapman." The man addressed Hank. He took a cigarette case out of his pocket and opened it.

"The pleasure is all yours," Hank answered, his voice hard.

The man smiled, but there was no mirth in his expression. "We didn't get to finish our conversation last night."

"I said all I wanted to say to you." Hank was not making eye contact with the man.

The man picked out a cigarette and tapped it twice against the closed case before tucking the slim silver box back in his inside pocket. He glanced around the table and caught Alice's eye and held it.

"Listen, doll," he said. "You got to make him listen to me."

"I don't have any control over him," she answered honestly.

"Leave her out of it," Hank growled.

"I'm just here to issue a friendly warning." No one said anything, so the man lit his cigarette and continued. "Be careful who you keep as friends, that's all I'm saying. Because if someone is going around shooting fishermen, you don't want to be next." He laid an embossed card on the table. "Come see me."

Shooting fishermen.

That was the phrase that stuck out at Alice. Who would do that? No one, probably. But it wasn't unheard of for fishermen to also be rum runners. Rum runners sometimes got shot. Rum runners were also likely to know where speakeasies were. And how to get in.

Of course, rum runners might not be so keen to spend time with police officers. It bore thinking about.

The dapper man walked away, and Hank leaned close to her and whispered, "You want to find out who killed Tomas Nagy? Check out that guy. Vince Salerno."

Vince Salerno. She'd be sure to do just that.

And she might do a little checking into Hank Chapman as well.

Chapter Ten

The damn thing was he liked her. He liked the way they were able to glance at each other in knowing amusement at Marty and Douglas. He liked the way she didn't seem desperate for a husband. He liked the pink tinge that came into her cheeks as she sipped more of her cocktail. He liked the way she was willing to have the drink, even though she was a lady cop.

Maybe she was someone he could spend time with, no strings attached. He maybe could do that. Maybe.

He wasn't at all disappointed when Douglas suggested they walk along the waterfront for a while before heading back. It would be a chance to talk to her one on one and see where things might go. He walked slowly, allowing Marty and Douglas to get ahead. Alice kept pace with him. So far so good. Apparently, she didn't object to spending time alone with him.

"So tell me about Vince Salerno," she said when the others were out of earshot.

Not who he wanted to talk about right now. There was a full moon reflecting on the water. Didn't that spark romance in most people?

"Why do you think he killed Tomas Nagy?"

It was his own fault. He shouldn't have said anything. By the same token, he'd like to see the man who killed Tomas behind bars.

"I don't have any specifics," he admitted. "Just a

hunch. Salerno has been rumored to be involved in some unsavory things. And I think he knows what happened to Tomas."

"And you don't want to say anything else," Alice said with amazing perception. "That's fine. I'll see what I can find out. Trust me, I want to catch whoever killed Tomas Nagy." He heard her take a breath as if to ask something else, but then she let it out and looked out at the moon. "Quite pretty, isn't it?"

He breathed a sigh of relief. He didn't want to answer questions that would surely get awkward quickly. Much better to enjoy the moon.

"What did Douglas and Marty tell you to make you ask me to dinner tonight?" Alice asked the question so abruptly and so candidly that he actually stopped mid-stride. Maybe he'd be better off talking about rum runners. That might be a less volatile topic of conversation.

He quickly recovered, continuing to walk beside her, and cleared his throat. The truth was definitely the best option here. She was a cop; she'd probably find out the truth sooner or later anyway. No need to be branded as a liar.

"Your sister is apparently concerned that you don't get out enough."

In the light of the moon he could see her cringe. She sighed.

"That's about what I figured. Thank you for taking pity on me and agreeing to go."

"It wasn't exactly a hardship." He couldn't let her go on thinking he'd only agreed because he felt sorry for her. "I had fun dancing with you last night. Maybe we can do that again sometime."

"I'd like that."

He was pleased to find that the thought did not fill him with dread.

"I do go out, you know," she added, conversationally, as they walked.

"I'm sure you do," he answered. "Younger siblings can be…well…I guess I don't have to tell you."

"No, you don't." She sighed. "They do lay it on rather heavy. Though they are sweet to be concerned. I'm sure you don't really see yourself as unfit for human companionship, as Marty tried to tell me."

Heat rose in his face. Why would Douglas tell that to Marty?

"No, they weren't exaggerating on that one."

"But why?" Alice turned to face him, and the moon shone in her eyes. "You seem perfectly sociable to me." She waved the question away as soon as she'd asked it. "I'm sorry. You don't have to answer that. It's really none of my business. And you hardly have to justify your feelings to me."

"It's hard to explain," he said, and they walked in silence for a while, listening to the water lap against the shore.

"You were in France."

It was not a question, and he saw no point in denying it.

"I was."

"One of the officers I work with was over there. He doesn't talk about it much, but sometimes he panics and acts as if he's reliving part of it. It must have been truly awful."

He couldn't express how grateful he was that she didn't ask him to tell her what it was like. He couldn't even begin, even if he had wanted to, which he absolutely didn't. It was also nice that she understood a little what it was like to have been there.

"I think I left my humanity over there." He hadn't really ever told that to anyone in so many words. Why would he choose to tell Alice?

"I think that the fact you think so just proves how very human you are. A human isn't supposed to deal with seeing their friends blown up."

Damn. She did understand.

"I have nightmares. I wake in a cold sweat, flailing around in my bed. I couldn't ask anyone to ever share my bed with me."

"I'm no expert," Alice said softly, "but I think that the right person might help you move forward. There's no reason to have to be alone forever."

"I like being alone," he said with a touch too much defiance. It wasn't strictly true. If he thought he wouldn't be burdening someone else with his demons, he wouldn't mind having someone to share his bed, his life. When the wives came to greet the married crew members when they got into dock, there was a part of him that was envious. When he saw his men pick their children up and swing them onto their shoulders, he felt a pang that he wouldn't have that kind of life to come home to.

"I don't." She said it softly, as if to even say it out loud was shameful.

The answer surprised him. He kept his tone light as he responded. "I thought you were a happy bachelor girl. A modern career woman."

"Oh yes. That's me," she said a little too brightly. "And I do enjoy my job. But I can't help but notice that the male officers are all married. There doesn't seem to be a reason you have to be alone if you have a job."

She had a good point there.

"So it's not your job keeping you from settling down."

"Actually, it is." She wrapped her arms around herself as if she were cold, and he wondered if he should offer his jacket, or put his arm around her. He decided, under the circumstances, to do nothing. "Men seem to have the idea that the woman they are married to will not work outside the house. I don't really want to quit."

"I always got the impression that taking care of house and children was a fulltime job." He didn't want to sound like one of those men she'd had to deal with in the past, but at the same time, there was reality to consider.

"Oh, I'm sure it is. And I'm very lucky that my mother takes care of me, really. I suppose it's rather like having a wife at home." She stooped and picked a pebble up from the beach and tossed it into the bay. "It's not how I thought my life would be."

"No? What did you envision for yourself?"

"Something like Trudy, I suppose. I figured I'd get married and have a houseful of kids. I'd keep the house spotless, of course, and cook wonderful nutritious meals every night, and have a loving husband to share my life with me."

"And what happened to that dream?" He knew what happened to his. When he was young, he'd had a similar dream. And then he'd been sent to France.

"My father was killed." She said it baldly, without emotion. That was different than passed away, which is what she had told him yesterday. Killed implied a crime and a culprit. He wanted to know more but didn't want to interrupt her. "And the department offered me a job in order to help Mama out. And slowly my other dreams kind of melted away."

"So what are you dreams now?" he asked.

"I want to be a detective. I want to do more than just pick up drunks and stick them in the holding cell, or comfort women who have been hit by their husbands. Not that those things don't matter. I'd like to really get a chance to solve a crime. To put the clues together and find the answer where no one else could." She had become quite impassioned, but now she paused. When she continued, her tone was softer, almost wistful. "I want to find out who killed Tomas Nagy. And why."

"I hope you do," he answered sincerely. "I want to know that as well." Partly because he didn't want to be the next victim, but he couldn't tell her that.

"Do you think it was more than just a random robbery?"

He had to be careful how he answered this. He might have information that would help her, but on the other hand he didn't want her poking around into what he did. Would she make the connection on her own? People don't just shoot fishermen, so the odds were that Nagy was involved in something else. It was no secret that fishermen doubled as rum runners. He was friends with Nagy and was a fisherman. Not too much of a leap to suppose he also smuggled. And then there was the fact that they had stupidly taken her to a speakeasy. Involved in one illegal activity, likely to be involved in more.

117

"I have no idea," he answered. "But you said it wasn't your case anyway, right?"

She sighed. "It's not. But if they gave me a chance, I'm sure I could show them I was just as capable as any of them. I'm good at clues. Heck, I even do the crossword puzzle in pen."

He grinned. Crossword puzzles were one of his weaknesses. "I love crosswords! I save up all the puzzles when I'm ashore and bring them with me when we go out to sea. They are great for the downtime."

"I like doing them when I get home from work. Something different to think about."

"Though some of the clues are kind of ridiculous." He was glad the conversation had moved away from criminal activity.

"That's what makes them fun."

A commotion rang out from the direction of the marina. A boat was coming in, and the crew was shouting something as people rushed in their direction.

"It sounds like they need a doctor." Alice started to walk in that direction.

Hank took hold of her arm to stop her. "You're not a doctor."

"No, but I do have some emergency training. I need to see if I can help." She shook free of his arm and headed toward the marina. Hank did the only thing he could—he followed her.

As they got closer, the crowd grew and so did the sense of urgency.

"Stan's been shot!" A hoarse voice shouted above the din.

The story became clearer as he drew near the boat. They'd been beset by pirates. When the crew put up resistance, they'd opened fire. One man had been shot, and the pirates took what they wanted and went on their way.

Hank grabbed hold of a young man, his work shirt stained and damp from days at sea, as he ran past. "Who was it? Who boarded them?"

"No idea. Let go! I need to find a doctor."

Could it have been the work of Salerno? Was the meeting in the restaurant a ruse to secure his alibi while he had his thugs targeting fishermen?

Several Perth Amboy police officers came on the run and parted the crowd like Moses and the Red Sea. He saw them confer with Alice, who had managed to make her way on board.

His natural instinct when it came to police being involved with rum runners was to scram, but he couldn't just leave Alice here. With a heavy heart and stiff back, he walked toward the boat. The police were trying to keep everyone back and out of the way, so he waited at the perimeter until Alice noticed him. It went against the grain, waiting here, while the woman was in the thick of the action. He should be there protecting her. Wasn't that what a man did? But right now, she didn't need his protection, and he didn't need to be associated with smugglers. He stayed where he was.

Douglas and Marty joined him.

"What's going on?" Marty asked. "Is Alice playing lady cop again?"

"She's not really playing, though, is she?" Hank answered. "I mean, it's what she does."

"I know," Marty said, sounding only slightly chastised.

"Someone on the boat was shot." Even as he said it

his mind reeled. Was this connected to what happened to Tomas? Was there a way to find out without somehow implicating himself?

"Dirty rum runners shot by pirates trying to steal their booze." Spat out a man in a bowler hat, standing nearby. "They got what they deserved. They're all a bunch of dirty criminals."

"Hmph," Douglas said, low enough that only he could hear him. "That guy was at the table next to us in Mulberry House. Where does he think the booze comes from? The rum fairy?"

"Undoubtedly," Hank murmured in response.

"We should get out of here," Douglas said.

"We need to get Alice back first." He wished she would hurry. Being here and unable to take charge of the situation was making him uncomfortable.

"She's coming," Marty said, and he saw it was true. Alice was walking down the gang plank and back toward them.

"He's still alive," Alice said, and Hank could see that her hands were shaking. "It's a belly wound, and the crew was able to stanch the bleeding. If they get him into surgery quickly, he may be okay. I hope so."

Hank gently touched her elbow and steered her toward Douglas's car.

"The crew said it had something to do with pirates," she said as they climbed into the car. "Do you think that was what happened to Nagy? Was it the man who came up to us in the restaurant?"

"Yes." How much should he tell her? How much was she going to figure out on her own?

"Of course, Salerno couldn't have shot the man, he was in the restaurant with us. Does he have a large syndicate?" She looked directly at Hank with her clear brown eyes.

"I don't know," he answered honestly. "Obviously he has people working for him. People like that don't do their own dirty work." He could see the wheels in her mind turning. "Keep your distance. He's a dangerous man."

"I'm a police officer. I'm paid to deal with dangerous people."

"I'm not kidding." He liked this young woman; he didn't want to see her entangled with pirates.

"Neither am I," she answered.

Douglas cranked the motor, and they drove away from the waterfront and back toward home.

"Does this happen often?" Marty asked, her voice sounding young and innocent. "These pirates attacking fishermen?"

"I doubt they were after the fish," Alice said, and Hank rather wished she weren't that astute.

"What then?" Marty asked. "Rum? Like that fellow said? Were they rum runners?" Her voice rose in almost childlike excitement.

"Most likely," Alice said, clipping the words. She stared out the window. What was she putting together in her head? He never should have mentioned Salerno in connection to Nagy; now she'd begin to wonder if Nagy had been a rum runner. And how long before she cast her net wider and caught him in a web of suspicion?

Douglas parked in front of the house on Green Street, and they escorted the women to the door.

They stood on the porch, under the pale illumination of the porch light. "I had a very pleasant time." Hank hated how stiff and formal he sounded. He had to loosen up a little, let her know this was not a pity date. "I'm glad Douglas suggested it. Next time it will be my own idea."

She gave him a sweet smile. "I'd like that. Thank you."

Douglas and Marty looked to be involved in a slightly more intimate goodbye. Hank cleared his throat and Douglas let go of Marty and the girls went inside.

"Drop me off at the *Mary B*," Hank said to Douglas as they got back in the car.

"Why? What are you going to do on it tonight?"

"I need to check on it. That's all. I'll be home before long."

Douglas didn't argue with him but dropped him where requested.

"Oh," Hank said as he was getting out of the car, "next time, don't bring a police officer to a speakeasy, you dunderhead."

"She's said she wouldn't squeal."

"You better hope not."

Douglas drove off and Hank climbed aboard. He didn't really have anything he needed to check here. He just felt better being on his boat. He took a lantern from the storage room and lit it, bringing it down into the hold. The fake bottoms he used for hiding the liquor, when he had a shipment, were ingenious and couldn't be discovered by the untrained eye. But it was an open secret that the *Mary B* was a rum runner. Was it worth the risk? Should he go out on a fishing run and not detour out to rum row? Should he simply fill up with scallops and leave the liquor to others? At least for a little while?

Nagy was dead. Stan might die. The rum running was lucrative, but it wasn't worth it if he lost crew members. If he were boarded, could they convince the pirates they had nothing? What if he changed the holding area? Could he make it more secure?

But if Salerno's people were convinced he had something on board, would they stop at anything until they uncovered it? And what would that mean for them if they truly were running empty? The only solution was to make sure they weren't boarded. Maybe he should do some target practice before heading back out to sea again.

He made his way up the newly painted stairs to the bridge and took his pistol out of the drawer he kept it in. If someone was shooting at fishermen, he wanted to be prepared to shoot back. Then he headed down to the working deck, where he sat and just let the moon and the lapping of the water and the sea air relax him. He closed his eyes and thought of the delightful pink of Alice's cheeks when she sipped her cocktail. He thought of the way she ran toward trouble instead of away from it. He thought of the way she understood about his demons and didn't make him explain. He'd like to spend more time with her. Too bad; if he did she was likely to find out he was a rum runner, and that would certainly be awkward for both of them. She'd feel compelled to arrest him, and that would put quite a damper on a budding romance.

Maybe he could stop rum running. He didn't need the money.

The thing was, he didn't do it for the money.

The peaceful silence of the night was broken by the creak and whir of a bicycle on the old dirt road leading to the marina. He opened his eyes and sat up straight, peering into the moonlit night to see who was coming this way. The sound stopped by his dock and he heard the clunk of the kickstand being put down. He put his hand on his pistol. If Salerno was coming for him now, it would be a foolish move. He had nothing on board to steal, not even fish.

Light footsteps approached his boat and stopped. His heart beat quickly.

Whoever it was climbed his gangplank and started onto the boat.

"I should warn you, I'm armed." His voice sounded loud and ridiculous in the silent night.

"So am I," came Alice's calm voice. "I don't plan on shooting you, though. I hope you return the favor."

His hand shook in relief as he put the pistol in his pocket and stood up to greet her. "What are you doing here, skulking around my boat?"

"Hoping to find you, actually," Alice said with succinct matter-of-factness.

He took her hand to guide her the rest of the way across the gangplank. Her hand was warm and soft in his.

"How did you know I'd be here?"

"Call it an educated hunch."

"And why did you want to find me?" He rather wished it was because she, as a woman, wanted to spend time with him, as a man. He suspected, however, that it had more to do with the fact that she was a cop and he was a fisherman who might be able to tell her more about Salerno and his pirates.

"Was Nagy a rum runner?" she asked without prelude.

"Yes," he answered. It would come to light before long. It was one thing to withhold information, but he wouldn't want to be accused of outright lying to her.

"And that's why he was killed?"

"It would seem like it." He sighed. If they were going to have a long conversation, they might as well go someplace they could sit. Problem was there wasn't exactly a drawing room he could bring her to. "Let's go to the dining room. It's more comfortable." He led the way and then lit the lantern on the table and waited for her to sit on the bench seat. "Can I get you a cup of coffee or anything?"

"No, thank you," she answered, looking around the cramped room. "If I have a cup of coffee at this hour of the night, I'll never sleep."

"I seldom sleep anyway." Maybe she didn't think this was a more comfortable option. To him the dining room said relaxation and refreshment, but maybe she only saw the Formica-topped table with the thin strips of wood designed to keep everything from sliding around while they ate. What the hell kind of life was he living, at thirty, that the best place he had to bring a lady was to this cramped little dining area?

"You should drink less coffee." There was a bit of a touch of humor in her voice.

If only that were the problem.

"Undoubtedly." He slid onto the bench next to her. "What do you want to know?"

"What can you tell me?"

"Touché." He laughed. He should have known she was no fool. "I can't tell you for certain who killed Tomas or why." He situated himself so they weren't touching, even though he'd really like to be touching her. "I can make a guess, but I wasn't there. I've no proof."

"And what's your guess?"

"What do you know about pirates?" It wasn't as much a non sequitur as it sounded like.

She tapped her fingers on the table top and he noticed her nails were short and neatly trimmed, with no lacquer on them. It suited her. She was a no-nonsense kind of woman.

"Frankly, I was ready to relegate them to the history books. I don't know too much about modern pirates."

He wished he could relegate them to the pages of the history books.

"Modern pirates are much like historical ones. They take what isn't theirs. And sometimes get quite nasty when thwarted." Like shooting people.

"So common thieves." She looked him straight in the eye and his blood tingled.

"More or less." Why did they have to be talking about pirates? He needed his own place. With a proper sitting room.

"Calling them pirates lends them an air of romance they don't deserve." Alice gave a definitive nod as if that settled that.

Be that as it may, they were what they were. He didn't care what they were called as long as they left him alone.

"Do you think pirates might have been involved in Nagy's death?"

"I suppose anything is possible. But don't even think of taking on the pirates on your own." He realized he sounded rather authoritative when he had no right to.

"Please. I beg you. I know these people. They will not respect either the title of police officer or that you are a woman."

At first, he thought she was going to argue with him, but she screwed up her face in thought. "Fine. I have a better idea. If I put a stop to the rum running in town, then the pirates would have no reason to come around here, would they?"

He wasn't sure what to say to that.

"You don't think I can do it?" She challenged him.

It was more that he thought she probably could, or at least make a good effort at it. He knew the reason he and the other rum runners thrived was that the law didn't look too hard for them.

"I'm sure you can," he said softly. "Are you sure you want to? You could make some pretty powerful enemies."

"I wouldn't be much of a police officer if I were afraid of people not liking me. Especially criminals. It's part of my job."

They were sitting so close together, he could feel the warmth from her body on his. Why did he have this desire to protect her? She clearly didn't want or need his protection, yet he wanted to reach out and take her in his arms and keep her safe from harm.

She turned to him, and their faces were inches apart. He reached up and touched her cheek and she didn't recoil at the touch, instead she sighed and closed her eyes.

He moved toward her and kissed her quickly, light as a butterfly's wings. When she didn't object, he moved his hand to the back of her neck and pulled her closer to him, kissing her long and deeply. Feelings coursed through him that he hadn't thought he'd ever feel again.

After forever he pulled back from her.

"I'm sorry," he said.

"I'm not," she answered.

"I should escort you home." He wanted to simply escort her to his bunk, right on the other side of the wall. But he was still enough of a gentleman to know that was a bad idea.

"If you must," she whispered.

Damn it, he must. Mustn't he?

Chapter Eleven

She couldn't get the kiss out of her mind. It was all she could think about as she lay staring at the ceiling, not sleeping, Saturday night. It was all she could think about during Mass at St. James Church on Sunday morning. And now, sitting at her desk, she could still imagine she felt his lips on hers even as she slipped paper into her typewriter to begin typing up the reports.

He'd pushed her bicycle as he'd walked her home from the marina Saturday night. Not able to hold hands because of the bicycle, not able to see each other because of the dark, they'd been able to talk. At first it was just silly small talk, but before they had crossed the causeway they were talking about their hopes and dreams.

She told him that she'd love to have a home of her own, overlooking the water, with a picket fence, and a child, perhaps a son named Sean after her father. He'd told her about wishing he could spend all his time at sea.

"I've never even been on a boat," she'd admitted. "Other than a ferry ride. Or, you know, just now when it was sitting at dock."

"We'll have to remedy that sometime."

She'd rather glowed at the thought of that and was glad he couldn't see how pink her cheeks undoubtedly were.

"But wouldn't you have to come ashore sometime?" she'd asked as they came to Berry Street and her thoughts automatically went to Irene Nagy, mourning her husband in their rented house.

"Now and then, I suppose." He was silent for a moment until the Nagy house was past them. "Might be nice to come home to a little house with a picket fence, overlooking the water, and a son named Sean."

She knew it was just talk. They barely knew each other, but her heart leapt in her chest anyway. It was the closest to someone saying they'd like to spend their life with her that she'd ever come. She wished she could see his face, so she could tell if he were serious or just humoring her. Or maybe it was better she couldn't. This way she could dream.

And dream she had. All day Sunday.

But in the bright light of day she'd wondered if she'd been too forward going out to his boat like that. She rather wished he'd stop by the house, but he didn't, and she didn't go back out to the marina. What had it all meant? Anything? She knew one thing, the kiss had awakened something in her, something that she thought was dead or long asleep. Her skin had tingled, and warmth had flowed through her, and all she could think was that she wanted more. Oh, so much more.

Was it a foolish hope?

Certainly, it was and the sooner she banished it the better off she'd be. For now, she had to get her head out of the clouds and concentrate on work. She had to tell the chief about the lead she had picked up in the Nagy case. If he let her, she'd investigate Salerno on her own, but at least she could make sure he had the information. The other thing she had to do, when he came into the office, was ask if he would consider hiring Mrs. Nagy.

Now it was just her and Rawlson in the office, though; the chief and Mark had already gone out on patrol before she made her way to her desk this morning.

It was closing in on lunchtime before they came back, a man in handcuffs between them. Murphy dropped a scribbled paper onto her desk as he passed. "Type this up, Grady."

She glanced at it. His handwriting wasn't much better than Mark's.

John O'Connor. Murder of Tomas Nagy. Apparent motive: common theft.

Mark was getting the criminal situated in the holding cell, and the chief was pouring himself a cup of coffee from the percolator kept on the electric ring. Alice got up and followed the chief into his office.

"What is it, Grady?" he asked, not unpleasantly. He was always in a good mood after they caught a perp.

"I had a tip about the Nagy murder this weekend."

He grinned and gave her a helpless shrug. "A little late to help us at this point."

"That's just it. I don't think it was simple robbery."

"Nagy had just been paid. And when the body was found he didn't have the money, so there's that. Witnesses saw this man running from the scene. And he confessed. Said it was robbery gone wrong. I know you want to solve the big case, Grady, but this one's already been solved. There will be others."

"But—"

"Hey, Chief, got a minute?" Rawlson called from the open doorway.

"Yeah. Better get that report typed up, Grady," he

131

said, and she knew she'd been effectively dismissed.

She sat down at her desk and typed the report, but something didn't seem right. It was too easy, too convenient. Or was she just hoping for something more exciting?

Why would Hank have told her about Salerno and the rum running if he didn't think that had something to do with it? She had to believe it did, but how could she ever prove it? And would anyone listen? After all, they got the man who shot him. Case closed. Why did it leave her with an unsettled, unfinished feeling? Was it just because she didn't solve it herself? Maybe that's all it was, a bit of professional jealousy.

She typed up a few more reports and went back into the chief's office.

"I'd like to do something to help the Nagys," she said without preamble.

"We caught the guy who shot him. Isn't that good enough?" he asked, shuffling some papers around on his desk.

"I was thinking that perhaps we could hire Mrs. Nagy to be a typist here."

The chief gave her a paternal smile. "Tired of typing up all the reports?"

"I can do so much more. You know I can."

He gave an almost imperceptible nod. "Can she type?"

"I don't know," Alice admitted.

"Does she want the job?" he asked, picking up his coffee cup and taking a sip.

Again, she had to admit she didn't know.

Murphy sighed and pushed the papers to the side. "Give me a few minutes to run over the budget and see if we can justify hiring someone. Then, and only then, you can go find out if she even wants the job."

With a lighter heart Alice went back to typing up reports. At least she might be able to make a little bit of difference to the family.

Half an hour later, Murphy came out to her desk. "We'll make it work, if she wants it. I'd have to interview her, of course. She has to be at least somewhat suitable for the job for me to justify it. Why don't you go talk to her? See what she thinks. See what else the family needs. Maybe the department can sponsor a spaghetti dinner for them or something."

Alice had to restrain the urge to throw her arms around Murphy's neck. Instead she grinned at him. "Thanks, Chief."

With a spring in her step which matched the warm May breezes, she walked around the corner to the Nagys' house. Once again it was the little girl who answered the door. "Is your mama here?"

"She's in the kitchen talking to some of Papa's crew," the girl said. "Come in."

Mrs. Nagy was sitting at the table with Snake and Patsy, who Alice practically regarded as old friends at this point. They were deep in conversation, but looked up, surprised, as she entered. Alice noted the fine china teapot on the table; it was not what she expected to see on the table of the wife of an immigrant fisherman. In fact, the whole kitchen was outfitted in modern appliances and looked fresh and sharp. Fishing was apparently a much more lucrative business than she had thought. Of course, that was not the only business Tomas Nagy was involved in. But regardless of how Tomas made his money, Irene must be concerned about where money was going to come from in the future. Alice hoped her news would help in that regard.

"Yes?" Irene's face took on a guarded look. She pushed her teacup away from her, as if it had suddenly lost its appeal. "What is problem?"

Patsy reached out and gave the widow's hand a comforting squeeze.

"Was it wrong man?"

Was it the wrong man? Interesting question, and from her point of view entirely possible, but no point in worrying Irene. "No, the killer is safely locked behind bars. I'm actually here for another reason. May I speak to you privately?"

"Yes, of course." Irene stood and led Alice into the living room; the little girl stayed close by her mother's side, looking up at Alice with her big brown eyes.

"I realize it may be presumptuous of me," Alice began, "but I thought you might be concerned about income, with Tomas gone."

"The fishermen are very generous," Irene said, her hand resting gently on her daughter's head. "The Chapmans are buying the *Katinka*. That helps."

"That is good." She looked around the tidy living room. Perhaps her help wasn't actually needed here. She'd offer anyway. "We need a typist at the police department, and I was wondering if you had those skills and would like the job?"

She didn't want the woman to think she was offering charity. People could get awfully bent out of shape about that.

But instead of Irene appearing insulted, tears pooled in the corners of the woman's eyes.

"You are offering a job?"

"If you'd like it. And of course, you'd have to meet with the chief and he'd have to agree you are suitable."

"Of course, of course."

"Can you type?" Alice asked, hesitantly.

Mrs. Nagy shook her head sadly. "No. But I could use job." She looked around her house as if for inspiration. "You have one of those machines? I learn how before meeting your chief?"

There was an old typewriter in the attic. She'd used it herself to learn to type when she was in high school. No one used it now, and no one would care if she loaned, or even gave it outright to Mrs. Nagy.

"I do," she said. "And I can give you lessons. I'll come by after dinner today and we can start. Is that good?"

"Is very good." Mrs. Nagy took Alice's hands between her own. "You are good person. Thank you. You like cup of tea, maybe?"

She really should get back to work, but at the same time, she also wanted a chance to speak to Snake and Patsy. If she could earn their trust, maybe she could find out more about rum running and pirates. A cup of tea might be just the thing.

"Thank you very much. That would be lovely."

Mrs. Nagy turned to lead her back into the kitchen but stopped. "I'm sorry, I don't know your name."

How had she never introduced herself?

"I'm Officer Grady. But, please, if I am going to teach you to type, call me Alice."

"Alice," she said in acknowledgment and smiled at her. "And I am Irene."

Back in the kitchen she introduced Alice to Snake and Patsy.

"We've already met." She took the fourth seat at the table.

"Ah, yes," Snake said, a smile lighting his face. "You make a lovely cup of coffee."

"One of my many skills," she said lightly, then let her tone grow serious. For after all, these three people had suffered a serious loss. "Let me say how very sorry I am about what happened to Mr. Nagy. At least the police have arrested the killer."

Snake and Patsy exchanged a covert look. Did they, like her, think there was more to the story? How could she find out what they did think without being crass? She may be a police officer, but she was also sitting at the table of the newly bereaved, she needed to proceed with caution.

"I'm told it was robbery and that the man confessed." She took the proffered cup of tea from Irene and shook her head to indicate she'd have neither milk nor sugar.

"Robbery, aye." Patsy took a sip of his tea. The delicate cup looked out of place in his work-hardened hand.

"You don't think so?" She looked back and forth between the two men. "I was told his pay was missing."

"And what pay would that be?" Snake asked, looking her straight in the eye. "Whatever he had left after paying his crew he locked in the safe in the *Katinka*. That wasn't touched. Not till we got it out and gave it to Irene."

How did Mark and the Chief not know that?

"You didn't tell that to the investigating officers?"

Snake shrugged. "Didn't seem no point."

She sighed. Why couldn't she be the one in charge

of this investigation? Then again, they caught the killer. And he'd confessed. What was it exactly she was looking to find out?

"Where does Jiggy fit into this?"

The atmosphere in the kitchen became tense. Snake and Patsy exchanged worried glances. Irene's expression became hard. Clearly, she'd stumbled on something here. No going back now.

"You told me he was a customer," Alice addressed the two fishermen. "But you sold your scallops at Martin's fishery. What did Jiggy buy from you?"

She was pretty sure she knew. After all, Hank had confirmed that Tomas had been rum running.

Again, the covert glances back and forth.

"*Folyadék*," mumbled Irene, nearly under her breath.

"I'm sorry?" Alice said. "What's that?"

"Don't, Irene," Patsy cautioned.

She waved his objection away. "Tomas is dead. What harm can come of telling now? Liquor. He smuggled liquor in from rum row and sold it to Chiggy." The look of defiance on her face dared Alice to make something of it.

Alice didn't let her expression change. It was as she thought.

"Do you think Jiggy had something to do with his murder?" Alice watched them all closely for some clue as to their thoughts. She knew body language was much more likely to give her answers here than words.

Irene frowned and seemed to contemplate the possibility.

Snake and Patsy froze and carefully didn't look at each other. They knew something and they didn't want her to know it.

"Not Chiggy," Irene said, definitively. "He was done with Chiggy."

"What do you mean?" Alice asked, ignoring Snake and Patsy, whose faces had gone disturbingly pale.

"He had new buyer. Salerno."

And there was that name again.

She looked at the two men. "Did he sell his haul to Salerno this time?"

There was an almost imperceptible nod from Patsy.

Snake cleared his throat. "We didn't think it was a good idea. We weren't sure we could trust Salerno."

"Do you think either one of them would kill him?" She studied them all over the top of her teacup.

Irene shrugged. "Tomas can't bring him any more liquor if he's dead."

"Where can I find either Salerno or Jiggy?"

Patsy's face colored, and he put his teacup down and leaned across the table toward her.

"With all due respect, miss, I don't think it's a good idea to go talk to either of them. They are dangerous men."

"I'm a police officer," she reminded them. "I can take care of myself."

"I'm sure you can, miss. Under normal circumstances. But if you want to talk to these men, bring backup."

But she'd get no backup. As far as the department was concerned, the murder was solved. If she was going to talk to them, it would have to be on her own.

"If you don't mind me saying so, miss," Snake spoke up. "Let it go. They caught the man who killed Tomas. That's all any of us really wanted."

Was that enough for them? It wasn't enough for her. There were too many questions. If Salerno was a buyer, why would Hank think he was a pirate? Why would changing buyers get him killed? Saying it was simple robbery seemed like taking the easy way out. There was something more going on here, and Alice felt she was close to stumbling on what it was.

For now, she'd get no more help from the people around this table. She finished her cup of tea.

"I had better get back. I appreciate the tea, and I'll be back after dinner with the typewriter."

Irene gave her a sad smile. "Thank you. You may be angel in disguise."

"Not likely, just someone trying to help." She wasn't doing that much really, just what she could.

At the door, out of earshot of Snake and Patsy she took hold of Irene's hands. "You wouldn't happen to know Jiggy's given name, would you?"

"No, miss." Irene gave her a sad smile. "Just know him as Chiggy Malone. He does business along the river."

That would have to be enough for now.

"Thank you, and I'll be back after dinner. Around seven, perhaps?" Suddenly she remembered the young children. "Is that too late? Will I be interfering with bedtimes?"

"Sari goes to bed at seven, but I'll have the boys do it. It will be fine."

This was why it was easier for men to get ahead; they didn't have to worry about who would care for the children. What Irene needed was a wife. Or a mother's helper. Or Marty. Alice smiled at the thought. Maybe she could convince her sister to help out tonight.

139

"If my sister agrees, and you agree, of course, perhaps she could watch the children while I teach you to type. She's quite good with little ones."

Alice could see the relief wash across Irene's face.

"That would be good. Yes. Thank you. If she agrees."

Alice was fairly certain she could get Marty to agree.

In the meantime, she needed to see if she could track down a Mr. Jiggy Malone or Vince Salerno.

She headed back to the office glad of something to do to help.

Chapter Twelve

The Nagy boys showed up so quickly after school that Hank wondered if they'd even bothered to stop home and tell their mother where they were going. He didn't want to be the cause of any extra anxiety for Irene. She had enough to worry about.

"Does your mother know where you are?" he asked as they clambered over the gangway into the boat.

"Yes, sir, Captain," Ernst said in his boyish treble, his dark hair falling into his eyes. "We even changed out of our school clothes. But we ran fast to get here. The more work we can do, the more we can make to help Mama, right?"

"That's right." Hank suppressed a smile.

"Should we swab the deck again, Captain, sir?" Kristof, the younger of the two, asked eagerly.

"Well, no. It doesn't need it again quite yet." He'd been thinking about what job he could have the two boys do. Obviously, they couldn't repair the knocking sound in the engine, and he couldn't have them inspecting the trawlers. "Today I need you to check our nets for holes."

Kristof frowned, looking at the net on the deck, which obviously was made mostly of holes.

"Extra holes that aren't supposed to be there," he clarified, and Kristof nodded.

"What do we do if we find one?" Ernst asked. "Do

141

we fix it?"

"Do you know how?" They might. They were Tomas's sons, after all.

"Yes sir, Captain," Ernst answered proudly, and then his face darkened. "I mean Papa showed us how, but we never really did it on our own."

Of course they hadn't; they weren't even ten years old yet.

"When you find a hole, you come and get me and show me how you'd mend it. I'll let you know if you did it right or not." He figured he'd have to do most of the mending himself but didn't mind it.

The rest of the crew took to the Nagy boys right away, treating them like beloved mascots. Before long he noticed Swede sitting by the boys, patiently showing them how to mend the nets. With the boys in good hands, Hank went up to the bridge to organize things for his next trip.

Even as he sorted through charts and polished the brass equipment, he couldn't get Alice Grady out of his mind. He never should have kissed her the other day; it made him want more, much more. And he couldn't have it. First of all, Alice deserved a whole man, not someone as beset by demons as he was, and second of all, she was a cop, and he was a rum runner. That was a recipe for disaster if ever there was one. Either he would have to lie to her, or she would have to ignore her duty to the law, if they were going to make things work. He didn't see either of those things happening.

Why had she come into his life? Only to remind him of the things he couldn't have? It had been so easy to talk to her. He almost, for a moment, imagined coming home to her in that little house with the picket fence and the boy named Sean. But it was a fantasy.

The best thing he could do was to not see her again. It shouldn't be that hard. Their paths had never crossed before this weekend. Why would he think they would cross in the future? He stared out at the sun sparkles on the water. Unless, of course, his brother continued to be involved with her sister. That could make things awkward. He sighed. It didn't matter anyway. He spent most of his time out at sea.

Another week and he'd be out on the ocean with his crew. By the time he got back, maybe his brother would have moved on, and there'd be nothing to worry about.

As the sun moved lower in the western sky, the shadows in the bridge lengthened. He'd have to light a lamp soon if he were to continue working. A tap at his door was followed by Swede sticking his blond head in.

"Captain, the Nagy boys are ready to be paid. They say they need to go home for dinner."

He snapped out of his reverie.

"Of course." He reached into his pockets for some coins to pay the boys.

"They're good workers." Swede leaned against the open door. "The guys and I were discussing other jobs they can help us with, if you don't mind keeping them around while we're in dock."

"Not at all." He sorted through his handful of change for a couple of quarters for the boys. "I just didn't want them getting in the crew's way. We do have real work to do."

"It shouldn't be a problem." Swede shoved his hands in his pockets. "Like I said, they're good workers, and quick learners. They'll help, not hinder."

"Good to hear."

He headed down the metal steps to the working deck where the two boys stood, hats in hand, looking up at him expectantly.

"We'd keep working," Ernst said, revealing a gap where one of his front teeth used to be, "but Mama expects us home for dinner, and we don't want to make her worry."

"Of course." Hank pressed fifty cents into each boy's hand. "Your mother has enough to worry about, you don't want to add to it, and you are quite right. Now, on home with you. And I'll expect you back here tomorrow, as long as your mother says it's all right. There's always work for two likely lads to do."

The grins that broke across their faces warmed his heart.

"Off with you now." He turned away, trying not to think of those boys growing up without their father. He started back up the steps to the bridge but turned to address his crew. "And off with the rest of you, too. Go have dinner. We made good progress today. I'll see you all tomorrow."

Soon he was alone on the *Mary B*. He inhaled deeply of the sea air and absorbed the silence around him. Not complete silence, of course—the water still lapped along the hull, sea gulls cried out as they circled and dove into the water, the breeze jostled the lines. These were all sounds that he could absorb, that he could sleep to if need be. Even the sounds of other people in the marina, muted conversations and hammering coming from somewhere, were still part of the silence.

He climbed the stairs back up to the bridge and

closed the door firmly behind him. He took the ring of keys from his pocket and sorted through the keys of various shapes and sizes until he found the small silver one that unlocked the storage area in the bench seat under the window. He extracted a half empty bottle of rum and poured some into a glass before returning the bottle to its hiding place.

He lowered himself into his captain's seat and sipped the rum, while enjoying the vista of the Arthur Kill and Staten Island. It was better when all he could see was water, but this would do. It was no surprise he liked the open feel of the water around him. It was a far cry from the trenches in France that still gave him nightmares. When on the open sea nothing could sneak up on you. No bombs could drop on your position from some hidden vantage point, obliterating the men to the left and right of you. You were safe at sea.

He hated these sojourns on land while waiting to set out again on the next fishing trip.

He drained his glass, waiting for the numbing effects of the rum to give him the courage to go home to the confining walls of his parents' house.

The clatter of feet on the metals steps startled him, and he slammed the glass down as someone pounded on the door.

"Captain! Uncle Hank! Captain Hank!" It was the clear high voice of one of the Nagy boys.

He opened the door to see both boys standing there, faces tear streaked, eyes panicked.

"What's the matter?"

"It's Sari. We can't find her. Will you help?"

"Sari? Your sister?" He was already following the boys back down the stairs. "When was the last time anyone saw her?"

"Mama put her in for a nap before we got home from school, and when she went to check on her later, she wasn't there. She's been looking everywhere."

"Okay, let me get you two home, and I'll find out where your mother has already looked. We'll find her. I promise."

He didn't know if that was a promise he was going to be able to keep, but he'd sure do his darnedest.

He could get back into town quicker with a car. He steered the boys toward his parents' house. "I need one of the cars," he announced as he walked through the door, the boys looking around at the grandeur that was the Chapman family home.

"Is something wrong?" His father came out of the den to meet him.

"These are the Nagy boys," he said. "Their little sister is missing. I need to look for her."

Douglas came down the stairs. "Come on. I'll take you where you need to go."

"I just need the car," Hank said, hating every moment they were wasting. "I am capable of driving."

"I know. But I can help look. Or whatever anyone needs. Let's go."

They piled the boys into the back of the car and Douglas drove them over the causeway into town. They pulled up in front of the Nagy house and the boys hopped out and rushed inside, heralding their arrival.

Hank hurried up the front steps two at a time and let himself into the house, following the boys. He stopped short when he saw Alice and her sister, Marty, standing in the living room with Irene.

"Oh, Hank! Thank God!" Irene rushed to him, and

he took her hands in his. They were ice cold and shaking. "Sari is gone! I look everywhere. I don't know what to do."

"You've called the police?" he asked, eyeing Alice, though he noticed she was not in uniform.

"No," Alice answered taking a step forward. "I was going to teach Irene how to type." A black typewriter case lay at her feet. "Marty was going to watch the children. We just got here."

Marty rushed to Douglas as he came in, clutching at him.

"We have to help her find her little girl."

"We'll find her," Douglas assured her, taking her in his arms. For a brief, crazy second, Hank wished Alice had rushed into his arms like that.

"Where have you looked?" he asked Irene. This was no time for petty jealousy. "Have you searched the house?"

"She wasn't in her bed and I called for her. I've looked in all the rooms."

"Did you search under the beds and in the cupboards?" Alice asked, with the authority and clear-headedness that came from being a police officer. "When Marty was little, she used to hide in one of those places and then fall asleep. She sent our mama into a panic any number of times."

"Boys!" Hank said in his best captain voice. "I want this place turned inside out. Look in any place Sari could fit. No stone unturned. If she is in the house, you will find her."

"Yes, sir!" The boys scampered off.

"Are there any places that Sari is likely to run off to?" Alice asked before he had a chance to. But it was exactly the question he would have asked, so he had no complaint.

"She doesn't go anywhere without me." Irene wrung her hands. "She's only five. I don't know where she would go."

"Where have you looked?" Hank asked before Alice had a chance.

"I've been to the neighbors' houses and the splash pool on School Street and even up to Main Street. I took her for a soda at Woolworth's last week, and she's talked about it since. But there was no sign of her all the way up to the Amboy Road."

Upstairs they could hear the boys scurrying around, looking in cupboards and under beds. Hank didn't think the girl was here, though, no matter how much he hoped one of the boys would suddenly proclaim that he'd found her.

"Would she have gone toward the marina?" Hank asked. "Did she know her brothers were going to be helping me?"

"I don't know." Irene could barely hold back a sob.

"Alice and I will check the causeway." He took charge, falling easily into his role as captain. "Douglas and Marty can check in town again. You wait here in case she comes back on her own."

Irene shook her head, grabbing at his hand. "No, no! I can't stay here and do nothing. I must go look."

Douglas unwrapped Marty's arms from around him. "You'll come with me," he said to the widow. "We'll check in town again. Marty will stay here with the boys."

The boys in question thundered down the stairs. "She's nowhere upstairs," they exclaimed breathlessly.

"We have to check downstairs. Maybe she's in a kitchen cabinet."

"Go," Marty said, with a light touch on Douglas's arm. "I'll keep an eye on the boys. And if she really is in one of the cabinets, we'll be sure to get word to you."

Douglas and Irene headed toward town, while he and Alice turned toward the causeway. The sun was setting behind them, lengthening the shadows.

"It will be dark soon." Alice stood straight and tall, all business, which made sense given the task at hand. "Perhaps we should get a lantern."

"I have one on the boat," he assured her. "If we get as far as that without finding her, we'll get it before turning around and looking some more."

"If she went this way, do you think she could have fallen in the water?" Alice kept her voice low, even though Douglas and Irene were already clearly out of earshot. "Do you think she can swim?"

If she came this way, it was very likely she could have fallen in the water. It was also very likely she did not swim. "We'll find her," was all he said.

They walked slowly, looking from side to side, calling her name, knocking on the doors of the few houses along the causeway to see if anyone had seen the child.

"Little Sari?" the old woman who lived in the last house asked. "I saw her skip past a couple of hours ago. Called out to her, I did. She's such a little thing, and I thought it was mighty odd she was out on her own. But then, you never do know with foreigners. They have their own ways."

Hank's fists balled up in anger at the way she spoke about foreigners as if the Nagy family, because they came from Hungary, were inferior in some way. With a featherlight touch, Alice put her hand on his arm.

"You say you called out to her," she said to the woman. "Did she tell you where she was going?"

"Something about the boats. She was going to help her brothers work on a boat. Some nonsense like that. I told her to go home. She was too young to be out and about on her own." The woman said with a definite air of self-righteousness.

"And did she go home?" Alice asked, and Hank was amazed at how calm she was able to sound.

"I assume so, if she was an obedient child she would have, but…" The old woman shrugged. "You never can tell with these foreigners."

Hank took a step forward, but Alice's gentle touch held him back.

"Thank you," Alice said and guided him away from the woman's front door.

"What were you going to do?" she asked as the door shut behind them. "Beat up an old woman?"

Realizing how ridiculous that would have been, he shrugged. "I suppose not, but…"

"No buts," Alice said, her voice firm. "We know we are on the right track. There's no time to waste."

Of course she was right. She was maddeningly right.

They walked side by side, alert to any clue that might lead them to Sari. Why had he decided he shouldn't see Alice anymore? Just because she was a cop and he was a rum runner? Because he didn't want to impose his damaged self on anyone? Nothing felt more natural than to be working with her. She was calm and organized, not at all like the fluttery females he often found himself spending time with.

They reached the bridge over the Woodbridge River, and he prepared to cross, heading toward Sewaren and the boats.

"Wait," Alice said, reaching out for his arm. "Would Sari know where the boats are? Would she have followed the river?"

It was a good point. If she had gone all the way into Sewaren and the marina they would have seen her on their way back into town, but no one had. Would a little girl, knowing that boats go on water, have followed the river instead?

To the north of the bridge the area was too swampy for even a child to get far, but there was a path on the south side. It was muddy and overgrown with brambles and nettles, and it led right to Jiggy's hut. The last thing Hank wanted to do was bring Alice to Jiggy Malone. But if there was any chance Sari might have gone this way they had to check.

"You're going to ruin your shoes," Hank said as they slogged along the path.

Alice looked down at her feet and picked one foot gingerly out of the mud. "I suppose so." She shrugged. "It really doesn't matter, does it? I can buy new shoes. Sari would be a lot harder to replace."

She stooped to study a thorn and called to him.

"Look, a scrap of cloth. Do you think it could be from Sari's dress?"

They hadn't even bothered to ask Irene what the girl was wearing. They should have asked.

"It might be." He called out the girl's name once more.

"A footprint!" Alice shouted jubilantly. "And it's about the right size!"

Hank breathed a sigh of relief. At least up to this point she hadn't fallen in the water. He called the girl's name again. Louder. And then paused, listening closely for any response. Perhaps she had fallen and gotten hurt. Perhaps they would hear a whimper from her instead of an answer. He had to be alert to anything.

But there was nothing. He couldn't imagine what Irene would do if she lost Sari so soon after losing Tomas. He had to make sure that didn't happen.

Ahead of him, Alice was searching the area diligently. She was putting her all into this search. Perhaps it was due to her job as a police officer. It was the kind of thing she was trained to do. But he rather felt that to her it was personal. That finding Sari meant as much to her as it did to him.

Alice called out Sari's name, but he was afraid her voice wasn't resonant enough to carry far. He echoed her call. This time they got an answer. But it wasn't the cry of a little girl. Instead a man's voice called out, "Ho! She's here!"

Alice looked back at him, startled.

"We've found her!"

They had, Hank realized as a wave of relief washed over him. To be more specific, Jiggy Malone had found her, for that was who had called out. There'd be no keeping Alice from meeting Jiggy now. He just hoped that in discussing Sari, there'd be no talk of rum running.

Chapter Thirteen

Alice broke into a run, following the voice that had called out to them. She rounded the bend and saw a stocky man with a long mustache standing outside a ramshackle hut on the edge of the river, a beat-up dock in front of it. There was a small motor boat, maybe a sixteen-footer, tied at the dock.

"You found Sari?" she asked, barely stopping to catch her breath.

"Small lassie, about five? Dark braids and a talkative nature?"

"That's her." Hank came up behind her and put a hand protectively on her shoulder. "Where is she?"

The man nodded toward the cabin. "She fell asleep about twenty minutes ago. First, she told me all about her life and her family, and of course, her favorite, Uncle Hank. She's Tomas's daughter?" The last bit wasn't entirely a question, more of a clarification.

"She is." Hank gave a slight squeeze to her shoulder and she couldn't understand the trepidation she felt coming from him. They'd found Sari. Everything was all right.

Alice held out her hand to the stranger, though clearly, he wasn't a stranger to Hank.

"I'm Alice Grady," she introduced herself.

The man looked her up and down in a way that made her feel distinctly uncomfortable. He took hold of her hand and shook it.

"Nice to meet you, Miss Grady. Jiggy Malone, at your service."

So maybe that explained Hank's reaction. She'd found Jiggy Malone. This wasn't the time to ask the questions she had, but now she knew what he looked like and where to find him.

"You would be Sean Grady's daughter?" Jiggy still gripped her hand

"I would." Of course he knew her father. Everyone in town had known him, or so it seemed.

"I was in the Knights of Columbus with him," he said, finally letting go of her hand. Somehow this didn't surprise Alice at all.

"You are in the Knights of Columbus?" Hank asked, astounded skepticism in his voice.

"I'm a deep man, Hank. A very deep man." He nodded toward the shack. "I suppose you want to see the little one."

"She's not hurt, is she?" Alice asked. Just because she was safely asleep now didn't mean she hadn't had misadventures on her way here.

"Tired and a bit muddy, a few scratches and scrapes, but those may have been from earlier, hard to tell." Jiggy grinned, showing one gold tooth off to the side. "She's fine."

He led them into the shack where Sari was curled up on a cot, sound asleep, her hands tucked under her cheek, looking like a little angel. One glance told Alice that Sari was unharmed, and then she spared some attention to look around. Bare boards, with chinks letting the light through, made up the walls, although with only two small windows, one in the front and one in the back, there was not a lot of natural light in the shack. A gas lamp on a Formica-topped table cast a cozy glow. A spirit lamp with kettle sat on the table, along with two teacups, one empty, one still half full.

"She was thirsty, and the best I had to offer her was a bit of tea."

"Very kind of you," Alice said.

"Not at all," Jiggy answered. "Just doing the Christian thing."

Hank went straight to the cot and gently picked Sari up in his strong arms. She settled against his shoulder, waking up only long enough to look at him and murmur, "There you are, Uncle Hank. I was looking for you." She patted his face with her tiny hand and drifted back to sleep.

Alice's heart softened toward Hank even more. He tried to put on this veneer of a hardened man of the world, but he was as gentle as a teddy bear with this little girl.

"I can take you down the river in the boat," Jiggy said, uncertainty in his words, as if he wasn't sure how the suggestion would be taken.

"Thank you," she said taking a step toward the dock.

"No," Hank said firmly. "It will be easier to walk. There's no place close to their house to tie up anyway."

Jiggy shrugged. "Suit yourself."

"Thank you very much." Alice held out a hand to him. "Her mother will be grateful to know you kept her safe."

The tips of Jiggy's ears turned red. "Least I could do, least I could do," he murmured.

"It's getting dark," she said to Hank as he turned to

head down the path toward home. "Don't you think it would make more sense to take him up on his offer of the boat?"

"No."

The answer was so short and curt that it took her by surprise. Clearly there was a reason Hank didn't want to spend more time with Jiggy than need be. Perhaps he knew of his involvement in rum running and disapproved of him. But he knew that Tomas was involved, and he thought of him as a brother. There was more here than met the eye, and she intended to find out what it was.

Hank walked quickly, and even though he was carrying the child, she struggled to keep up with him.

"You know Mr. Malone?" she asked, when the path narrowed, and he had to slow down some. It wasn't precisely a question.

"I've met him before," Hank admitted.

"I've heard rumors about him." Alice tried to keep her voice neutral as she pushed branches out of her way.

Hank's head jerked toward her and his brows came together in consternation. "There are rumors about everyone if you listen hard enough. Probably even about you."

Her eyebrows shot up. She wasn't expecting that sort of response. She figured he'd ask what kind of rumors and that would lead into a discussion about rum running and pirates and maybe give her some clues as to where to look for the reason for Tomas's death. She didn't think it was as simple as robbery.

He was trying to divert her. He wanted her to ask what rumors there could be about her. But she knew these kinds of tactics. She'd interviewed enough suspects, and the ones she hadn't interviewed personally she'd typed up the reports of their conversations. And while it was natural for her to wonder what rumors there were about her, if any, she could probably guess. After all, she was a woman in what was traditionally a man's role. There would be speculation that she had slept her way into her position or that she was too manly a woman to interest a real man. But rumors were just that, only rumors. She gave them no credence. Besides, she knew the truth. Anyone else could as well, if they cared to investigate.

Maybe a direct approach was better when dealing with Hank.

"Do you think he had anything to do with Tomas's death?"

"I thought they caught the man who shot Tomas." It wasn't exactly an answer.

Was he hiding something from her? He clearly knew Jiggy, and presumably knew his activities. He knew that Tomas was a rum runner. What else did he know?

"How do you know Jiggy Malone?"

Hank sighed and shifted the sleeping child in his arms. "He has a boat. I have a boat. You get to know people."

Undoubtedly that was true, but she suspected there was more to it than that.

Sari stirred, and raised her head, opening her eyes and looking around. "I want to go home, Uncle Hank."

"We're going there now," he said gently.

Alice's shoulders slumped slightly. So much for getting any information from him about Jiggy. But it didn't matter. She knew where to find Jiggy herself now. It was enough.

The silence was now broken by a newly energized Sari.

"I had an adventure! I wanted to help Ernst and Kristof work on the boat. It sounded like fun. I wanted to swab. I bet I could swab. Do you think I could swab, Uncle Hank?"

"I think you'd be a master swabber," he answered cheerfully.

"But I didn't find your boat. I looked all along the river but didn't see it."

"You should have waited for someone to take you." There was no censure in his voice. "It's not on the river, but on the Arthur Kill."

"Oh." Sari took a moment to absorb this information. "Next time?"

"We'll see."

"Jiggy gave me tea. He's nice. He says he has the gift of blarney. Do you think I can get that gift too? I like gifts. What's blarney?"

Alice smiled as the girl prattled on and on and Hank answered when she paused long enough. Walking behind him, she enjoyed the view of his lean, muscular body. He moved with the grace of an athlete. She could appreciate it now that they had found Sari safe and sound.

It didn't take them long to get back to the house, where Marty was keeping the boys occupied by playing poker with them. She threw down her cards when they came in carrying Sari.

"Oh! Thank goodness she's okay. Where was she?"

"She was by the river," Hank answered, and it was not lost on Alice that he didn't mention Jiggy's hut. He set Sari down and she was immediately besieged by her brothers, who wanted to know everything. "I'll go find Douglas and Irene and tell them Sari is safe."

Marty pulled Alice into the kitchen, leaving the door open so they could keep one eye on the children. It wouldn't do if they lost one of them now. Marty poured a cup of tea for Alice from the waiting pot and then put the kettle on the stove. "Irene will want a cup, I'm sure, when she gets back. She'll appreciate a fresh pot."

"And I don't?"

"You let your tea sit so long before you drink it, it's usually lukewarm by the time you get to it anyway. The old tea will do fine for you." Leave it to a younger sister to not pull any punches. "She was by the river?"

"An old fisherman found her and kept her safe in his hut. She was trying to get to Hank's boat but followed the river instead of going to Sewaren."

"Lucky that old fisherman was around."

Alice held the cup of tea in her hands and took a sip. She nodded absently. Lucky indeed. But the real luck was that she now knew who Jiggy was and where to find him. His secluded hut on the river would be a perfect spot for rum runners to bring in their contraband, if that, indeed was what he was up to.

"Alice?"

By the way Marty said her name, Alice suspected she'd said it more than once.

"What?"

"You were a hundred miles away."

"Sorry. Just relieved we found Sari."

"Right. I suppose spending some quality time with

159

Hank didn't hurt either."

Alice's face flushed, and she knew her cheeks were turning red, but there was no point in trying to lie to her little sister. "No, it didn't."

Before long, Hank was back with Douglas and Irene. Irene scooped her little girl up and held her tight, speaking rapidly to her in Hungarian. Alice didn't know what she was saying but based on tone and body language she suspected it was along the lines of "I was so worried. I'm glad you are all right. I love you. Don't you dare scare me like that again."

There would be no typing lesson tonight.

"I'll leave the typewriter here and come back tomorrow," Alice said to Irene, who was ensconced on her sofa, still holding Sari tight.

"Not tomorrow. The viewing for Tomas is tomorrow, and the funeral Wednesday. Maybe come back Thursday?" Irene said, looking up at her with entreating eyes.

"Of course." How could she not have taken the wake and funeral into account?

"I'll drive you girls home," Douglas said, already standing in the doorway.

Hank held up one hand to hold his brother off and turned to Irene.

"Have you had dinner?"

She looked up at him as if startled by the question.

"I didn't think so," Hank said and turned to his brother. "You take Marty home. Alice and I will cook Irene and the kids some dinner."

Douglas and Marty didn't waste any time leaving.

"I can't actually cook," Alice said to Hank, following him into the kitchen. It was rather embarrassing to admit it, but it would be silly to hide the fact.

"That's okay, I can." He handed her an apron. "You can be my assistant."

Happy warmth flooded her as she put the apron on.

"Okay, chief, what can I do?"

"That is the key question. You say you can't cook. Can you cut up vegetables?"

"Aye, aye, Captain." She gave him a salute which he returned with a grin. "And I am not completely helpless in the kitchen. It's just that I'm out working every day, and Mama makes dinner. I don't really have the opportunity."

He handed her some potatoes he found in the pantry.

"What are we making?" she asked, gripping the potatoes.

"Nothing that has to simmer too long," Hank said, apparently thinking as he went. "It's late and they're hungry." He peeked in the icebox and took out some ham. "We'll fry up some ham and potatoes. It's a bit lacking in the greenery department, as my mother would say, but it will get something in their bellies, and it won't take long to do."

Alice peeled and sliced the potatoes while Hank melted some lard in a frying pan and cut the ham. Frying ham and potatoes was something she probably could have managed on her own. She wondered how much of a cook Hank really was. How much did he have to cook for himself?

She couldn't imagine any of her fellow officers even knowing how to melt lard, but yet she also couldn't picture a more masculine man than Hank. He was a bevy of contradictions. Would she ever really get to know him?

"Where did you learn to cook?" Alice asked as Hank layered the ham and potatoes in the frying pan.

"We take turns when we are out at sea," he explained. "Can't say I do gourmet meals, but I won't starve."

"Most men look for a woman to do the cooking for them."

"I'm not most men." He stirred the food around a bit as it sizzled.

That much was clear.

"Don't want to share your kitchen?" she teased. He intrigued her, and she wanted to understand him. He was a puzzle to solve. And there was, unwanted, in the dark recesses of her mind, a picture of her sharing his kitchen. It wasn't such a bad thought.

"Don't want to share my life," he answered shortly, not returning teasing for teasing.

Alrighty then. The door slammed on that unbidden image in her mind.

"Because of the nightmares?"

"Among other things."

"You know," she said, suspecting she was entering very dangerous territory and should perhaps back off, but forging ahead nonetheless, "some married couples have separate beds, or even separate bedrooms. You don't have to be alone just because of nightmares."

Would it sound like she was angling for him to propose to her? She certainly hoped not. She just wanted him to know he didn't have to be alone.

He sighed and leaned against the sink, crossing his arms. "I'm a person who is better off alone. That's all."

Then why had he kissed her? Why had he awakened all these feelings in her if he wasn't going to follow through on them?

"Why? Do you turn into a wolf on the full moon?"

"Something like that."

Alice studied his face. He wanted to be forbidding and off-putting, that was clear from his words and his stance. He wanted her to think he didn't want her to come close to him. But there was something in his eyes. Something just a little needy or inviting. Maybe she was imagining it, but maybe not.

She looked straight into those eyes and said, "I rather like wolves."

A smile tugged at the corner of his mouth, and if he was trying to repress it, he failed.

"I suspect you do."

Their moment of connection was broken by Ernst and Kristof running into the kitchen.

"That smells good. We're hungry!"

Hank's attention shifted to the boys. He put on a big smile.

"Good thing, because I wouldn't want this food to go to waste."

"Wash your hands," Alice said automatically as the boys started to sit at the table. They groaned, but obediently went to the sink to wash up.

Irene, holding Sari by the hand, came into the kitchen, a look of delight on her face.

"I can't remember the last time someone cook for me. Thank you so much."

Alice took plates from the cupboard and brought them to Hank, who filled them with ham and potatoes. Then she placed one in front of each member of the family. She had brought a plate for Hank as well, but he dished up all the food before he got to his.

"Aren't you going to eat?" she asked.

"I'm not taking food from them. I'll get something when I go home. And you?"

"Ate before I came over." The food smelled good and she wouldn't mind a taste, but she was not taking food from the family either. She pulled Hank aside and said quietly, "Should we stay and do the dishes?" She felt they should finish what they started, but yet it seemed odd to simply stay here and watch the family eat.

"No, no!" Irene looked up from her meal. "The boys, they will wash the dishes. Thank you for all you have done!"

"Our pleasure." Hank unwrapped the apron from around his waist. "If you need anything else, you know where to find me."

"Can we come work on the boat again tomorrow, Uncle Hank?" Kristof asked, before shoving another forkful of food in his mouth.

Hank hesitated, looking at the boys and then at Irene, whose mouth was set in a thin straight line.

"Maybe not tomorrow. Stay here and play with Sari. Keep her out of trouble so your ma can get things done around the house. That is a way of helping too, you know."

"But we can come again, sometime, right?" Ernst asked, eyes bright and eager.

"I'll work it out with your ma. But now eat up, and then I'm sure you'll have to go to bed soon. Tomorrow is a school day."

Alice hung her apron beside Hank's and smiled at

Irene. "I'll come Thursday. Same time. And we'll have a lesson."

"Thank you, Officer Grady. Thank you."

"Please, call me Alice. It will be so much nicer working together if we can be friends."

"Thank you, Alice."

With that, goodbyes were said, and she and Hank left the family to settle in for the night.

"I'll walk you home," Hank said as they stepped out onto the front porch.

She started to say that it wasn't necessary, she lived only a few blocks away, and it wasn't that terribly late. But yet she rather wanted to continue this time with Hank, even if he had said he didn't want to share his life with anyone. They could still share tonight. She had no problem letting him walk her home.

"I'd appreciate that."

The night had turned chilly and it felt like it might rain, even though the moon shone brightly. Alice shivered a little at the thought of what might have happened to Sari had they not found her, or rather, had she not stumbled upon Jiggy and his hut.

"Are you cold?" Hank asked.

"No, a mouse just ran over my grave." Her mother's expression came naturally.

"Sounds unpleasant," he deadpanned.

Alice laughed. "I suppose so. Just thinking how glad I am that Sari is okay."

"It would have just about killed Irene if she hadn't been."

That was undoubtedly true.

"You are a good friend to the Nagy family." Alice wondered if perhaps Hank was a bit sweet on the widow? Was that why he was so helpful?

"You are as well. I'm sorry I gave you a hard time about it the other day."

She'd almost forgotten their first encounter, when he'd been so rude.

"You were upset about your friend." She reached out and gently touched his sleeve. "I understand."

They turned down Pearl Street and watched as a train pulled into the station, disgorging passengers from New York City.

"Would you like to come in for a cup of coffee, or even some food?" Alice offered as they neared her house. "You must be starving." It wasn't so much that she felt compelled to feed him but rather that she didn't want her time with him to end.

"I'm fine. I had better get back on home, though. Thank you."

So he didn't care if their time together ended. She took a deep breath. She could deal with that. She was used to being alone, after all.

"Afraid of the full moon?" she asked, one eye skyward.

He looked confused.

"What with being a werewolf and all?" She quirked an eyebrow at him and tried to keep from smiling.

He grinned. "Yes, that's it. Must get home before I change."

They walked up the steps to the wraparound porch, the yellow light by the door casting a welcoming glow. She would like him to kiss her good night, but he was hanging back, and that didn't seem like it was going to happen. She opened the door.

"I'd better be going," Hank said, and took off into the night.

Maybe he really was a werewolf. Whether he was or not, he clearly was not the person for her, as much as she might like to daydream about it. Time to move back to reality. She stepped inside and shut the door.

Chapter Fourteen

He had to warn Jiggy. He'd known that from the first time Alice spotted the hut. The thought had come crashing back at him while they were preparing dinner. She was tenacious, and she was determined, and she would bring them all down if given the chance.

He headed straight back to the shack. The full moon kept the path fairly well lit, but he still wished he were in a boat, approaching Jiggy's place by water instead. He always felt much more confident on the water. No light pierced the darkness, and as he got closer, he had to acknowledge that Jiggy wasn't there.

He breathed a sigh of relief. If he wasn't there, then Alice couldn't confront him tonight. He still had to warn him, though. He'd have to head into Perth Amboy and see if he could find him at one of his other haunts.

Hank walked out into the night, back toward the causeway. The night air was cool and crisp, and the full moon shone brightly overhead. He thought of Alice's remark about werewolves and grinned to himself. She wouldn't mind a wolf, she said, but what would she think of a criminal? Bet that wouldn't be so attractive to her.

Maybe he should stop rum running. The risks were starting to outweigh the benefits, and he'd rather like getting to know Alice a little better without having to worry that she was going to arrest him. He got to the road and headed east toward Sewaren and home, as the night birds accompanied him with their music.

But would it be fair to his crew if he stopped the rum running? Many of them depended on that extra money. They couldn't make that kind of cash from scallops alone.

Maybe he'd buy a schooner, see if Slim and Swede wanted to crew for him, and sail to the Caribbean. There he could drink rum on the beach and think about nothing all day.

He kicked a stone out of the street. That would be running away from his problems, and he didn't do that. Then again, what were all those weeks spent at sea but a way to escape the nightmares left over from the war? Maybe he did run away from his problems after all. What would be wrong with doing it one more time?

Would Alice enjoy lazing on a Caribbean beach? He shook his head to clear it of the thought. Alice would never run away with him; he might as well just get that stupid thought out of his head right now.

Back at the house, he raided the icebox for leftovers and then joined his mother in the drawing room, where she was reading a book. He'd have to see if he could borrow his brother's car to head into Amboy.

"When do you take the *Mary B* back out again?" she asked, marking her place with her finger.

"Trying to get rid of me so soon?" He kept his tone light but still wondered if perhaps he should take offense.

"Hardly. Rather the opposite, I want to know how long we'll have you home for."

"Probably go out again on Friday."

"You should wait another day or two. Another weekend at home to relax and enjoy yourself."

"I don't enjoy myself at home." He wondered if that was still true. He'd actually had a good time dancing with Alice, and dining with Alice, and kissing Alice.

Why did everything keep coming back to Alice? He needed to get back on the *Mary B* and out to sea before she took over his mind completely.

"Douglas seemed to think you had a good time the other day." His mother gave him that raised-eyebrow all-knowing look that mothers have.

"Douglas doesn't know anything," he said, as if he and his brother were kids again and caught in some argument.

"I think I know quite a lot, actually," Douglas said as he came into the room, a half-eaten cookie in his hand. He leaned against the door jamb. "What is it I supposedly don't know anything about?"

"If I had fun at the club," Hank answered, wishing he could go out to his boat right now. Everything was so much easier on the boat.

"Of course you had fun at the club. In fact, I'd even go so far as to say you are falling in love with Miss Alice Grady."

He jumped up from his seat and stalked across the room.

"And I say, again, that you don't know what you are talking about." He strode down the hall and out the front door, shutting it behind him with a satisfying slam.

He kept walking, heading automatically toward the *Mary B*. The one place he could get some peace.

It wasn't long before he heard the slapping of shoe leather on pavement. He didn't break stride. There was no reason to make it easier for his brother to catch up with him. When he did, he put one hand on Hank's shoulder, panting as if he'd just run a marathon.

Hank pushed the hand away. "You spend way too much time sitting behind a desk," he said, "to be winded that easily."

"Yeah. Whatever. Where are you going?"

"Where do you think?"

"Come with me to Mulberry House."

"I want to go on the boat." Though what he really needed to do was go to Amboy. Mulberry House was in Amboy. That could work out for him.

"I could use a drink," Douglas said.

Hank sighed. He could provide a drink for Douglas on the *Mary B*, but maybe it was better if Douglas didn't know that.

"Fine. We'll go to Mulberry House."

They were silent as they walked back to the house and Douglas cranked the car to start it.

"You should buy a car." Douglas settled himself in the driver's seat.

"Why?" Hank answered. "I spend more time on sea than on land."

"When you settle down. Won't it be nice to have a family car?"

Hank had to stop himself from hopping out of the car right then and there. If he did, he knew Douglas would only follow him. Might as well see it through and get a drink.

"I am as settled as I'm going to be."

"I don't know." Douglas grinned at him. "You and

Officer Grady make a sweet-looking couple."

"No." He clenched his hands. He would not think of her that way. He would go back out to sea. He would get away from people. It was for the best.

But he did have to see her again. He needed to get her off Jiggy's trail. If not for his sake, for her own.

Douglas parked his car down the block from Mulberry House, and once again, a few words to the man at the door had them ensconced in the back room, this time sitting at the bar. Hank ordered a martini and Douglas a Tom Collins, as always.

"Glad the kid was all right tonight," Douglas said as they watched the bartender mix their drinks.

"She gave us quite a scare but seems none the worse for her adventure."

The bartender handed over their drinks, and they laid their money on the bar.

"Dad's buying the *Katinka*," Douglas said, and Hank nodded, sipping his drink. Dad had told him he was planning on doing that.

"He wants me to skipper her."

Hank spit his mouthful of martini across the bar, to the disgusted look of the bartender and other patrons. He grabbed a napkin and wiped it up and turned to his brother.

"You?"

"Yeah, crazy right?"

"Do you want to?"

"No. I have no interest in spending weeks at a time with only men around. There is nothing about that which appeals to me."

"It's not as bad as all that." He rather enjoyed the time in the company of men, when he could simply be himself.

"I suppose it might be worth it, if the only business being conducted wasn't in scallops." Douglas gave him a searching look, and he strove to keep his expression neutral.

"I have no idea what you're talking about," he said.

Douglas let his glance sweep the speakeasy to make sure no one was paying any attention to them and leaned closer to Hank. "Oh, come on, everyone knows Tomas was rum running, and that it was lucrative. How could I get into that business?"

Hank stared at his younger brother. He did not want him involved in the rum running. It was getting too dangerous, and there was no reason why Douglas should take risks like that. He should stay working in the office of Chapman & Sons and marry cute little Marty Grady and have pretty babies. That's what he needed to do. He did not need to get involved with pirates or dodging the law.

He finished his martini in one long swallow.

"I don't know what you're talking about," he lied.

As he put his glass down on the counter, he spotted Jiggy at a table in the corner. "I got to talk to someone," he said to Douglas, and without further explanation he headed for Jiggy.

Jiggy raised one eyebrow but didn't put down his drink, when Hank approached.

"Fancy meeting you here," he said. "We can't talk here, though. Come into the back with me."

Hank had always figured this was the back of Mulberry House, but Jiggy stood up and led him to a storeroom filled with crates of wine and barrels of liquor. Jiggy perched on a barrel marked Rum and leveled a steady gaze at Hank.

"I trust the little girl is fine."

"She is."

"Good. Now, about that lady cop you brought to my place."

Hank steadied himself against one of the barrels. He knew. Jiggy already knew Alice was a cop. Okay. That was good, really. It meant he would take the proper precautions. He'd been going to warn him anyway.

"You knew she was a cop?"

"Like I said, I knew her father. I've taken an interest in her career."

"I didn't think she knew who you were."

Jiggy sipped his drink. "She doesn't. Or didn't, until you brought her by."

"She was helping me search for the girl."

"All very noble and good." Jiggy put his drink down on the barrel, pulled his pipe out of his pocket, and lit it. "Keep her away from me." There was a definite warning tone in his voice.

"I don't have any control over her," Hank protested. "She's a cop! Who knows who she might tell her suspicions to?"

Jiggy took a long drag on his pipe. "If she busts me, I'm taking you down with me."

Frankly, Hank expected nothing less.

"About that." Hank cleared his throat and stood taller to show he wasn't intimidated. "I'm done."

"What do you mean 'done'?" Jiggy took the pipe out of his mouth and glared.

"Not making any more runs." If Nagy's death had anything to do with his rum running, it might make sense to step back a bit. He didn't have to think only of himself, but his crew, and some of them had families to consider. And now his brother wanted to get involved. It was too much.

"You can't stop."

"What do you mean, 'can't'? I can do whatever I like."

A small, almost evil smile came to Jiggy's face. "I wouldn't say that. You stop, I can't trust you anymore."

"Of course you can trust me."

Jiggy pointed his pipe at him. "You brought a cop to my hut. I'm not even sure I trust you now."

"That was not intentional."

"Regardless, it was a dangerous move. So I'll expect my next shipment from you when you get back in to port. What will that be, two and a half weeks or so from now?"

"I told you, I'm done. I'm not going out to rum row anymore."

"Listen." Jiggy stood up and got nose to nose with him. "The last person who told me he wasn't supplying me anymore was Nagy." He paused long enough for Hank to absorb that information. "Understand?"

Hank took a step back, though there wasn't much room to maneuver. This tiny space wasn't much bigger than one of the trenches. One of the trenches that could collapse on you at any minute when a bomb hit it. Suddenly it didn't seem as if there was enough air. He tugged at his collar and tried to concentrate on what Jiggy had told him.

"You telling me I'm going to end up dead if I don't supply you?" The thought was chilling, and it pissed him off.

Jiggy didn't answer right away, just looked deep into his eyes as if trying to read his soul. Slowly he smiled.

"No. I'm not telling you that. You wouldn't give a damn. You've been dead inside since the war. I'm telling you that someone you care about is going to end up dead. Maybe your mother, or your brother, or that cute lady cop. You want that on your conscience?"

The blood drained from Hank's face. His whole body went cold. "For God's sake, what are you saying?"

"I thought I was pretty clear." He put the pipe back in his mouth and puffed casually on it.

"Fine," he said. "I'll go out on another run." He couldn't risk anyone getting hurt on his behalf, especially not Alice.

If anything, Jiggy's grin became more sinister.

"Care about the lady cop, do you?"

"No." Hank said, too quickly.

"Then it really shouldn't matter to you what happens to her. But in case you do care, you might want to warn her that nosing about my place could be bad for her health. Savvy?"

"I told you, I don't control her," Hank repeated. How on earth was he going to keep Alice from visiting Jiggy if that's what she got it in her mind to do?

"Too bad for her." Jiggy's shoulders relaxed a little, and he took a sip from his drink.

"I'll keep her away," Hank promised, because it did matter to him what happened to her. Because, dammit, he did care about her. A lot.

Chapter Fifteen

Alice inserted paper into her typewriter and opened the top folder on her desk. She would teach Irene to type and then she would be freed from this endless paperwork. Free to do actual police work. Like track down Jiggy Malone. She knew where to find him now, so it was only a matter of having the time to get there.

She squinted at Mark's handwriting before beginning to type.

She couldn't just tell Malone that she wanted to know what his involvement in rum running was. He'd lie. People don't usually admit to illegal activity without a bit of coercion. But what coercion could she supply? She couldn't say it was under the guise of the Nagy murder, because as far as the department was concerned that case was closed. In fact, the report was somewhere on her desk waiting to be filed away.

But she could be simply investigating the illegal smuggling of alcohol in the township. Malone didn't have to know she suspected him of being involved, but again, he would be suspicious, especially if he was involved, and then he would pick up and run and she'd never find out anything.

Maybe the better thing to do would be to stage a stakeout, at night, when someone was likely to smuggle something in to him. If she saw it happening, she'd have proof that she could take to Chief Murphy and then maybe a real investigation could take place.

She rather liked the idea of conducting the whole investigation on her own and presenting it as a *fait accompli* to the department, but she wasn't a fool. In order to pull this off, she'd need the help of others. That didn't mean she couldn't get started on her own. If she could get away from her typewriter.

For now, she tuned out the sounds of the office, the phone ringing, the background conversations, and concentrated on typing up reports. It might not be the most exciting work, but that didn't mean it wasn't worth doing well. That was a lesson she'd learned from both her father and her mother.

She remembered one time a neighbor child had brought a torn doll's dress to Mama for her to sew it. Mama, of course, had plenty of real, paying work to do, but she took that small dress, and brought it to her machine and fixed it up good as new, giving the little girl a cookie along with the dress when she was done.

"You could have just whip-stitched it," Alice had pointed out.

"I could have," Mama agreed. "But why shouldn't I do my best work, even for a small thing?"

Lesson learned.

"Grady!" Chief Murphy's gruff voice cut through the background noise.

She looked up from her typewriter to see him standing over her desk.

"Yes, Chief?"

"Go out with Piccolo. There's been a bit of disturbance on New Street."

She didn't have to be told twice. She grabbed her hat and followed Mark out of the office.

"What's the call?" Alice asked him as they headed into the spring sunshine.

"Neighbor called to report the sounds of a fight next door. She says there are little children in the house and she's worried for their safety."

She figured as much. A bit of a disturbance, where her help was required, usually meant a husband was beating his wife. Mark would handle the husband, she'd comfort the wife, and see if she could convince her to press charges. They usually didn't.

"Anyone we've dealt with before?"

Mark nodded. "George Evans."

Alice sighed. George Evans was a violent man, but a charmer. His wife Matilda was meek and lacked any kind of self-confidence. Their children were still too young for school. If Alice couldn't convince Matilda to file a complaint, perhaps she could at least convince her to get her children to safety. But based on past experience, that wasn't likely.

They got to the house and Evans answered their knock. He was breathing heavily, but other than that didn't seem too out of sorts. He could have just been doing some heavy lifting, or perhaps he rushed to answer the door. Alice peered behind him and saw his wife, her back to the door, busy with a dustpan and broom, sweeping up some broken pottery. A picture on the wall was askew, and a chair was off center, as if righted quickly after being over turned. The children sat, huddled together on the sofa.

"What can I do for you, officers?" Evans asked jovially. "Collecting for the officers' ball?" He reached for his wallet.

"Actually, Mr. Evans," Mark said, making a move

to step past him into the house. "We were called to investigate a disturbance at this address."

"Nothing wrong here," Evans said and started to close the door. Mark used his foot to stop it from closing all the way and then pushed it open again.

"Just the same, we need to investigate." He looked past the man to his wife, now standing in the shadows, watching. "Officer Grady here is going to speak to your wife out back, while I have a word with you."

The man went to slam the door again, but Mark held firm, this time grabbing his arm as well to keep him there. Alice hurried around to the back of the house and could only hope that Mrs. Evans had taken the hint and gone out the kitchen door.

She had and was nervously wrapping her hands in her apron when Alice got there. She had a bruise forming on the side of her face and a trickle of blood ran down from a cut on her forehead.

"Sit down," Alice said, indicating the porch steps. She was afraid the woman would fall over if she didn't sit. "Can I get you a cold cloth for your face?"

Mrs. Evans let one hand drift up toward her face, but then let it fall again as she shook her head. "Better to not go inside."

"What happened?"

"I fell," she answered, rather woodenly.

A lie. Or perhaps the incomplete truth. She might well have fallen after her husband hit her.

"Your neighbor called, said they heard a commotion. Do you know what that might have been?"

"George was angry that the coffee wasn't ready. Sometimes he gets a bit loud."

"Ah." Alice sat on the steps next to the woman.

"He likes his coffee, does he?"

"Doesn't like to wait for anything is more like. And coffee takes time to brew. Can't do it in a minute. Not with the children to take care of."

"He's an impatient man." Alice kept her voice neutral, hoping to draw the woman out a bit.

Mrs. Evans gave a mirthless laugh. "That's one word for it."

"Say the word, and Officer Piccolo will bring him down to the station right now. We can charge him with assault."

"And then what would I do?" The woman asked, almost angrily. "I've got two children and no skills. We'd be thrown out of the house and then we'd starve."

"There are organizations that can help."

"Charity? No. I don't take no charity and neither do my children."

"You wouldn't get hurt anymore," Alice tried one last time.

The woman put her hand to her face. "This? This ain't nothing. Besides, he'll go out on the fishing boat again soon and I'll have a couple of weeks' peace."

"Fisherman, is he?" Alice asked, her interest piqued. She hadn't remembered that detail. "Who does he work for?"

"Just started with some man named Salerno. Been with him a couple of months now. Pay is steady. I was hoping that would make things better. I just have to be faster about the coffee."

Alice didn't think the problem could be solved by getting coffee ready faster, but she held her tongue. In the end she took the children to Woolworth's for ice cream while Mark sat down with the husband and wife in the hopes of getting them to talk through their difficulties. Alice didn't think it would matter much, but the kids enjoyed the ice cream, and they had no problem telling her all the details of the fights their parents had, complete with bad words and what piece of furniture got thrown most often: an ash tray.

She'd have to try again with Matilda, perhaps go there when George was off at sea, and convince her to press charges, or at the very least to leave.

Maybe it wasn't so bad that she'd never gotten married. Better to be single and occasionally lonely than to feel trapped in an abusive relationship for the sake of security. She thought of Hank insisting he couldn't live with someone else. Was he afraid he would be violent? If anything were to come of their friendship, would this be what she had to look forward to? She shook her head to clear it. No. Hank would never hurt her, she was sure of that. At least not intentionally.

She dropped the children back home only to find that Mark had left. There was no reason for her to rush back to the office, the reports could wait. For now, she'd play "beat cop." She strolled down Main Street, keeping an eye out for anything out of the ordinary.

She stopped to say hello to the grocer setting a display of fresh fruit on the sidewalk. She nodded to Mr. Parson the mail carrier as he left the post office on his rounds. She saw Patsy come out of the hardware store and quickened her pace so she could come even with him.

"Good morning, Mr. Finley."

He stopped and looked confused for a moment before a grin split his impish face. "Everyone calls me

Patsy, I almost didn't know you were talking to me. Irene says you've been real helpful to her. Thanks for that, on behalf of Tomas."

"I don't feel like I've done nearly enough," Alice admitted.

"At least they caught the guy who killed him," Patsy said. "We can all sleep a little easier in our beds at night."

"Can you?" Were they really safe now that an arrest had been made, or were they all still involved in rum running which would end up with them encountering pirates who apparently stopped at nothing to get what they wanted?

She watched as a variety of emotions flashed across his face. Finally, as if coming to a decision, he nodded his head.

"I'll buy you a cup of coffee."

She had a feeling this wasn't a case of him flirting with her. He had something to say, and she wanted to hear what it was. She followed him to the cafe.

They took a seat in the corner, well away from the window, and when the waitress came over, Patsy held up two fingers. "Two coffees," he said, then turned to Alice. "Do you take cream or sugar in yours?"

"A little cream," she answered.

"I'll have mine black." The waitress walked off and Patsy turned to Alice with an odd intensity in his eyes. "You don't think they got the real killer."

She was taken aback by this statement. It wasn't what she was expecting.

"As a matter of fact, I do think they have the real killer. But I don't think they have the whole story."

The waitress came with their coffee, and they fell

silent until she was out of earshot. Alice poured some cream in her cup and absently stirred. He had something he wanted to tell her, and she could wait here until he did.

Finally, Patsy sighed, pushed his hands through his hair and had a sip of his coffee.

"Ma'am, me and Snake, we weren't a hundred percent honest with you."

"When?"

"Ever," he said with a shrug.

She waited. If he'd admitted that much, chances were he was about to come clean. Marty said she had the patience of a saint, and while she wouldn't go that far, she was good at silent waiting.

"Jiggy was Tomas's buyer, it's true. Or he had been, but Tomas had a new buyer. Vince Salerno."

"The pirate?" She couldn't help herself from asking. Patsy had already told her about Salerno, when they'd been at Irene's. What had he held back?

"I don't know if he's a pirate or not. He did buy the lot, and a pirate would steal it, but maybe he dabbles a bit in piracy on the side." He took another sip of his coffee. "We unloaded the wine with Salerno and then Snake, Forster and I headed to a little place we know where we could get drunk. As you doubtless remember."

Yes. She remembered.

"Forster wanted to tell Jiggy that Tomas had a new buyer. He didn't think it was right to just leave him in the lurch. Snake and I thought it was best to leave well enough alone. Anyway, we argued, but Forster went to tell Jiggy anyway. Snake and I were arguing about what to do next, if we should warn Tomas or not, when you stumbled upon us."

Her hand shook as she put down her coffee cup. "If I hadn't brought you in, you would have warned Tomas and he might not have been killed?" Pain squeezed her heart. "Is that what you're saying?" Tears filled her eyes and she willed them away. She couldn't cry. She was a professional. But had she aided in Tomas's death in some way?

"No, ma'am," Patsy answered, reaching out to touch her hand. "I thought we shouldn't say anything, and I'd won the argument. Locking us up made no difference."

That didn't really make her feel better.

"So you think Jiggy had something to do with it?"

"Jiggy's the kind of man who will smile and pat you on the back with one hand while stabbing you in the back with the other."

"I have to stop him."

Patsy shook his head. "He's too slippery."

"What if I had proof of him accepting contraband?"

Patsy shrugged. "Aye, maybe that. If you can catch him."

But she knew where the hut was. The hidden hut on the water that would be perfect for hiding shipments of illegal liquor until he could move it out. She knew who and where and what. Now it was just a matter of when. She could do this. She could shut him down.

The bell in front of the shop jangled as two women came in, chatting amiably. They took a seat near the window. Patsy looked at his empty coffee cup and tossed a few coins on the table. "I have to go," he said, standing.

Alice stood as well.

"Thank you for the coffee, and the conversation," she said. "If you find out anything new, please let me know."

He nodded, his Adam's apple bobbing in his throat. "Aye, and you'll do the same."

"I will, Mr. Finley," she said and headed toward the door, Patsy following close behind.

That evening after dinner she and her mother and sister put on somber-colored dresses and headed across the street to Greiner's funeral home to pay tribute to Tomas Nagy. There was a large crowd, mainly of men who looked uncomfortable in ill-fitting suits.

Irene greeted Alice and her sister like old friends and thanked them for coming and being such a help.

Mama took Irene's hands in hers. "I, too, lost a husband. It is very difficult. I know. If there is anything I can do for you, please let me know. Even simply a cup of coffee and a listening ear."

Tears spilled over in Irene's eyes. "Thank you. Thank you so much."

They moved on to let others comfort the widow, and paid their respects to the deceased, kneeling in prayer by his coffin before moving toward the back of the room.

She couldn't be in the building without thinking about her father's funeral. Sometimes the pain was as fresh as if it had all happened only yesterday, and other times it seemed impossible he'd ever been a part of their lives at all. She remembered standing in the front of the room, by the coffin, accepting the greetings of well-wishers. She'd stood stoic and dry-eyed, sure she had to be strong in order for him to be proud of her.

Her eyes weren't dry now, and she was old enough and wise enough to know that didn't make her weak.

Mama was in conversation with a neighbor, and Douglas appeared from nowhere and made off with Marty. Alice looked around for Hank, sure that he was here someplace. Of course, since he was a good friend of the family, she couldn't expect Hank to have time for her tonight, but she would like a chance to say hello.

When someone tapped her on the shoulder, she turned, a smile on her face, expecting to see Hank. Instead she found herself face to face with Jiggy Malone. The smile stayed frozen in place, although now she didn't feel at all like smiling.

"Miss Grady, may I have a word with you? We can step outside on the porch. Get a bit of air."

This wasn't how she'd expected to encounter him, but she'd take what she could get.

"Of course." She followed him out into the cool evening, where a light mist was falling.

"I knew your father," Jiggy started to say, his eyes showing nothing but compassion. "As I said, we were in the Knights of Columbus together. He was a good man, and a dedicated one. I suspect you are a lot like him, and you want to get to the bottom of a mystery. You want to understand why someone would shoot a humble fisherman like Tomas Nagy."

She hesitated before answering. Was this a trick? And if so, in what way? She supposed there'd be no harm in admitting she wanted to know more.

"Yes. I would like to know that."

"And you don't think it was simple robbery."

Alice was confused. If this man had anything to do with it, why would he be bringing all this up? That made no sense. "I think there may be something else involved, yes."

"And, like your father, you won't rest until you get answers."

She supposed that was true, but she said nothing.

"I have answers."

"Yes?"

"You need to investigate a man named Vince Salerno."

A chill ran down her spine. There was that name again.

"You think he has something to do with it?"

"I can't say for sure, of course, but I do know Tomas had gotten involved with him lately. I'd warned him against it, but he was one for taking risks, was Tomas. In this case, it doesn't appear the risk paid off."

"So you think the answers lie with Vince Salerno?"

"I'm sure of it," Jiggy said. He put a finger to the side of his nose, in a goodbye gesture and slipped down the steps and out into the misty night.

Alice watched him go, wondering how she could discover who was telling her the truth.

Chapter Sixteen

The room was hot and stuffy and crowded, and the flowers smelled of death. Maybe not death, but that overly sweet smell that is meant to counteract death in the funeral parlor. It was oppressive.

Hank tugged at his collar and looked around the room for Alice. He'd seen her come in but had been involved in a conversation with Patsy Finley and hadn't been able to go to her. Now he wanted her and couldn't find her.

His palms were starting to sweat, and his heart was beating too fast. The body of his friend, looking as if he were sleeping peacefully in the front of the room, mocked death. Death did not look peaceful and serene. Death looked like mutilated bodies and despair.

"You don't look so good," Patsy said to him. "You should get some air."

Hank didn't need any further urging.

He stepped out onto the porch in time to see Jiggy striding down the street, and Alice, standing by the railing watching him go.

Alice and Jiggy? Had they been talking? He grabbed the side of the door for support. He'd had no chance to warn Alice to stay away from Jiggy. What had happened? What had been set in motion that he couldn't stop? No. He had to stop it, whatever it was. For now, Alice was safe and Jiggy was gone and that was all that mattered.

She turned and saw him then and her eyes widened as she rushed toward him.

"Hank! Are you quite all right? You don't look well."

He took a deep breath, gulping in air as if he were emerging from a deep-sea dive.

"I'm fine." His clammy hands perhaps proved that a lie.

She took his hands in hers.

"We'll go to my house. I'll make you a cup of tea. You can sit and relax."

"I should stay…"

"And pass out? Making more stress for poor Irene. No, come with me. I'll just pop back inside and tell my mother we're going."

"Tell mine as well," he said, for once thinking to spare his own mother some worry.

Alice wrinkled her brow. "I'm afraid I don't know your mother. I'll tell Douglas. Will that work?"

He nodded, suddenly finding himself incapable of speech as she hurried inside. Maybe he was going to pass out. That would be inconvenient. Head between the knees stops that, right? Wasn't that what his mother always told him? He sat on the damp front steps and lowered his head.

He'd seen friends scattered in little pieces around him, but he couldn't stomach seeing one laid out neatly in a coffin? What was the matter with him? What kind of a man was he?

The rushing sound in his head began to subside and a bit of warmth returned to his fingertips. Where was Alice? Certainly, she should have found her mother and

Douglas by now. Deep breath. He would be okay. Another deep breath. He was not in France. It would be okay.

The door opened, and he glanced up to see Alice looking down at him.

"Can you make it across the street?" she asked, her voice full of compassion.

"Should be able to. Feeling a bit better."

"Lean on me," she instructed as he stood up.

As much as he was loath to lean on anyone, and especially a woman, he found himself doing just that. She led him across the street and up the stairs to her own porch. Then she settled him on a damask-covered davenport in the sitting room and turned on the lamp, giving the room a cozy glow.

"I'll make you a cup of tea and be right back," she promised.

He nodded meekly and looked around the room, finally able to breathe again away from the cloying closeness of the funeral parlor. It was a nice room, fairly feminine in nature, with lots of pastels and florals, but that wasn't surprising seeing as three women lived here alone.

There were pictures on the mantel, and he felt steady enough to stand and look at them. Framed snapshots of young girls with their father and mother. A wedding portrait in a silver frame and a portrait of a smiling Sean Grady, in police uniform, nestled in a black-bordered frame.

Alice came back into the sitting room, carrying a tray with two cups of tea and a plate of gingersnaps. She set it on the coffee table.

"You seem to have your color back. Feeling

better?"

"Yes, thank you." He sat back down on the couch, leaving room should she choose to sit next to him. She handed him a cup of tea but didn't sit. He took a sip and was pleasantly surprised to find a taste of whiskey within. He looked up at her, one eyebrow raised in question.

"Medicinal, of course. You looked as if you needed it."

He wasn't sure what to say to that. He preferred if people thought him invincible. He took another sip of the tea and Alice sat beside him.

"I understand, you know," she said, her hands folded loosely in her lap. "Ever since my father's funeral I get heart palpitations when I go in a funeral home."

"Do you think we're the only ones?" he asked and was rewarded with an endearing smile.

"I doubt it. Perhaps some people are just better at hiding it." She picked up her own teacup, and he couldn't help wondering if she'd given herself some medicinal whiskey as well. "Have a gingersnap. Mama made them this afternoon."

He did as he was told and found that gingersnaps went quite well with whiskey-laced tea.

"Will you be at the funeral tomorrow?" He wouldn't mind having someone to lean on, in a purely figurative sense, tomorrow.

She shook her head. "I have to work."

"I'd rather be at work," he said under his breath.

"If you are at work aren't you out at sea?"

"Exactly."

She reached out and put a comforting hand on his

knee. "You know how much your being there will mean to Irene and the children."

"Too bad I have to be there sober." As soon as he said it, he wished he could pull the words back. This wasn't his brother or one of the crew he was bantering around with. She was a cop and he was an idiot.

"Some things just have to be dealt with sober."

"Most things these days."

She laughed. "Oh, I don't know, you and your brother seem to have your ways."

Laughing was a good sign. Her hand was still on his knee and he put his hand over hers.

"Ways I probably shouldn't tell you." He winked at her.

"Probably not," she agreed, but there was no reproach in her voice.

He put down his teacup and took her hand in both of his.

"How is it our paths never crossed before this?"

"I think we ran in different circles." She smiled, and he noticed a dimple in her cheek. It was completely endearing. "You were probably a few years ahead of me in school."

This was true. She'd said she was twenty-seven and he was thirty. Three years can be a lifetime difference when you are school age.

"I suppose that's true."

"And let me guess," she continued. "You were on the football team and maybe even the baseball team, and all the pretty girls gathered around you and sighed, hoping you'd notice them."

He remembered playing baseball in high school. A lifetime ago. He'd been a pretty decent pitcher. "I did play baseball and one season of football," he acknowledged. And the rest of it? Was that true? His ego would like to think it was, but his own memory didn't quite jive. "And what about you? Let me guess. You were in the band?" He took a stab in the dark.

She shook her head and her eyes shone. "Can't tell one note from another."

"You were in the cooking club?"

"Already told you I don't cook," she pointed out. "You're very bad at this."

He hung his head in mock shame. "You're right. I am. What did you do in high school?"

"Read, mostly. Hung out with Trudy and Mark and some other friends. I wasn't one of the shining lights."

"I wish I'd known you then," he said. All those wasted years when they could have been spending time together.

"You wouldn't have looked twice at me! I was awkward and skinny and completely tongue-tied if some boy tried to talk to me. I was much happier reading my books."

"I'm not so shallow that I only think about looks," he protested.

"Not now," she agreed. "But at seventeen?"

He wasn't even going to argue that his seventeen-year-old self wasn't shallow. Of course, he'd been shallow. That pretty much went with the territory of being seventeen.

"Did you go to college?" she asked. "Before you went off to war?"

"I did a couple of years at Rutgers but would have rather been out on the boat. Mother wanted me to get an education, though, so I obliged. When the chance came to enlist, I jumped at it, fool that I was."

"I think it was noble and brave."

He was oddly touched by that. He pulled her close to him and kissed her. To his relief, she happily and eagerly kissed him back, putting down her teacup and putting her free hand behind his neck and running her fingers through his hair.

How had he gone so long without knowing her? How had he even thought that he could do without seeing her anymore? He would do anything to keep her in his life. He had to.

The door opened, and they jumped apart so quickly that Alice knocked over her teacup.

"Oh dear," Mrs. Grady said, taking in the scene, and rushed to the kitchen for a towel, Alice following right behind her.

He pulled a handkerchief out of his pocket and tried to wipe up some of the spilled tea with that, but it wasn't terribly effective.

Alice came back with a towel and wiped up the tea. Her mother followed her back in.

"I certainly didn't mean to interrupt anything," she said, and he got the distinct feeling that she was rather glad there was something going on worthy of interruption. "I'll just go upstairs now and let you two have some privacy."

"No!" Alice protested. "Don't be silly, Mama. We don't want to chase you out of your own sitting room."

Hank wasn't sure he agreed with that sentiment. He wouldn't object at all to a little more privacy. But then, he had a perfect place to take her if he wanted privacy, even if it wasn't nearly as comfortable as the sitting room. He finished his tea in a few long gulps, no point in wasting the whiskey, and stood up.

"Alice, would you care to go for a walk with me?"

"I'd be delighted," she said, and then started gathering up the tea tray things.

"Leave it, dear," Mrs. Grady said. "I'll tend to it."

"Thank you, Mama." She kissed her mother on the cheek and then tucked her hand into Hank's and they headed out the door.

"Mind walking down to the *Mary B*?"

"It's a lovely night for a walk," she said.

It wasn't. It was still misty and damp and all in all a night better spent cozily in a sitting room rather than walking the causeway, but if he was with her, it would be lovely and supposed she must feel the same way.

"Why do you not think you are good company?" Alice asked with surprising candor. "I enjoy spending time with you."

He was glad it was dark, and she couldn't see the blush he was sure came to his cheeks.

"Even after my breakdown at the funeral home?" He'd rather forget the whole incident, but maybe it was better to get it out in the open.

"What about it? So you needed some air. It happens a lot at funeral homes." Alice seemed to genuinely not see the problem. He certainly did; how could she not?

"It's not just funeral homes. It can happen any time. I hate enclosed spaces."

"Isn't your boat an enclosed space?"

"I suppose, technically. But there is wide open space all around me, and that's what counts."

"You saw horrible things during the war." It wasn't a question and Hank didn't bother answering it. Of

The Rum Runner

course he saw horrible things during the war. War was full of horrible things. "But you've seen nice things since. Doesn't that count for anything?"

"No."

With a featherlight touch she put her hand on his arm. He forced himself not to shrink away. He wanted her to touch him. He wanted to touch her. But he wanted to keep up his walls more. His walls kept him safe.

"I disagree."

"What do you disagree with?" he snapped and now he did pull back from her. "How can you disagree with how I feel? It's my mind. They are my demons. You can't tell me how to act toward them."

"I have demons, too," she said softly.

He scoffed. "You weren't in a war."

"No. Bad things happen other places than war."

He wanted to argue with her, but really, she was right. He reached out and touched her hand and she let him wrap her fingers in his.

"What are your demons? Is it from when your father was killed?"

"No." Her voice was soft, and he wondered if she had as hard a time sharing hers as he had sharing his. If so, they had that much in common anyway. "I wasn't there when it happened. I didn't see it. Of course, that doesn't stop me from imagining it and having nightmares about it, but no. That's not it." She was silent for so long that he thought she wasn't going to tell him more. Now he wished it wasn't dark. He wanted to see her face, to try to divine her thoughts from her expression.

"It was a few years ago," she finally said. "When

197

they were opening the new town hall. Pole sitting was all the rage."

Oh God. He knew what she was going to tell him. He remembered the story. The crazed man who climbed the flag pole outside the new town hall. He'd fallen to his death. It was quite the talk of the town when he'd come in to port the next time.

"You saw the man fall?" Hank asked gently. It wasn't the same as being in the trenches in France, but he could see how it might give one nightmares.

"He didn't fall. He jumped." Her tone was flat as if something inside her had died. "And it was because of me."

"He jumped because of you? Did you know him?" Was this some spurned lover? He'd never heard that part of the story before.

"I didn't know him. I was the one who spotted him up there. I tried to talk him down. And...it didn't work." She paused, and he waited for her to continue. "He landed at my feet." Another pause, and he imagined she was picturing the scene.

"It wasn't your fault," Hank assured her. "If he was going to jump, I'm sure he would have done it whether you were there or not."

"And the bombs would have hit the trenches whether you were there or not," Alice countered.

Wow. She really pulled no punches.

"Doesn't make it any less horrible," Hank said.

"Exactly." Alice squeezed his fingers. "I didn't bring that up to depress us, though it certainly did have that effect. I wanted to let you know that I understand having seen horrible things. I get it. I also know it is possible to move on. It was for me, and it can be for you. If you want to."

"You think I don't want to?"

"You tell me."

Of course he wanted to be able to live a normal life. This wasn't a matter of choice. He didn't choose to have panic attacks or nightmares. But maybe he didn't have to let them control him quite so much. Maybe there was a way to move on.

And maybe he could do that with someone who understood to help him. They had reached the *Mary B*, and Alice was shivering beside him.

"Tea?" he asked as he guided her over the gangway, her hand warm in his.

"Brandy?" she asked, one eyebrow quirked. "Medicinal, of course. It would warm us up quicker."

He grinned. "I may have some on board. For medicinal purposes."

"Naturally."

He led her into the galley and lit the lantern, casting the small wood-paneled room with a cozy glow. They actually kept a bottle of brandy in the galley. She was right that there was nothing quite like it when someone had a chill, and that tended to happen when they were out at sea. He poured a little into two glasses and sat down beside her at the table.

"When do you go back out?" She took a sip and looked at him over the top of her glass.

The question hit him like a dagger in the heart. He was going out to sea, soon, and for two weeks. Never before had he wanted to stay on land instead of going. There'd never been a reason to stay before.

"A couple of days." Was there a way to delay it more? Maybe he could wait until after the weekend, take her out on Friday or Saturday.

"And you'll be gone for a couple of weeks."

Two weeks suddenly felt like an eternity. "Ten days to two weeks, depending on the haul."

"So if you catch a lot early on, you get to come home sooner?"

He smiled at her eagerness.

"Something like that."

She took an appreciative sip of her brandy. "This is quite good. I suppose I better not ask where you got it."

"Better not," he agreed. He took the glass from her hand and put it on the table. He pulled her close and kissed her, hoping to pick up where they had left off in her sitting room.

She responded eagerly, and he wondered if there were any non-awkward way to get her to his cabin. It wasn't the most comfortable place in the world, but it beat the galley.

Before he could formulate the words, the boat shifted and there was a thump from the working deck. He pulled back from Alice, all his senses alert. Someone had boarded.

"What's the matter?" Alice asked, eyes wide.

"Nothing, I hope," he said and stood up. No one was expected on board tonight, but it was possible one of his crew members had come looking for him. They knew that in a pinch this was usually where he could be found. He'd better see who it was and what he wanted.

"I'll be right back," he said and headed out to the working deck. He wasn't terribly surprised to have Alice follow right behind him.

The man on deck, dressed in dark clothes, with a black wool cap pulled low over his eyes, looked up, eyes wide when Hank burst upon him.

"You there! Who are you? What do you want?"

"That's George Evans," Alice said, with certainty, behind him.

Hank turned to her, confused.

"Who?"

"He works for Salerno."

"Damn."

The man took advantage of Hank's distraction to jump off the boat and run into the night.

Alice moved as if to follow him, but Hank grabbed her arm, stopping her.

"Where are you going?"

"I can arrest him for trespass. Clearly he wasn't meant to be here." She tried to pull her arm free, but he was stronger than she was.

"I don't want you messing with Salerno's gang."

"Hank, I'm a police officer. It's what I do."

"Leave it." The words came out a lot more strident than he'd intended. He tried to lighten his tone. "You're not dressed for a pursuit."

She looked down at the heels and black dress that she'd worn for the wake. "I know where he lives. I can go there tomorrow and arrest him."

Hank let go of her arm, since the immediate threat of her taking off seemed to be past.

"Don't. I won't press charges. Let it go."

"Why? I know he works for Vince Salerno. Jiggy Malone warned me that Vince Salerno is probably behind Nagy's murder. Patsy thinks Jiggy is. Either way, I don't like that guy sneaking around on the *Mary B*."

"I don't like it either," Hank said, and he also

201

didn't like the fact that Alice had apparently already collected an awful lot of information. How long before she traced things back to him?

"Is that what Jiggy was talking to you about at the funeral home?"

She nodded.

"Stay away from him." He couldn't forget the threat Jiggy had made against Alice. He needed to keep her away from him at all costs.

She crossed her arms and looked him straight in the eye.

"Either Vince Salerno or Jiggy Malone, or both, are involved in rum running in this town, and I intend to put a stop to it."

"Don't mess with them."

"Don't tell me how to do my job." She tapped her foot, and he suspected he was on dangerous ground here.

"I wouldn't dream of it, but stay away from them. Especially Jiggy."

"I can take care of myself."

She turned toward the gangway, and his heart filled with panic. He had to make her understand that she was putting herself in harm's way. He rushed to intercept her, grabbing her arm once more.

"I'm telling you, if you don't stay away from Jiggy you'll be sorry."

The hard look in her eyes startled him.

"Is that a threat?" She jerked her arm free.

He took a step back as if she had actually slapped him.

"No! It's a warning. You could end up like Nagy."

"I can take care of myself, Henry Chapman. Thank

you very much."

She climbed off the boat, and like a coward he watched her walk away into the darkness.

Chapter Seventeen

He didn't try to follow her. She wasn't sure if she was happy about that or not. She should have known he was no different than any other guy, thinking that because she was a woman she couldn't do her job.

She trudged back up the causeway, wishing she had on more comfortable walking shoes. They hadn't bothered her while she was walking with Hank. The way back seemed twice as long as the way there. She'd let her head be turned by a handsome man and gentle kisses. She was a fool.

She had a job to do, and he wasn't going to stop her. Maybe she couldn't arrest George Evans for trespass if Hank refused to sign a complaint, but she could still ask him what he was doing on Hank's boat late at night. She wouldn't go now; it would be better if she waited until she was on duty and in uniform.

She got across the causeway and glanced down at the Nagy house. There were lights on, and people silhouetted against the windows. Good, Irene wasn't alone. Every day was going to be a struggle, but at least she had people to help her through them.

Right now, she just wanted to get home and take a hot bath and not think about anything. The problem was that she knew she wouldn't stop thinking. About Hank. Was she too rash in running out on him? He hadn't followed her, so maybe not.

It had all been a pipe dream. A fairy tale wish brought on by dancing with him at the club, and somehow that long-ago dream of having a home and family of her own seemed to be possible. Silly of her.

As she approached the police station, she decided her bath could wait. There were things she needed to find out.

She pulled open the door, and McGrath, the night sergeant, looked up in surprise.

"What are you doing here, Grady? Chief give you the night shift all of a sudden?"

"I want to look at some files."

McGrath picked up his coffee cup and nodded toward the cabinets.

"You know where they are, help yourself."

Not only did she know where they were, but nearly every damn piece of paper put there in the past few years had been put there by her. But she didn't have a photographic memory, and there were plenty of papers put there before her time.

"Want a cup of coffee?" McGrath asked as she headed straight toward the drawer marked S.

"Yes, please." She flipped through the folders. Sabo, Sacco, Saffron, Sakowski, Salgado. She stopped and looked again, but there was no file on Salerno.

"You ever hear of a Vince Salerno?" she asked McGrath as he handed her a cup of coffee.

"Can't say as I have. No folder on him?"

She shook her head and took a grateful sip of the mud-like coffee.

"That's good, then, right? Kept his nose clean."

She supposed that was true. At least in Woodbridge.

"Who made this coffee?" She grimaced as she took the second sip.

"Those of us on the night shift need a higher octane to keep us going." He gave her a self-deprecating shrug. "Who's this Vince Salerno guy? What you want with him?"

"I don't know," Alice admitted. "I think he's involved in rum running. His name keeps popping up when people talk about Tomas Nagy's murder."

"Thought we arrested the guy who killed Nagy." McGrath perched on the edge of a desk.

"We got the guy who pulled the trigger."

"And your gut tells you to dig deeper."

"Pretty much."

McGrath grinned and shook his head. "You are your daddy's girl, that's for sure. The Chief ever gives you a chance, you'll put us all to shame."

She didn't want to put them to shame, she just wanted to do her share. She put down the vile cup of coffee and checked another drawer. Her heart nearly stopped when she found a file for Chapman, Henry. She hadn't wanted to find a file for him. She wanted him to have kept his nose clean, as McGrath would say.

She opened it and found only one piece of paper, nearly ten years old. Apparently, he'd been involved in a fist fight shortly after coming back from the war. She put the folder away. That certainly wasn't something she would hold against him.

On to the next drawer. Malone. The problem, of course, was that she didn't know Jiggy's given name. She felt fairly confident that he hadn't been named Jiggy by his mother. Though who knows, weirder things had happened. She'd gone to school with a girl named Ladybug. That girl had insisted everyone call her Charlotte.

She found several folders for Malone and brought them back to her desk. She sipped the coffee and pored through what she found inside. One was for a woman, a Bridget Malone caught shoplifting from Christensen's a few years before. That clearly wasn't Jiggy. The next was for a Walter Malone, and it was a complaint he had issued about the neighbor's cow getting into his garden. The paper was yellowed with age, and Walter had been about eighty at the time of the complaint. This was not the Jiggy she was looking for.

The last file was for a James Malone, and Alice let her hopes rise. Surely Jiggy could be a nickname for James. But the James in the file had been the victim of a deadly carriage accident fifteen years before. This was not Jiggy either.

She had struck out.

"No luck?" McGrath said, looking up from his desk.

"Afraid not."

"What are you looking for, anyway?"

"I have no idea." Alice closed the last folder. "I was hoping something would jump out at me."

"Not a bad method but doesn't always work. Go home, get some sleep. There are other avenues you can explore in the morning."

"Like what?" she asked, feeling defeated.

"Good old-fashioned police work. Go out and talk to people. That will tell you a lot more than old reports."

"I suppose you're right." She returned the Malone files to the cabinet, but one of them didn't fit in smoothly, blocked by something that had fallen between the files. She fished it out. It was a small pocket notebook. The kind her father used to always carry with him.

She took it back to her desk, ignoring McGrath's questioning look. As soon as she opened it, she knew it had been her father's. She recognized his handwriting and his cryptic note-taking style.

She read through the notes that would have made perfect sense to her father but were a puzzle to solve for her. On one page were lists of times and days which she suspected related to high tide and low tide. Some of the times were starred. She wasn't sure what that star meant. Was it a time he needed to check something? A time he knew something was happening?

What had he been investigating? Some snippet of conversation from way back then made her think he'd been trying to stop rum running. If that were the case, the tide time tables would make sense.

There were lists of boat names. She perused them and her heart stopped when she saw the *Mary B* listed there.

It didn't have to mean anything, though. Maybe it wasn't a list of rum runners, just possible suspects? It wasn't proof of wrongdoing. Just the same, she wished it hadn't been there. But maybe Hank hadn't even been the skipper of her then. How long had he been captain?

On another page the word Jiggy was circled.

Jiggy.

In that case it was almost certain her father had been investigating rum runners. And maybe he'd gotten too close for comfort. Could it be that his murder, like Tomas Nagy's, wasn't quite as cut and dried as it appeared?

She tapped her fingers on the page in front of her.

She needed to find out more. To find out more, she needed to get out of the office. Can't do good police work sitting behind a desk. For now, she needed a good night's sleep.

She tucked the notebook into her desk drawer and stood up. "Good night, Sergeant, and thanks for the coffee."

"Good night, Grady," he answered. "Get some sleep. You'll find what you're looking for in the morning."

However, in the morning what she found was a foot-high pile of reports to type up.

"Are you kidding me?" she asked no one in particular when she got a look at her desk. They hadn't been there last night. Where had they been hiding them all before dumping them on her?

"It's been a busy couple of days," Mark said. "I thought you were getting us a new typist."

"Yeah, as soon as I get a chance to teach her to type." Which wouldn't happen today, because today was the funeral, and she certainly wasn't going to be giving typing lessons to a widow on the day of her husband's funeral.

At home that night, she avoided Marty, who was getting ready to go out with Douglas, and snuck through the back yard to Trudy's. Trudy made a fresh pot of tea and put some sponge cake on the table. Then she chased the children outside and told Mark to keep an eye on them.

"Now, tell me. What happened?"

It was good to have a best friend.

"He tried to tell me what to do."

Trudy sighed. "Clearly he doesn't know you well enough yet to know that is not allowed."

Trudy's tone was light, but Alice realized she might have a point. Maybe it wasn't fair to judge Hank based on something he wouldn't realize was wrong. But then again, wasn't it wrong of him to boss her around at all? Of course, it was.

"He thinks he needs to protect me." She took a bite of the sponge cake, which was, naturally, delicious.

"It's a guy thing," Trudy said. "It makes them feel important. Mark thinks he needs to protect me, too."

"Mark's a police officer, trained to protect," she pointed out.

"And?" Trudy held her eye, teacup poised half way to her mouth. "Do you think only police officers want to protect women?"

"But I'm an officer! I can protect myself."

"And you don't sometimes want someone to take care of you?"

"No." She knew she was lying, and Trudy knew it too.

Trudy laughed out loud.

"You are such a liar. Tell me what is really bothering you about Hank."

"I think he's a rum runner." Once she said it out loud, she knew it must be true. Of course he was a rum runner. Tomas had been, and Hank was involved with all the same people and he didn't want her to investigate. What other answer could there be?

Suddenly Trudy got serious.

"Oh. It would seem you have incompatible careers."

Alice nearly choked on her tea. Trudy handed her a napkin.

"That's one way of putting it," she said when she could breathe again. "So what do you think I should do?"

"Quit your job, of course," Trudy said and winked at her.

Alice sighed. She supposed that would solve one problem, but it really wasn't an answer and they both knew it.

"Short of that?"

Trudy got up and went to the window, where she could look out on her children and husband playing in the yard.

"To me, nothing is more important than Mark and the kids."

"I barely know Hank." She put down her teacup. He couldn't be that important to her yet.

"I know. I was just thinking out loud."

"If he doesn't want me to be able to do my job, he's not the man for me."

Trudy nodded.

"If he's involved in illegal activity, he's not the man for me."

Trudy nodded again.

"If he thinks I need him to protect me and can't take care of myself, he's not the man for me."

For the third time, Trudy nodded, but this time she said, "If he's not the man for you, you wouldn't be trying so hard to convince yourself he wasn't the man for you."

Damn it. She hated when Trudy was right.

Chapter Eighteen

He was going back to sea. Land held nothing for him. He thought Alice would prove a reason to stay, but clearly, he'd been wrong. As soon as he could get the *Mary B* provisioned, he'd be out on the waters where he belonged.

He would have gone today if he hadn't had to go to the funeral. The funeral and the pain on Irene's face as she laid her husband to rest was another reason to get back out to sea as soon as possible.

When Alice left last night, he fought with himself as to whether he should follow her or not, but she had been so clear that she didn't want or need his advice or interference in her life that he thought it best to let her go.

He'd closed himself up in the bridge and poured himself a few fingers of whiskey. He'd downed it quickly and poured himself some more. Why had he let himself feel anything for that lady cop? It was a mistake. He should have known that from the first time Douglas suggested going to the club. He didn't need anyone. Life was much easier that way.

He'd taken the bottle with him to his quarters. He'd thought he'd have Alice in here. He was a fool.

He'd spent the night huddled in the trenches dodging bombs and woken in the morning to a raging headache, a sore hip, where he'd been lying on the bottle, and someone pounding on his door.

He'd stumbled out of his berth and opened the door to see his brother standing there.

"I was hoping to find you here. Mother is beside herself."

"I'm thirty years old. I don't have a curfew."

"No, but you do have a mother who worries when you don't come home at night." Douglas peered past him into the small room. "I'm surprised to find you alone, though. I thought you'd have the lovely Miss Alice with you."

"The lovely Miss Alice wants nothing to do with me. And the feeling is mutual." He wished his head would stop pounding.

"You had to go and mess that up, did you?" Douglas scolded. "She was perfect for you. Why couldn't you see that?"

"I'm not perfect for her." He clutched the door frame. "And keep your voice down, will you? There's no need to shout."

"I'm not shouting." Douglas grinned. "But you're hung over." Douglas grabbed his arm, but Hank shook him off. "Come on." He lowered his voice to a more soothing tone. "Let's get you home to some breakfast and coffee."

Hank let himself be led out to Doug's car and driven home. His mother came out of the drawing room and shook her head and sighed. "There's breakfast in the dining room."

Several cups of coffee and a few eggs later, Hank was beginning to feel human again. And then he went to the funeral and he felt worse than ever.

In the afternoon he borrowed Doug's car to get

word to all his crew that they would be leaving at high tide on Friday.

"I can't," Swede said. "My kid is turning three on Friday. I promised my wife I'd take them all down the shore for the day."

He didn't want to wait. He wanted to get out on the water. "You good with cash if we go without you?"

"No worries," Swede answered. "I wouldn't mind a small vacation."

If he stopped rum running, his men would have worries, but for now it was nice they didn't.

There were always men looking for a crewing gig hanging around the fishery, so he knew he would have a full crew.

The rest of his crew was available, and he went to the market to stock the larder for what they would need for two weeks at sea. He placed his order with the butcher for fifty pounds of ground meat and another fifty pounds of a variety of steaks and chops, to be delivered to the *Mary B*. He called Cooper's Dairy and ordered thirty gallons of milk. He filled the water jugs they kept on board so that each man would have plenty to drink. He ordered coffee and beans and rice and potatoes and forty tons of ice. He had the provisioning of the boat down to a science.

Next stop was to the office to talk to his father.

"I hear you are short a man," Father said, shuffling some papers on his desk.

"I'll get someone." That was really the least of his concerns these days.

"Take Douglas."

Across the room, at his own desk, Douglas's head shot up.

"He's not an experienced crewman." Hank protested.

"I want to set him up as captain of the *Katinka*. He's got to get practice somewhere. Why not with you?"

Why not? Because he didn't want his little brother to know about his side business. That was why not. Not that he could exactly tell that to his father.

"Mother will be lonely if we are both gone," Hank said, knowing the protest was lame.

"Your mother has me." His father winked. "You don't have to worry about her being lonely."

Douglas was up now, striding across the office. "I told you, Father, I don't want to captain the *Katinka*. I'm happy working in the office."

"I put in my time as a fisherman before I started worrying about the paperwork side of it. If you want to take over for me, you need to put in your time as well." Father looked over his glasses at him. He was not going to be put off.

Douglas wasn't ready to give up, though. "I've got a date with Marty this weekend. Maybe I can go out on the *Mary B* another time."

Father's brows came together in a frown. "Hank is short a man now. Marty is going to have to learn that you won't be available every day. Understood?"

Douglas paled slightly, then stood taller and swallowed hard, his Adam's apple bobbing.

"Understood."

"It's settled then," Father said. "It will be good for the two of you to work together." With that, Father walked back out of the office.

Douglas snarled, "What am I supposed to tell

Marty? She's expecting me to take her out."

"Tell her you'll see her in two weeks. It's not that big a deal." Hank picked up an anchor-shaped paperweight from the desk and turned it around his hands. "We leave at dawn day after tomorrow. Get your stuff on board tomorrow. It will be easier that way." He put the paperweight down and left his brother alone.

Whether Douglas ever skippered his own ship or not, it would be good for him to have a working knowledge of what went into it. Also, it would be nice to work with his brother. The only problem was the whole rum row thing. Douglas was going to find out about that side of the business too, and Hank would have greatly preferred to keep it from him.

He could simply skip rum row, as he had originally planned. The problem then was keeping his loved ones safe when Jiggy found out. He rubbed his temples as a headache threatened to take over. Fishing, and even smuggling, used to be so simple. What had happened?

The next day, Smitty came on board and together they went through the checklist of maintenance issues to make sure everything was seaworthy.

By late afternoon he found himself alone once again, waiting for his deliveries. It was a sparkling clear spring day, as if the rain the night before had scrubbed the skies. He sat on the working deck, his feet up, his face tilted skyward, enjoying the afternoon sun and a few minutes to do nothing but relax.

The problem with relaxing was it gave him time to think. And now that all the work had been done, his thoughts turned to Alice. He didn't want to think about Alice. He wanted to forget her. But he kept seeing her bright, alert eyes, and the way her hair swung by her face and the smooth assurance she had when she walked. He liked that she was so helpful to the Nagy family, people she didn't even know. He liked how she had struck right in to help find Sari. He liked the way they had moved together when they danced and how she had tasted when they kissed.

From the road behind him came the sputtering of an engine and the whirr of tires on gravel. He opened his eyes and stood to see which of his deliveries had arrived. But he was faced not with a truck but a long low Cadillac. His heart jumped when Vince Salerno, in a dapper pinstriped suit, stepped out.

"I'm not even provisioned yet," Hank called to him. "I've got nothing for you to steal."

Salerno put his hand to his heart as if the words had wounded him. "I'm afraid you misapprehend me. I'm not a thief," he said as he boarded the *Mary B* with no more than a by-your-leave. "I'm here to make a deal with you."

"Not interested." He folded his arms and glared at Salerno. He was not intimidated by this man, though he was wary.

"You don't even know what it is yet." Salerno didn't drop his avuncular persona.

"Still not interested."

Salerno walked around the deck, stepping carefully over lines and nets. "I think you will be when you hear what it is."

"I doubt it."

"I want you to sell your next shipment to me."

"Didn't know you needed a load of scallops," Hank responded.

"You know full well what I mean." The jovial

persona was starting to slip a bit.

"I'm a fisherman. I sell scallops. It's what I do. If you are not interested in buying scallops, I suggest you move along. I've got work to do."

"Listen, Hank, and listen carefully. I know you sell to Jiggy, and I know what you sell to Jiggy. He's got a stranglehold on the business right now, but there is no reason he should. I can do better for you." He paused to let that sink in. "And I'm a safer business partner."

Hank stared out into sparkling diamonds rippling on the water. He couldn't argue that Jiggy was a dangerous business partner; the problem was that stopping doing business with him was even more dangerous. He couldn't risk it. Not unless he knew there was a way to keep his family—and Alice—safe.

For now, as intriguing as this possibility was, he'd have to let it go. Jiggy had too much of a hold on him.

"I'd be happy to sell you as many scallops as you need," Hank said with finality.

Salerno nodded. "So that's how it's going to be, is it? You'll regret it."

"Possibly," he answered. "I have lots of regrets in my life. What's one more?" If Jiggy hadn't threatened his family—and Alice—he would have seriously considered Salerno's offer, but while he was willing to take risks for himself, he wasn't willing to risk others.

Salerno started to head back over the gangway.

"By the way," Hank called after him, "why did you have someone sneak aboard the *Mary B* the other night?"

Salerno froze mid-step but waited a beat too long before turning around. A beat that Hank was sure he used to compose his expression.

"I don't know what you're talking about."

"Luckily, I scared him off before he could steal anything, but I'm seriously thinking about filing a criminal trespass complaint against George Evans. You wouldn't want that to come back and bite you. Rein in your goons."

"I'm not the one with goons around here," Salerno answered and stepped off the boat.

He watched as Salerno drove off in his fancy convertible. He couldn't settle his mind down. Would he be sorry he had not reached an agreement? Was he a pirate, like rumor had it? If so, why would he offer to buy the shipment? Wouldn't he just steal it?

The thing was, he had no intention of having his shipment stolen. He had stockpiled enough rifles to arm the whole crew if it came to that. He was not going to be a passive victim of pirates. He had survived in the trenches against the German guns. He could survive Vince Salerno. The key was being prepared. Tomas had apparently been taken off guard. That would not happen to him.

What he didn't like was that Salerno had clearly pegged him as a target. He'd have to make sure some of the crew was always standing guard once they left rum row. He wasn't taking chances with either his shipment or the lives of his men.

Douglas arrived, with Marty in tow, laughing together as they stepped out of the car.

"Can I give Marty a tour of the *Mary B*? Last time I tried I couldn't bring her very far because you had just painted the steps." He looked so young and eager that it was impossible to say no.

"Of course."

They stepped on board.

"This is the working deck," Douglas said with an air of proprietary pride. "Those nets get dragged through the water and hauled up using the hoists. Then the scallops are dumped on the deck here and shelled." Douglas led her away, narrating as he went.

The sight of Marty had brought Alice back into his mind. He didn't want to think about her. She complicated his life, and he wanted to be done with her. But yet, unlike other women he had danced with when he was on shore, there was something about Alice that intrigued him, that made him want to know more, that made him want to spend time with her. But it was impossible and a ridiculous idea. She'd made that very clear the other night. He had to forget her. Once they were out at sea, he'd be able to do that. He could hardly wait for the morning's high tide to arrive, so they could cast off.

Douglas and Marty came back to the working deck. "Did you have a fight with my sister?" Marty asked.

"Not intentionally," Hank said, putting his book aside.

"She was pretty upset with you."

"She apparently doesn't like it when people are protective of her."

Marty grimaced.

"No, she doesn't like that at all." She paused, as if thinking that over. "Actually, I suspect she would really like someone to be protective of her, but she doesn't want to admit that she could possibly be protected, if you know what I mean."

Strangely, he thought he did.

"You should try again with her," Marty said, in her

clear, cheerful, optimistic voice. "I think after two weeks she'll have cooled down and be ready to forgive you."

Hank shook his head. "I'm not good for her. She knows that. I know that."

"I think you're wrong," Marty said with a backward glance as Douglas led her off the boat.

He wasn't wrong. He only wished he was.

The dairy truck pulled up then, followed closely by the butcher and the ice truck, and Hank had to put all his energy into getting the ship stocked.

He went home for one last home-cooked meal and to collect his personal belongings before heading back to the *Mary B*. He'd spend the night on her, because he didn't like to leave her unoccupied when she was stocked full of everything they would need for the next two weeks.

His mother pressed a box of homemade cookies on him before he left the house. "So you don't forget us while you are gone," she said and wrapped her arms around his neck.

"I never forget you," he assured her, patting her awkwardly on the back.

"I wish you could find peace with your demons," she said into his ear. He hadn't realized she'd known about his demons.

"They stay away when I'm at sea," he answered.

"I know." With one final squeeze she let him go. "Have a safe journey and take care of Douglas."

"I will."

Back on the *Mary B*, he got the captain's quarters in order and settled down on deck with a book. Usually when he was anticipating a fishing run, he had no hesitations at all. This time there were too many things pulling at him: Jiggy and Salerno's threats, a reluctant Douglas, and Alice. Always it came back to Alice.

He hoped that once he was at sea, the problems that had accumulated on land would all wash away like they usually did.

Chapter Nineteen

Thursday evening, after dinner, Alice and Marty headed back to the Nagy house. Marty had once again agreed to watch the children while Alice gave Irene a typing lesson. Alice was surprised to see the typewriter set up on the kitchen table when she got there, a piece of paper already inserted and half-filled with letters.

There were rows of fs and ds. Clearly Irene had started out with the book. After a few orderly rows, there was a row of random letters and symbols and it seemed that perhaps Sari had taken over. After that there was, in all capital letters "ERNST IS A GOFFBAL" which Alice suspected was supposed to say "goofball" and had been typed by his brother.

"I get started," Irene said proudly. "I want to learn." She looked at the addition to her paper and blushed. "The children…they help."

"You're off to a good start."

The children appeared as if from nowhere. The boys clearly remembered their time with Marty because the first thing they asked was if they could play cards again.

"Not this time. We need to let your Mama have quiet, so she can learn to type."

"She learned already!" Sari tugged at Marty's dress and pointed to the paper in the typewriter. "We helped."

"Well, she needs to be able to do it without your

help."

Alice loved the way Marty was able to handle children. She would make a fantastic mother someday.

"Have you all finished your homework?" Marty asked.

When they promised they had, and Irene agreed, Marty took the three of them out for ice cream.

Once in the quiet of the house, Alice sat beside Irene at the table and with a fresh piece of paper walked her through the first few typing lessons.

"You really don't need me," she said when they had gotten through nearly half the book. "You're quite good. You just need to practice so you can do it without looking."

Irene seemed skeptical. "I can't look?"

"You can, but it goes faster if you don't have to."

"When can I get the job?"

Alice appreciated her eagerness but didn't want her to ruin her chances by not being ready.

"I'd say practice for a week and then come into the station to meet with Chief Murphy."

Irene nodded, tears glistening in her eyes. "You have been so kind. I thank you. Much."

The front door swung open and the children burst through followed by Marty. Alice wasn't in the least surprised to see Douglas with her.

"Did we give you enough time?" Marty asked.

"We were just wrapping up," Alice said, finding her heart was searching for Hank to be with them. But clearly, he wasn't. She put on a smile. "Your timing was perfect."

The children rushed to their mother, eager to tell about the ice cream and about an adventure they had with a stray dog that tried to get Sari's ice cream, but Uncle Doug saved everyone.

"It wasn't nearly as dramatic as it sounds," Douglas said, with endearing humility, "but I don't mind being thought of as a hero."

"Doug is going out on Hank's boat tomorrow," Marty sounded like a proud mother. "He's being trained to be the new captain of the *Katinka*!"

"And when I'm big enough I'm going to be first mate!" Ernst proclaimed.

Douglas tousled the boy's dark hair. "That's right, mate."

Alice felt frozen to the floor. Hank was leaving. Tomorrow. Without saying goodbye? Of course, she had walked out on him. But he hadn't even attempted to apologize or anything.

She'd almost fooled herself into thinking that maybe he cared about her, and that was why he was being stupidly protective of her. Clearly, she'd been wrong. It didn't matter. She had bigger things to worry about than emotionally stunted sea captains.

Somewhere there was a link between Jiggy Malone, Vince Salerno, her father, Tomas Nagy and maybe even Hank Chapman. That link had to do with rum running. She needed to do some good solid police work and figure it out.

Douglas and Marty took off to spend a few precious hours alone, and Alice turned to Irene.

"Could you perhaps do me a favor?"

Irene's eyes opened wide. "Is something I can help you with? Only ask!"

"I want to talk to Tomas's men. Did he keep a list of his crew?"

"Not always same men," Irene said, uncertainly. "Some go with him all the time. Patsy, Snake, Benji. Some go only sometimes. I do have a list. You give me a minute?"

"Of course."

Irene hurried to a back room, while Alice waited with the children. Sari took a paper from a cupboard and approached Alice with it. It was clearly a picture she had drawn. It showed a man and a woman, with a little girl between them.

"That's you and Uncle Hank when you found me when I was lost," she explained. "It's for you."

Alice's heart melted a little. Trudy's children sometimes drew her pictures, and she was always touched to receive their artwork. This picture made her both happy and sad, though, because it showed the possibility of there being a future between her and Hank, when in reality there was none.

"It is lovely," she exclaimed, surprised to find tears in her eyes. "I will treasure it."

Sari beamed proudly as Irene arrived with a penciled list of names and addresses. "These are the men on the last trip." There were stars next to two names. "Those men. New for that trip. I not know them."

Interesting. Maybe those were the men that got Tomas to switch buyers. Maybe they were the place to start.

"Thank you, Irene. I'll come by Monday and see how you are getting on."

With the drawing and the list of names safely stowed in her handbag, Alice took leave of the Nagy house. It was too late now to deal with this, but she'd go straight after work tomorrow. Since it wasn't her case, or an official investigation, it would probably be best if she wasn't in uniform.

But Friday after work, Trudy invited her for dinner, and she could hardly say no, especially not if she didn't want to have to explain her extra-curricular investigation to Mark. Saturday her mother recruited her for work in the garden, while the day was bright and sunny.

It wasn't until the afternoon that she finally had a chance to investigate. Before going through the men on the list, she decided to stop in and see George Evans. Hank might not want to file a complaint, but that didn't mean she couldn't ask him why he'd been sneaking around on the *Mary B*.

As she approached the Evans' house, she could hear raised voices inside. Perhaps it was serendipitous that she was stopping by now. She paused on the porch, hand raised to knock on the door, as she tried to get a sense of what was going on inside.

"You are useless!" George Evans shouted, presumably at Matilda. "Look at this place. It's a wreck. What do you do all day?"

"What do I do all day?" Matilda shouted back. "I cook your meals and watch your children and you sit around on your ass drinking. A little help would go a long way."

Alice knocked before the fight could escalate to blows, which she was sure wouldn't be far off at this point.

The silence inside was instantaneous. The door was opened by an innocent-faced George Evans. He saw Alice and scowled. "Who called the cops on us this time?"

"No one. I'm off duty. I wanted to ask you some questions, though."

"The wife and I were just having a disagreement. No crime in that." He started to shut the door and Alice knew she wasn't going to be as good at forcing the door to stay open as Mark was. Then again, she wasn't here officially; she had no right to force the door open.

"I completely agree. But I would like to talk to you, if you have a minute."

He stepped out on the porch.

"What is it?" He wasn't gracious, but at least he hadn't slammed the door on her.

"What were you hoping to steal from the *Mary B* the other night?"

"I wasn't going to steal nothing!"

Which was an implied admission that he had been on board the boat.

"Were you going to sabotage her for Vince Salerno?"

His brow wrinkled in confusion. "Why would Salerno want to sabotage her? She can't bring in cargo if she don't work."

"So why were you there?"

"I wasn't," he said, a bit belatedly.

"I was there. I saw you. Might as well tell me, when it's all unofficial and you're not under arrest for trespass."

He looked nervously up and down the street as if expecting someone to jump out and arrest him at any moment.

"If I talk to you, that means there will be no arrest."

"Yes." As long as Hank didn't change his mind

about filing the complaint.

"Okay, listen. I wasn't gonna do no harm. You can tell Chapman that. I wasn't gonna hurt the *Mary B*. I wasn't gonna steal nothing. I just needed to see how she was outfitted. How much she could carry."

"How many scallops? Why would Salerno want to know that?"

"Not scallops. Hams."

"Hams?" She might not know a lot about fishing or farming, but she was fairly sure you didn't fish for ham. Why would a fishing boat need to store any?

Evans scratched his nose. "It's what you call a bundle of wine bottles. Six of them, wrapped in canvas. Kind of looks like a ham."

"So Salerno thinks Hank is a rum runner."

"Lady, Hank *is* a rum runner." He let out a mirthless laugh. "Quite the mismatch—the cop and the rum runner."

"There's no match, mis or otherwise," she said firmly.

She ignored the pain in her heart. She'd suspected it for a while; she just didn't like to have it confirmed.

"Anything else?" Evans asked, impatiently.

"Why did Salerno want to know how many hams he could carry?"

"I don't know, lady. You'll have to ask him."

"Where can I find him?"

"Probably Perth Amboy. That's where his boat is." Without another word he went back into his house and shut the door firmly.

Alice walked slowly down the porch steps. At the very least, she hoped her interruption had cooled tempers down and there'd be no punches flung today.

She took out her list from Irene. The first man, a Mr. William Forster, lived only a few blocks away. He was one of the starred men, and as good as any a place to continue her investigation. He was also, if memory served, the man Patsy had said decided to tell Jiggy about Tomas's new customer.

There were several men sitting out on the steps of the New Street house when she got there, all smoking cigars, and passing around a flask. She wasn't in uniform. She'd ignore the flask. They looked up when she approached, but none of them seemed particularly welcoming.

"I'm looking for a William Forster."

A slim man sitting on the top step, leaning against the porch railing, spoke up.

"I'm Will Forster," he said. "You collecting for charity or something?"

"No." If it weren't for the obvious drinking, she would introduce herself as an officer, but she didn't want to scare them off before she had a chance to ask any questions. "I'm a friend of Irene Nagy's." When the name didn't draw any immediate recognition, she continued. "Tomas Nagy's widow."

He nodded and his mouth turned down in a frown. "Damn shame what happened to Tomas. He was a good guy. But what you want from me? I did donate to the fund the guys got up to help them. Can't help no more than that, especially since now I'm out of work."

"The *Katinka* will sail again soon," she assured them.

"Hopefully we'll be on it."

"You all worked with Tomas?" This could be better than she had hoped.

"No, just me and Shorty are fishermen." He indicated a tall man sitting on the porch.

She wondered which of the names on her list belonged to Shorty.

"What is it you want?" Will asked.

"I had a few questions about the day Tomas died." She had to be careful here. How much was reasonable to ask when she wasn't officially investigating anything?

"Don't know much." Will took a big draw from his cigar and breathed the smoke out slowly. "What I did know, I already told the cops. We got in, unloaded the fish, Tomas paid us off, and we went our separate ways."

Alice already knew that wasn't the full story. Patsy had told her about unloading the liquor for Salerno and the argument about telling Jiggy, but for now she'd play along with the story Will was telling her.

"Any idea where he was headed next?"

Will studied her carefully, taking a few more draws on his cigar. Finally, he said. "What did you say your name was?"

"I didn't," she answered. "But I'm Alice Grady."

"A cop."

Damn. She didn't think she was that well known in town. Clearly, she'd never be allowed to do undercover work.

A man in a paint-speckled shirt with the sleeves rolled up, shoved the flask behind his back. She pretended she didn't notice.

"I thought they caught they guy who shot Tomas," Shorty said.

"They did. But I have some questions.

Unofficially." She stood, hands at her sides, trying not to look threatening or impatient. She needed information from them. If they had it.

Will stood up, rested his cigar on the porch railing, and came down the steps to her. "What is it you want to know?" he asked, quietly, his voice not carrying back to his friends on the steps.

"What did Jiggy say to you when you told him Tomas sold his shipment to Vince Salerno?"

He glanced back up at the house before giving her a curt nod. "Let's walk," he said. When they were a few houses away, he answered her. "Who told you about that?"

"Does it matter?" She wasn't going to snitch on Patsy.

He rubbed a work-scarred hand over his face. "No, I suppose it doesn't. Jiggy wasn't happy about it. And he said so. In words that wouldn't exactly be good for mixed company, if you get my drift."

She sighed. She was a police officer. Why anyone thought foul language would offend her was beyond her. Though she supposed it was nice to see some vestige of chivalry left.

"Do you think Salerno had anything to do with Nagy's death?"

Will couldn't hide his surprise at the question, his eyes widened, and he took a step back from her.

"Salerno?"

So he wasn't surprised by the insinuation that someone was behind Nagy's death, just surprised by who she had suggested. Interesting.

"Yes. My sources seem to think he is a pirate and had something to do with it."

"He ain't no pirate. At least I don't think so. After all, pirates steal, and he was buying."

That was a fairly valid point. She needed to talk to Salerno or Jiggy. Those were the names that kept coming up, one or both of them were the lynch pins here.

"Know where I can find him?"

"Salerno?"

"Or Jiggy Malone—when he's not at his hut, that is."

Will looked taken aback that she knew about the hut. More than knew about it, she'd spent several hours staking it out the other night, with nothing to show for it. He obviously only used it as needed.

"Can't say for certain for either of them."

"If you had to take a guess."

Will shifted his feet and seemed to consider whether he was going to answer or not. "Perth Amboy. But I wouldn't advise talking to either of them."

Alice stopped walking and turned to face him. "I'm a cop, as you pointed out. I can handle it."

"I don't think so."

"Damn it. First Hank tells me to stay away from Jiggy and now you think I'm too weak to talk to him or Salerno."

"Whoa!" He put his hand on her arm. "I didn't say you were weak. But they're dangerous."

"I'm aware of that," she said, her voice a bit snippier than she intended. "At least one man is dead, after all."

"Is there more than one?" Will suddenly sounded worried.

"My father," she said, because the more she turned

it over in her mind, the more she was convinced that was the case. "Thank you for your time." She walked away without a backward glance.

It was time to go to Perth Amboy.

She walked up New Street, passing girls jumping rope and boys playing stick ball, everyone taking advantage of a nice spring afternoon. At Amboy Avenue she waited for the bus that would take her to Perth Amboy, digging in her bag for change for the fare. The bus, when it came, was nearly empty. A woman and a little boy sat on a bench near the front. A pair of high school-aged boys sat in the back, whispering behind their hands. Alice took a seat near the middle.

Twenty minutes later she exited the bus by the Tottenville Ferry. From here she could easily stroll the length of the developed waterfront and see if Vince Salerno or Jiggy Malone happened to cross her path.

The air was cooling down as evening progressed and the breeze lifted the hair at the back of her neck, which felt quite refreshing after the rather stifling bus ride. What would it be like to be a fisherman? To spend long days at sea? She'd never even been on a boat ride, other than a ferry. How had that happened? They lived so close to the water. Every town had a marina, yet she'd kept her feet on dry land. It always seemed rather extravagant, taking off on an ocean voyage, or even just a speedboat trip. She didn't have the time for something like that. Or the person to do it with. She sighed. She could do these things alone, she supposed, but they'd be much more fun with someone else.

She stopped to admire the boats docked in the marina. Scruffy, utilitarian fishing boats, sleek runabouts with polished wood that gleamed in the evening sun, sailboats with cabins for sleeping.

"You like boats, do you?"

Startled, she looked to her right, where Vince Salerno himself was standing next to her as casually as anything.

"They are pretty to look at," she admitted, her mind whirling. Here he was, the object of her search. Now she just had to steer the conversation in the direction she needed without arousing suspicion. "I've never been out on one, though."

"Seems hard to believe. Your father never took you out on a pleasure ride?"

"He never had the time," she admitted.

"That's a shame. The best times of my life are spent out on the water."

"Oh?" She affected a look of interest that she suspected bordered on the flirtatious. "Tell me about it."

"You don't want to hear about me."

"I asked, didn't I? Which kind of boat did you have?"

"I can show you. Come with me." He started walking down the dock, and against her better judgment she followed. Don't go with strange men was common advice she'd had drummed into her head since she was small. But she was a police officer investigating a crime, and if she wanted to get answers, she needed to take risks. He led her through the gate on the dock to the boats below, stopping in front of a gleaming wooden boat with a cabin and red leather seats. "Would you like to come aboard?"

"Sure." She accepted his help as she gingerly

stepped on the deck. Instantly she tottered as the swaying of the boat caught her off guard. He steadied her.

"You'll get used to the movement in no time."

She knew that was true. She'd had the same experience when she'd visited Hank on his fishing boat. This boat was smaller, but more luxurious. The *Mary B* was designed to be functional. This boat was clearly designed for pleasure and comfort.

"Can I get you a drink...um..." He paused, awkwardly. She might know who he was, but they'd never exchanged names. Did he recognize her from their brief encounter in the speakeasy? She rather hoped he did not.

"Alice." That was all he needed to know for right now.

"Nice to meet you, Alice." He bowed slightly. "You can call me Sal. Now, would you like a drink? I've got some juice in the galley."

Staying long enough to have a drink would give her an excuse to stay and talk to him. She agreed.

"I'll be right back. Have a seat." He ducked into the cabin.

Alice sat on the plush leather bench seat. Not that she was letting her guard down, but Sal seemed quite nice and gentlemanly, hardly the dangerous person Will warned her about. Or that people thought was a pirate. He hardly seemed like the kind to be involved in Tomas's death. But then again, Jiggy had been perfectly nice when she'd spoken to him as well. But she'd dealt with all kinds of people in her job. She knew that psychopaths could be very charming. She had to be careful.

He came back out of the cabin with two drinks. She took a first, careful sip, but it tasted only like fruit punch. If he had added anything it was tasteless. She took a bigger sip.

"This hits the spot." She wasn't just being polite. The afternoon had been warm, and she hadn't stopped for refreshment. He sat down across from her and stretched his arm across the polished wood on the side of the boat. "Do you go out often? On your boat?"

"As often as I can." He looked dreamily out to the open sea. "Nothing quite like being out on the water."

"I suppose your day job gets in the way," she said, trying to be coy and conversational.

"Not too much. I'm not exactly a desk jockey, tied to an office. I can come and go as I please."

"A man of leisure." She tried to sound approving instead of censorious.

"Indeed." He looked quite proud of that designation. She would almost say he preened, the way he brushed his fingers alongside his lapel.

"If you like, I can take you out for your first boat ride. How about tomorrow? Say ten? We can have a picnic on the high seas."

She laughed. "So very tempting. But my father taught me to have a little more sense than to go out on the ocean with a man I just met."

"Smart man, your daddy, and he raised a smart daughter."

"Is this your only boat?" She had to approach questions carefully. After all, he hadn't introduced himself with his full name, so it would be awkward to say she knew anything about him.

"Oh yes. It's all I need."

She frowned. How was George Evans working for him as a fisherman if he didn't own a fishing boat?

Was she wrong about who this was? She'd only seen the man once, after all; perhaps it wasn't him. There was only one way to find out. It was time for a little judicious flirting.

"So, Sal…that's short for Salvatore?"

"No, no. Just a nickname. Name's Vince. Vince Salerno." He held out his hand in the manner of a formal introduction and she really had no choice but to give her full name as well.

"Alice Grady," she said as she shook his hand.

"Sean's daughter."

Why was she surprised he knew her father? Everyone else seemed to.

"Yes. You knew him?"

"Never met him, but I have all his case notes."

She put down her drink as the gears in her mind tried to process this new information. And if this were true, he didn't have all the notes. He didn't have the little notebook. But maybe those notes were transferred to something else. And maybe he was lying. Her gut wasn't giving her any clues.

"Rum runners." She leaned forward, elbows on knees. Her suspicions were being confirmed, she needed to find out more.

"That's right. He was on the trail of the local boss but got killed before he could bring him down."

So it hadn't been an arrest gone wrong. That's what that notebook had proved.

"Jiggy Malone," Alice found herself saying.

Sal nodded. "He's a hard man to track down. Even harder to pin anything on."

238

"He says you're responsible for Tomas Nagy's death."

Sal's head shot up, his eyebrows raised. "All I did was buy Tomas's shipment."

"Why?" Alice took another sip of her juice, rather wishing it had been spiked with something.

Sal sighed and stood up, pacing back and forth on the small deck before answering. "To get the alcohol out of the system. If we buy it, it doesn't get distributed to the sellers. Keeps it out of the hands of the people."

That was one way to deal with the problem of illegal booze.

"Isn't it easier to just confiscate it?"

"Sure." He sat back down opposite her and leaned his elbows on his knees. "We confiscate one shipment and that guy warns all his buddies about us and we're out of business."

It made a certain amount of sense. Except it didn't answer all her questions.

"What about George Evans? He says he works for you as a fisherman."

Caught in a lie about having only the one boat, Sal rubbed his hand through his hair before continuing. "Ah. Yes. Easier to get into the inner workings of the ring if I've got people on the inside, so we leased a boat."

It was a much bigger operation than she would have imagined.

"Are you working with the department on this?" She'd feel like quite a fool for thinking he was some criminal when all the time he was working with Mark and the others.

Sal shook his head. "The police department? No.

They don't know about me. This is a federal thing. Can't let the locals know or they'll blow my cover."

"But yet you told me."

"Out of respect for your father. Besides, if I didn't fill you in, you'd end up having me arrested. That wouldn't work, now would it?"

Alice picked up her glass. If he were telling her the truth, he'd be a wonderful ally in trying to stop Jiggy and his whole network, but if he weren't telling the truth…then what?

"How did you get his notes?"

"The department handed them over to the feds years ago." He reached into his pocket and pulled out a small leather wallet. He opened it so she could see the federal badge there.

"I'm on your side."

Her father was killed because of the rum running. Tomas Nagy was killed because of the rum running. Hank was involved in rum running. She didn't want to see him killed. She wanted to stop it. To stop all of it, and here was someone who was trying to do just that. She breathed a sigh of relief. It felt so good to have allies. "What can I do to help?"

He shook his head.

"Nothing. Just stay out of my way and let me work."

"You think because I'm a woman—"

He held up his hand to interrupt her. "It has nothing to do with you being a woman. It's because you're involved with Hank Chapman. You wouldn't be able to be impartial."

She wanted to say she wasn't involved with him any longer, but she supposed it was true that she wouldn't be able to be impartial with something regarding Hank.

"Why? What do you have planned?"

"We're trying to buy his next shipment, that's all. Nothing sinister."

"Except if he does business with you, Jiggy will have him killed, like Tomas?" It was a shot in the dark, but it was where things logically led.

"That would be unfortunate."

"Unfortunate?" She jumped up from the seat, but there really wasn't any place to go. "You can't just play with people's lives like that. Not even for the greater good!" Hank was not just some incidental point on the way to a larger goal. It would be much more than unfortunate. It would be tragic. It would be unimaginable. Unfortunate didn't even begin to describe it.

Sal stood too and reached out his hand to placate her. "Of course, we'll do our best to make sure nothing happens to him. What happened with Nagy…That never should have happened. I'm doing everything I can to make sure that doesn't happen again."

She wrapped her arms around herself, not really caring about Sal's attempt to assure her. She really did care about Hank. Who cared if he was a rum runner? Who cared if he was overprotective of her? She wanted to protect him, so they were even in that regard.

Steady footsteps sounded on the wooden dock, approaching the boat. Alice looked up to see George Evans. He looked as surprised to see her as she was to see him. He stopped short, and although it looked like he'd been about to say something, he kept silent.

Sal turned to face him. "Well, man, what is it?"

241

Evans shifted his eyes back and forth.

"You can speak in front of Miss Grady."

"She's a lady cop."

"I'm aware," Sal answered.

"It's Jiggy. He's going after the *Mary B*. He says he's got to protect his investment."

Sal turned to Alice. "You armed?"

Her service revolver was in a shoulder holster under her jacket. Even off duty, she hadn't wanted to go into the lion's den unprotected.

"I am," she admitted, bracing for whatever was going to come next.

"Good. Get in, Evans." Sal turned back to Alice. "Looks like you're going to get your first boat ride."

"Where are we going?"

"To stop Jiggy, and rescue Chapman."

Yes. That was all right, then.

"Let's go."

Chapter Twenty

Behind the wheel of the *Mary B*, Hank was more relaxed than he'd been in a week. There was only water in all directions, and he could breathe again. All the anxiety that had been building up inside of him over the past few days washed away. He was out on the water, where he belonged, where nothing could touch him, nothing could hurt him.

From the working deck he could hear the purr of the motors and the grind of the winches as the dredges were lowered into the sea. He could feel the boat's motors strain as they worked to pull the rapidly filling nets through the water. He slowed the boat to a crawl, letting the dredges hit bottom, to allow them to scoop up any scallops in the area.

Douglas came onto the bridge.

"Things under control?" Hank asked, glancing at his brother before bringing his attention back to the controls in front of him.

"Seem to be. They lowered the dredge again. The last haul brought up an octopus. Ugly thing."

"They got it back overboard safely?"

"There was some talk about keeping it for dinner, but that was vetoed."

"Good." Hank didn't mind keeping the lobsters or some of the other fish that got caught in his dredge net, but the octopus and starfish he preferred to return to the sea.

Douglas shut the door to the bridge with a firm click. "Now," he said. "Tell me about the false bottoms in the storage deck."

Hank sighed. He knew this moment would come. Anyone on the crew was going to be involved in the rum running one way or another. It could not be kept secret.

"They are for my side business."

"So you are running rum."

There was no point in denying it anymore. "Yes."

"I knew it!" Douglas flashed him a triumphant grin. "This makes having to be out at sea worth it!" He leaned against the control panel and peppered Hank with questions. "How long have you been doing it? Do you make a lot of money at it? Is the *Katinka* outfitted the same way? What do I have to do to get started? Just head out to rum row? Is it like going to the market? Tell me everything!"

Hank sighed and sank into his captain's chair.

"I don't want you involved in it."

"Why?" Douglas crossed his arms and narrowed his eyes at his brother.

"It's too dangerous." Hank turned to look at the bright expanse of ocean in front of him. He hadn't minded the dangers when it was just him, but to have his family and Alice threatened? That he didn't go for. And if Douglas got involved, who would Jiggy threaten then? Marty? Where would it end?

"You think you're the only one who can handle danger? Just because you were in France? I'm not a baby anymore!"

No, you're a petulant, spoiled brat. He slammed

his palm on the control panel. "Don't talk about France."

"Why not? You never do. Maybe you should!"

"You don't want to hear about it."

Douglas came and stood by him, putting a tentative hand on his shoulder. "I do. And I think, more importantly, you need to talk about it."

He shrugged off his brother's hand and got up, walking to the other side of the bridge before turning to glare at him. "What do you want to hear about? The rat-infested trenches? The body parts strewn about after a bombing? The look in the enemy's eyes when he realizes the bullet from your gun is going to kill him? Which of those things do you want to hear about?"

"Whatever you want to tell me," Douglas said, though his face had paled, and his bravado was gone. "You've been trying to kill yourself, one way or another, ever since you got home from the war. I want my brother back again."

"The brother you remember died in the trenches of France. I'm who you've got, and you have to live with it."

"But you didn't die." Douglas looked so young and earnest Hank had to look away. He couldn't stand the sadness on his brother's face. "You came back. You were one of the lucky ones."

"Lucky?" The word exploded out of him. "No. The lucky ones were the ones who took a direct hit and never knew what hit them. I watched my friends get blown to pieces. I was not one of the lucky ones."

"Hank...Henry..." Douglas faltered, as if unsure how to proceed. "Don't let the bombs kill you now. For your friends' sake you need to let yourself live."

"Don't lecture me. You weren't there. You don't know."

"I realize that," Douglas admitted humbly. "I can't know. But I want to help."

"You can't." Hank turned back to his controls, looking out at the bright expanse of the sea.

"Let me take some of the danger."

"You don't understand." It was time to explain. "I want to stop. I told my buyer I was done, but he threatened me." He cleared his throat. "More specifically, he threatened Mother, and you, and Alice."

Douglas crossed his arms and frowned. "What kind of threats?"

"Death. To be blunt about it."

"And you think this guy can follow through?"

"I think he ordered Nagy killed."

There was silence while Douglas absorbed that information. Hank waited him out. Waited for him to panic or insist he didn't care and wanted to get involved in this stupid business anyway. Instead Douglas straightened up, put his hands on the control panel and said, "So what are we going to do about it?"

"We?"

"Of course, 'we.' You're not in the trenches anymore, brother. You don't have to go it alone."

A weight lifted off his heart. Maybe things would be okay.

Smitty came up to take his turn at the wheel.

"Got a good load. Feel like going down to help them sort?"

"Yeah, actually." Right now, he wanted the mind-numbing job of sorting the scallops from the other sea creatures that got caught in the dredge. He left Smitty in charge of the bridge, and he and Douglas went down to the working deck, where the crew was ankle deep in scallops, throwing back starfish and other incidental creatures caught in the netting. Ahab was struggling with a bass that was as long as his arm.

"This will make a good dinner tonight, Captain, don't you think?"

"Absolutely. Cook it up."

The scallops were scooped into buckets and brought into the shelling room, where Junior and Curly got to work opening them and discarding the shells. The shells were dumped back into the sea; the scallops were rinsed and bagged. Fifty pounds of scallops to a bag. Then the bags were put on ice in the storage area.

"Everything happens so quickly," Douglas commented as he watched the activity.

"It does, and your extra pair of hands would make it go even faster," Hank pointed out. "Go help Junior and Curly. A little scallop shelling will do you good."

"Aye, aye, Captain." Douglas gave him a friendly salute.

Maybe it wasn't so bad having Douglas on board.

****

Hours later, back up on the bridge with Douglas, he poured them both a dram of his hidden whiskey.

"Guess I'll have to give up my secret stash." With a sigh he returned the bottle to its hiding place.

"Why did you get involved in the first place?" his brother asked him.

"I liked the thrill of it. The danger. It made me feel alive."

Douglas clapped a hand on his shoulder.

"Maybe there's another way to feel alive."

247

Hank shifted to remove his brother's hand from his shoulder. "There is no other way. Even this isn't working anymore."

Another pause, long enough that Hank finally turned to face his brother.

"Being with Marty makes me feel alive," Douglas said, a faraway, wistful look in his eyes.

"That's nice for you," Hank responded shortly and stared back out at the sea.

"I had the impression the same thing happened when you were with Alice."

His shoulders tensed. Yes, he felt alive when he was with Alice, but it didn't matter. She deserved better than him, and besides, she wasn't speaking to him anymore.

"No." He boosted the power to the engine as he felt the boat slow with the increasingly full dredges. Soon they'd be winching them back up again and dumping their contents on the working deck. "Listen, I'm happy for you that you and Marty get along so well. I wish you many years of happiness. I'll play the doting uncle when I'm on shore. But that's not the life I want for myself. It's not the life I get to have."

"Why not?" Douglas asked bluntly. "You deserve happiness as much as anyone else. If not Alice, then maybe someone else. Let yourself be happy."

"I do not deserve happiness," Hank spit out the words. "You did not see what I did during the war. You did not do what I did. You don't know. Just leave me alone."

Douglas moved to the other side of the bridge and sat down but didn't leave.

The thoughts Hank was always trying to push out

of his mind refused to leave as well. He stared into the open space. He could breathe when he concentrated on the open space. But in his mind the walls of the trenches were closing in.

He could see clearly the face of McGuire sitting next to him in the mud as shelling went on all around them and dirt and pebbles rained down on them. They were joking. Gallows humor, he supposed. They were being deliberately crude, something about he'd rather be buried in a woman than in a damn hole in the ground.

It was the last thing McGuire said before the shell landed damn near on top of him. When Hank looked again, there was nothing left of his friend and the walls were collapsing around him. He was afraid he'd never see open sky again.

He looked out at it now and breathed deeply.

It was over.

It had been over a long time, Douglas was right.

Why couldn't he put it behind him?

Would it help if he had someone to share his life with? But who would want to share his terrors with him? Or would the terrors go away? It was impossible to know. He'd felt safe when Alice had been in his arms. He'd kissed her, and she'd kissed him back. And then they'd fought. It was almost like he'd held the chance for a real future, a happy future, in his hands and he had thrown it away.

Douglas would probably say that's what he'd been doing ever since he got back from the war.

Maybe it was true.

Maybe it was time to try to live again.

It had been almost ten years.

He looked back over at his brother, sitting, waiting, as he always was. Waiting for him to finally come home from the war. It was time to move forward.

"How are we going to get me out of this deal with Jiggy without getting you or Mother or Alice shot?"

Douglas didn't seem to mind the shift in conversation. "I've been thinking about that. The most obvious thing seems to be to turn him in and have him arrested."

"On what grounds? I don't have proof he set up Tomas's murder."

"On smuggling."

Hank finished the rest of his drink and put the glass down.

"I'd have to implicate myself."

Douglas nodded. "Probably true."

"I could go to jail."

Douglas, annoyingly calm, nodded again. "Possibly. Or you could cut a deal. What do they say? Turn state's evidence?"

"I can't take that chance. I don't want to go to jail. I couldn't survive it." It would be worse than being in the trenches. No open space. He might as well just shoot himself now.

"We could fake your drowning and you could start over somewhere new."

Clearly his brother spent too much of his free time reading pulp fiction.

"I suppose it would get Jiggy off my case, but I'm not sure I want to go to that length."

"There's got to be a way." Douglas tapped his chin in contemplation. After a few minutes of silence, he shrugged and said, "Well, we have almost two weeks to think of it."

Right. Everyone was safe for at least two weeks, because Jiggy wouldn't expect him back before then anyway. That gave them time to come up with a plan.

The put-putting of a motor made Hank look up. He cocked his head to get a better idea where the noise was coming from.

"Sounds like a boat." Douglas was also listening to the foreign sound.

"It does." It did not sound like a fishing boat, and no one would come that close to another working boat anyway. Then with a sinking feeling he realized what it must be. "Pirates."

"But you don't have anything to steal," Douglas protested.

"They don't know that." He looked out the surrounding windows until he spotted the boat, a sharp looking runabout with a small cabin on the deck. And then he spotted Jiggy.

"What the hell?"

Douglas stood up to look as well.

"Who is that?"

"Jiggy Malone."

"Then I guess we don't have two weeks, do we," Douglas said with maddening calmness.

"No. I guess we don't."

Damn. What was Jiggy doing here? There was only one way to find out, and that was to go down and confront him. Hank cut the motor and let the boat drift. Time to find out what was going on. He got his pistol from its hiding place.

"There are rifles in the crew quarters. Go see that the men are armed."

"Will do," Douglas answered.

By the time he got to the working deck, Jiggy had already climbed a rope from his boat to theirs and was standing on the deck.

"What are you doing here?" Hank asked, making sure that Jiggy could see the pistol in his hand.

"I need to protect what's mine."

"Nothing of yours on the *Mary B*," he answered.

"We'll just see about that. Get rid of the gun," he said, showing that he had his own, which he now pointed at Douglas, who was still standing beside Hank. "Or I shoot him."

Hank didn't hesitate, he dropped the gun to the floor.

"What's all this about, Jiggy?" Hank asked, arms folded, shoulders tense. His only hope was that some of the men would remember the rifles and take Jiggy by surprise.

"I've come to get what's mine."

"As I said before, I have nothing of yours on board."

"I don't believe you, Chapman." He kept his gun trained on Douglas and ordered the men he'd brought with him to search. "Keep your crew where I can see them."

Hank shrugged. "There's not much place to hide here. A couple of my men are sleeping in the crew quarters."

"Wake them up."

"I will not. They've earned their rest, and there is nothing they can do for you except get in the way."

Jiggy didn't seem inclined to argue with that.

"Let's see what you've got in the hold."

"Scallops." Hank said, while his mind raced. What was Jiggy trying to prove? Why hadn't he waited for him to come in?

"Stay where I can see you," Jiggy ordered, and since he was holding a gun, Hank and Douglas preceded him down the steps to the fish hold.

Jiggy's men wasted no time. They started with the holds that didn't have any fish in them yet, dumping the ice indiscriminately to the floor until they found the secret compartments. But, as Hank had tried to tell them, each compartment was empty. Finally, they dumped the bagged scallops on the floor as well and shoveled out the ice in that hold.

"You must have other hiding places. We'll find the stuff. I know it's here," Jiggy said, turning on Hank. "I know you wouldn't risk not making the pickup."

Hank leaned against the door frame, arms crossed. "It's not that big a boat. There is no other hiding place. There's nothing to find. Now, would you mind putting my cargo back?"

"Screw you," Jiggy said and pushed past him. "Do it yourself. We'll search the galley and the crew's quarters."

"I wouldn't recommend you wake sleeping fishermen," Hank called after him.

Jiggy made a rude gesture, but other than that didn't answer him.

Hank straightened up and addressed the crew members who had followed him to the hold. "Better get that cleaned up, or the fish will spoil. Leave the false bottoms out. We won't be needing them."

To Douglas, whom Jiggy seemed to have forgotten, he said, "Better see if you can get to those rifles."

In the galley, Jiggy and his men were wreaking havoc.

"Enough," Hank demanded. "There's nothing there."

"I'll be the judge of that."

Hank sighed. "You're wrecking the place. You found my hiding place. It was empty. Why can't you accept that?"

"Because I don't trust you," Jiggy said.

Hank let out a snort. "Nothing like the pot calling the kettle black."

Jiggy stopped rooting around in a barrel of coffee beans.

"Okay. So if the stuff isn't here, it's because you haven't picked it up yet. That's troublesome, because you told me you always pick up the order on the first night out. Planning on skipping out?"

"My routine varies," Hank answered, though honestly, he almost always made the run the first night. Much easier to pack it away before the holds were full of fish. "Why couldn't you have just waited until I got in to port?" This was the sticking point.

"Because when you got into port you were going to sell to Salerno."

Hank didn't even have to fake his surprise.

"I was?"

"Don't play dumb with me. I have my sources."

"Your sources fed you faulty information."

"We'll see about that. Let's go." Jiggy headed back out onto the working deck and Hank followed him.

"Go where?"

Once again Jiggy had his gun in his hand and pointing at Hank.

"To rum row."

Where was Douglas with those rifles?

"I can't go there with your skiff tied to mine like a barnacle."

"That is no skiff."

"I don't care if it's the bloody *Mauretania*," Hank countered. "I can't sail with it dragging behind."

Just then the distinct roaring of a boat moving at high speed became clear to them.

"Weren't going to sell to Salerno, huh?" Jiggy sneered.

"No."

"Then why is he coming this way?"

And here he had thought things couldn't get worse.

Chapter Twenty-One

Alice held tight to the edge of the seat as the runabout sped out into the open waters, jumping waves and generally behaving much more like a thrill ride at an amusement park than she had expected. The saltwater spray chilled her, and she was glad she had on a jacket.

"You okay?" Sal sat next to her. "Warm enough?"

"I'm fine," she answered through chattering teeth.

"You can go into the cabin if you would be more comfortable."

That would be a good idea. She probably would be more comfortable in the cabin, if she had started out there. Right now, she was afraid to move.

"I'm fine where I am," she insisted.

Sal grinned as if he didn't quite believe her, but he didn't argue.

They were out of sight of land now, and behind them the last of the sunset spread warm pinks and oranges across the sky. If her heart weren't pounding, both in anticipation and fear that she might fall overboard, she'd almost want to stop and paint a picture.

Soon the colors in the sky faded to gray, and the moon and stars were their only illumination. Without any of the town lights to compete with them, they were surprisingly bright, but it was still too dark to see much around them.

"How will we find anyone in this vast ocean?" she asked. "It seems worse than trying to find a needle in a haystack."

"Not as hard as all that. The fishing boats go where they have the best luck. They tend to frequent the same general areas time after time. Evans knows where that is. He will find them."

But would they find them in time?

And what exactly had Jiggy meant that he needed to protect his investment? He didn't own the *Mary B.* He didn't deal in scallops. He was a smuggler and his investment would be illegal goods. That meant Hank was smuggling goods for Jiggy. But if he brought them in, then why would Jiggy go after him? Unless, he thought, like Tomas, that Hank had found a new buyer and he was going to get to him before he could sell his goods to someone else.

Tomas had ended up dead.

She wished the boat would go faster. She needed to get to Hank.

On the horizon she spotted some lights. At first, she thought it was just an extra bright star, but then she realized it was too low for that.

"There they are!" George Evans yelled back from the wheel.

"Can you be sure it's them?" Alice asked.

"We'll find out soon enough," Sal answered and hollered back to Evans, "Get us there as fast as you can!"

"Can't go much faster than this!"

In one way, as Alice clung to the seat, she was glad they couldn't go any faster; on the other hand, she really wanted to get there.

As they got closer, Sal lit a spotlight which clearly showed that it was the *Mary B* they were approaching. There was a smaller boat close beside it, as if tied there.

"Damn it!" Sal slapped a hand against the cushioned seat. "Looks like Jiggy beat us here."

Everything went fuzzy for a moment while the blood rushed from her head. Jiggy was already there. They were too late.

"You okay? You look a little pale."

Alice forced her eyes to focus on Sal, who was looking at her like a concerned uncle. She reached in and removed her service gun from its holster. She wasn't giving up without a fight.

"I'm fine." She nodded firmly. "Let's get them."

Sal handed her binoculars, and she was able to make out the fisherman aboard the ship. There was Hank and Douglas. And Jiggy. Holding a gun.

She tossed the binoculars back to Sal. "He's got a gun. Get us as close as you can!"

She could fire at him from the moving runabout, but that was a sure recipe for disaster. The boat was moving too much to be sure she could get anything like a clear shot at him. She would be just as likely to hit Hank or any of the other men on board. She couldn't take that chance.

The runabout came within yards of the *Mary B* and Alice sat down and hung on tight, afraid they were going to collide. But Evans cut the engine and threw it into reverse, and they came to a stop several yards from the fishing boat.

Alice could clearly see the men on board. Jiggy had spotted them. He looked over into the runabout and aimed his gun straight at her. She aimed back, only slightly intimidated, and then he turned abruptly and fired at one of the fishermen.

She didn't hesitate but got him in her sights and pulled the trigger. By the time she lowered her weapon Jiggy had already fallen.

"Good shot, Grady," Sal said. "Let's board her and see what's going on."

Her hand shook as she re-holstered her weapon. Who had Jiggy shot? Was it Hank? Was he okay?

Without her even realizing it, the runabout had pulled in next to Jiggy's small boat and tied up to the *Mary B.* A rope ladder was dropped and soon Sal was instructing her to climb it.

She looked uncertainly at the flimsy ladder and then down to the churning blackness of the sea beneath it. But if she wanted to see this through, she had to get onto the *Mary B*, and this seemed to be the only way. She put her hands on the rope ladder and took a deep breath. The wood of the step was slick beneath her palms. Or maybe it was her palms that were sweaty. She held tighter and put one foot on a lower rung. So far so good. But when she put the other foot on, the ladder swayed and turned. Her heart beat double time and her stomach clenched. Then Sal was there steadying the ladder.

"Go on, now," he said, his voice surprisingly gentle.

Hand over hand, foot over foot, she made her way up the ladder, not looking down at the dark, swirling waters of the ocean below her. As she neared the top, hands reached down to help her on board. She looked up into Hank's eyes.

259

"You're alive!"

"I am."

She let herself be enveloped in his arms for a brief moment. "Who did Jiggy shoot?"

"Doug." The answer was curt. Behind her, Sal had boarded the *Mary B*, and she could feel Hank tense up when he saw him. "Why are you with this pirate?"

Sal pulled out his badge and opened it at the same time that Alice answered.

"He's not a pirate, he's with the Feds. Now, let me see Doug. I have medical training."

"I'll take care of Malone," Sal said.

She glanced over to see him sitting against the side of the boat clutching his arm. She'd never shot a man before and couldn't say she was sorry she hadn't killed him. She had winged him, though. Not bad for being on a moving boat.

Doug was on the other side of the working deck, surrounded by the other fisherman.

"He got hit in the leg."

"Do you have a first-aid kit?" Alice asked, as the men made room for her.

"Right here," someone answered. They were already stanching the bleeding and cleaning the wound.

Alice knelt down beside him and brushed his hair out of his face. He was grimacing in pain, and there were tear tracks on his cheek.

"You'll be fine," she assured him. "You're in good hands."

"You know..." Hank squatted beside her and held his brother's hand. "I spent over a year in France and never got shot."

"It hurts like hell," Doug muttered through gritted

teeth.

Alice looked up at Hank. "Maybe some medicinal brandy?"

Hank shot a glance at Sal and Alice shrugged.

"I don't think he'll give you a hard time about that."

"Come with me," he said and took her hand as he stood up.

She didn't even hesitate. As soon as they got to the galley, he took her in his arms and kissed her hard and long. She wanted to stay in his arms forever, but she thought Douglas needed the brandy more than she needed the kisses. Gently she pushed back from him.

"We should bring the brandy to your brother."

"Of course."

Hank looked alarmingly pale.

"You haven't been injured too, have you?" She asked, unable to keep the note of concern out of her voice.

"No. I'm fine. I just…"

She took the brandy bottle off the shelf where she'd seen him hide it the other day and poured some into a glass and handed it to him. "That's for you," she said and poured another glass for Douglas.

He drank it without argument.

"What are you doing here?" he asked when he'd drained the glass.

"I'll tell you everything, but first get this to Douglas."

She sent him out of the galley and poured some brandy into the glass he'd left behind. She drank it down before hiding the bottle away again and putting the glass in the sink to be washed.

Damn this prohibition. She could really get used to a touch of medicinal brandy from time to time.

When she walked back out to the working deck she nearly collided with Sal. "You got Jiggy right above the elbow. No serious damage, but enough to stop him shooting anyone else. Good work." Alice looked past him to where Hank was helping Douglas drink the brandy. "I've placed Jiggy Malone and his cohorts under arrest," Sal continued.

"What about Hank?"

"What about him?" Sal looked sincerely confused.

"You're not going to place him under arrest, are you?"

"No cause," Sal answered with a shrug. "I've been assured he has no contraband on board...and I will do my own search shortly to confirm that."

"So he's not a rum runner?" Her heart soared. She'd never been so happy to be wrong.

"Oh, darling, he most certainly is. Or at least was. But right now, in this moment, I've got no cause to arrest him."

And she thumped back down to earth. Maybe she could quit her job as Trudy suggested. She could be a rum runner's wife. Might not be such a bad gig. She could have all her fill of the medicinal brandy she wanted.

Who was she kidding? She could never do that. She swallowed a lump in her throat and gazed at Hank again. At least he wasn't going to be arrested today.

"I want to talk to Jiggy."

"He's already under arrest," Sal reminded her.

"Understood."

"Don't shoot him again." There was a twinkle in

Sal's eye as he gave her this warning.

"No promises," she said and enjoyed the shocked look that came over Sal's face.

Jiggy was still on the working deck, propped up against a locker, his arm bandaged, his face pale.

Alice stood above him, enjoying the advantage his disadvantage gave her. He glared at her and she glared right back. Finally, she said. "That was for Tomas Nagy and my father."

Jiggy didn't seem surprised.

"You're a lot like him."

"I'll take that as a compliment."

"Take it however you want, but it nearly got you killed."

"I could say the same for you."

Jiggy chuckled at that. "Sean would be proud."

"Why'd you have him killed?"

Jiggy winked. "You're a smart girl. I'm sure you can figure it out."

And he wasn't dumb either, Alice acknowledged. He wasn't going to come right out and admit to arranging for her father's murder, though it wasn't too hard to read between the lines.

"I guess he got in your way."

Jiggy touched his nose with his uninjured hand. "Like I said, you're a smart girl."

Hank and Sal joined them.

"We need to get Douglas to the hospital." Hank glanced at Jiggy. "And I guess him, too."

"My thoughts exactly," Sal said. "I can take them in my runabout."

"That won't work. Neither of them could navigate the ladder. No, we'll head in now and get them to shore."

It was arranged that the *Mary B* would head straight to port, while George Evans took Sal's boat in and Hank's first mate, Smitty, brought in Jiggy's boat. Alice and Sal joined Hank in the bridge while he navigated toward home.

"So," Hank said to Sal, "you were trying to undermine Jiggy this whole time?"

"It would have worked, too. Eventually. Although, thanks to Alice's steady hand, we got him a bit sooner."

"How did you know he was going to be here?"

"I've got informers around town."

Now Hank looked at Alice, and she was afraid she could get lost in those eyes. "And how did you get involved?"

"I was employing a little good old-fashioned police work and trying to figure out the connection between Sal here and Jiggy."

Hank raised an eyebrow.

"I told you Jiggy was dangerous."

She grinned back at him. "And I told you I could take care of myself."

****

Traveling at full speed, directly back to the marina, it didn't take long before they were docked. Alice wanted a chance to talk to Hank, to spend time alone with him, to kiss him again. But that opportunity didn't present itself.

Hank had used his two-way radio to call the marina, so when they got in, not only was the chief there with his police car, but there were two ambulances as well. Alice disembarked as soon as the crew put out the gangplank.

"What did you get yourself involved in, Grady?" the chief asked with a shake of his head.

"We've arrested the key figure in the rum running in this area. The man who called for the murders of Tomas Nagy and of my father."

As she was speaking, Salerno escorted Jiggy off the boat.

"This the man?" The chief asked, with a jerk of his finger toward the injured man.

"Yes, Jiggy Malone."

The chief shook his head sadly. "Alistair Malone, your mother will be turning over in her grave to see what you've come to."

"Alistair?" Alice repeated, disbelieving. She never would have gotten that from Jiggy.

"You know him?" Salerno asked.

"Knew his parents." The chief introduced himself to Salerno. "Take him down to the hospital. Grady and I will meet you there and you can brief me."

"I've got these two as well," Salerno said, as a couple of Hank's crewmen escorted Jiggy's helpers off the boat. "Can you hold them for me until I can get someone down here to pick them up?"

"Fine. We'll bring them to the station and then meet you at the hospital." He supervised the loading of the men into the back of the car. "Come on, Grady. No time to waste."

She didn't want to leave. She wanted to talk to Hank, but he was helping his brother into the other ambulance and had no time for her now. She got in the passenger side of the police car and the chief drove across the causeway into town and to the police station.

Once they entrusted the prisoners to McGrath for

the night, they were back in the car on the way to the hospital in Perth Amboy.

"Might as well tell me everything," the chief said.

So she did, filling him in on where her research had led her and to the real identity of the mysterious Vince Salerno.

"Good work, Grady," Murphy said with an approving glance in her direction. "I suppose after this you'll want to get out on the beat more often?"

"I would like to, yes, sir."

"Well, get that Nagy lady into my office so I can see if I approve of her."

"Yes, sir. Monday morning." She wanted to hug herself and cheer. She was finally getting what she wanted.

"We only wanted to protect you, you know. On account of your father."

"I know." It was rather sweet of them, if a bit stifling.

"But I suppose you proved you can take care of yourself."

She grinned. *And don't you forget it.* But she was smart enough to keep that comment to herself.

At the hospital, Sal met them in the lobby.

"Jiggy's in surgery, so I don't suppose he'll go anywhere for the next hour or so. Let's get some coffee."

Seated in the cafeteria, at a white-topped wooden table, with burnt coffee in thick white cups, Salerno told the chief basically the same story Alice had already told, with a few extra details Alice hadn't known about, like the smugglers he'd already managed to buy out, and the extent of Jiggy's network in town.

"He had something on nearly everyone and wasn't afraid to use it," Sal said. "I'm still not sure how many people he had working for him, but we'll find out. In the meantime"—he gestured toward Alice with his coffee cup—"be careful. I don't know how many of his people did his bidding because they felt they had no choice and will be glad to be free of him and which ones will be angry that their boss has been caught."

"I can take care of myself," she reminded them.

"I've no doubt," Sal answered, but the chief didn't look so sure.

He looked at the clock on the wall and finished the last of his coffee. "Let me take you home, Grady, and I don't want to see you again until Monday. Rest and relax. Understand?"

"Yes, sir, Chief." She gave him a mock salute. She would have liked to find out how Douglas was doing, but the chief seemed in a rush, so she hurried after him.

"Lay low for the rest of weekend," he said as he pulled up in front of her house. "I want to get a feel for how much of a threat this network of Malone's is."

"I'm not afraid," she said.

"You shot their boss. Maybe you should be afraid."

There was a place for bravado and a place for caution. Caution might be called for here. "Relaxing day at home it is," she assured him and went inside.

Mama and Marty were in the sitting room with the Victrola playing. Marty was curled up on the davenport with a novel and Mama was embroidering ladybugs on a handkerchief.

"Where have you been?" Mama asked, the worry evident in her voice. "You never even made it home for dinner."

That reminded her that she hadn't managed to get an evening meal, only some fruit juice, medicinal brandy, and coffee. She should be hungry, but she wasn't. Instead she was thinking how she was going to tell Marty what had happened to Douglas tonight. At least his injury didn't appear to be life threatening.

"I thought maybe you went over to the Nagys'," Marty said, looking up from her book. "But Irene said she hadn't seen you. Her typing is coming along really well, though!"

That was good. Murphy would be happy to hear it.

Now they were both looking at her, expectantly, and she didn't even know where to begin.

"I, um, was working on a case," she said. "Things got a little out of hand, but we arrested the man who ordered Daddy's murder."

Mama dropped her embroidery to her lap. "What are you talking about?"

Alice perched on the edge of the davenport, next to Marty, and told them everything she could. When she got to the part about Douglas being shot, Marty was ready to call a cab and head to the hospital immediately.

"It can wait until tomorrow, dear," Mama said. "Visiting hours are going to be over by now anyway." She turned to Alice, her brow wrinkled with concern. "Would you like me to draw you a bath?"

Alice let out a happy sigh. "That would be heavenly! Thank you."

"What about Hank?" Marty asked when Mama had gone upstairs. "Is he a rum runner?"

"He had no contraband on his boat. But he did have secret compartments built into his storage holds, so I think so."

"So what are you going to do?"

The hundred-dollar question.

"Why do I have to do anything?"

"Because you love him," Marty answered.

Yes, she did. And that made this even worse, because she really didn't know what she was going to do about it.

In the morning, after church, she went with Marty on the bus to Perth Amboy so she could visit Douglas. She hoped this didn't go against the chief's directive to lay low. All the way there she thought about what she would say to Hank when she saw him.

Should she tell him she didn't mind if he was a smuggler and she'd promise not to arrest him, even though it meant throwing out all her ethical standards? Should she ask him to give it up? Was it right to ask someone to make a change like that?

In the end, it didn't matter. They walked into Douglas's hospital room, where he lay with his leg swathed in bandages, and Hank wasn't there. Marty rushed to the side of the white cast-iron bed, and Douglas opened his arms to her and embraced her. Alice started to back out of the room to give them privacy, but Douglas stopped her.

"I need to thank you. You saved my life."

"I wish I could have been faster. Then you wouldn't have been shot at all."

"Well, I know one thing. Hank can have the adventure. I plan on sticking with my desk job."

"Will Hank be by later?" Alice asked, hating the eagerness in her voice, hating that she was asking at all. She should be stronger than this, right?

Douglas shook his head. "He went back out last night. They were already provisioned, and he said it would be a waste to not finish the trip."

Her mind went immediately to rum row. Would he make that trip after all? But he had no buyer. Jiggy was arrested and Sal turned out to be the Feds. But surely there were plenty of people willing to buy illegal booze.

"Will he…?" she started to say, and Douglas seemed to divine her meaning.

"No. He says he's through with that."

That was good, anyway. But her heart hurt. He'd gone out again without even a word to her. She thought that last night he had been glad to see her. He had certainly kissed her ardently enough, but maybe she'd read more into it than she should have.

"He'll be back in about ten days," Douglas said. "And he wants to see you. I know he does."

She could only hope that was true.

Chapter Twenty-Two

The days at sea had never dragged like this before. Always he'd felt the time moved too quickly and he would do anything to prolong the time on the water. Now he wanted nothing but to finish filling the hold and get the boat, and himself, back to land.

When they'd first gone back out to sea, after making sure Douglas was taken care of, he'd called his crew together.

"I won't be making any more runs out to rum row. If you guys want to crew for other guys who are still making the run, then you are free to do so."

"We'll stay," Smitty said, with a glance around to the other members of the crew. "Besides, no one has a buyer now that Jiggy's been arrested."

"It's because of the lady cop, isn't it?" Slim asked, a wicked grin on his face.

"No." Hank stopped himself. Why deny it? "Yes, it is."

"You got it bad for her," Mack said with a shake of his shaggy head.

"She's a damn good shot, though," Smitty admitted.

There was general consensus around the crew that this was true.

"Not bad-looking, either," Slim added.

No, she wasn't. In fact, as far as he was concerned,

Christine Marciniak

she was beautiful, but this was not something he wanted to discuss with his crew.

"Okay, that's enough of that. We've got work to do."

And now, several days later, all he could think about was getting back to her. He should have said something to her before leaving, but he couldn't talk to her about his feelings in front of Salerno. That guy might not have wanted to arrest him, but he still thought it was better to proceed with caution with the Feds, and he still couldn't shake the feeling that he was a pirate, despite evidence to the contrary.

So he'd gone back out to sea without a word. Would she know from their stolen kisses that he wanted more from her? Did she want the same? Did she only fall into his arms because she was in a state of shock over shooting Jiggy? Would she have been as susceptible if the circumstances had been different?

He looked out at the endless sea keeping him from Alice and sighed. He just wanted to be back with her. Was that too much to ask?

Finally, the day came when Slim told him the holds were full.

"We've got a little over eight tons. Let's head in."

Hank was never so glad to head west.

The sun was high overhead when he maneuvered the *Mary B* in to the dock at Martin's fishery. The activity and noise were a welcome change from the silence of the sea with only the machinery on board ship to break the monotony. He hurried across the gangway to greet Jack Martin.

"Got eight tons for you."

"Great job, son." He took his hand in a hearty

272

shake. "Saw your brother earlier. He's getting around with a cane, and may be a bit gimpy for a while, but he's taking it all in stride. That was some action you got involved in. Didn't think scallop fishing was such a dangerous trade." He cocked one eyebrow at Hank.

"Life's a funny thing, isn't it?" He would admit nothing. That part of his life was behind him, but no point in giving people things to use against him.

"It is indeed. Come inside and we'll settle up."

Once the money was in his pocket, he helped his crew unload the scallops. The rhythm and familiarity of the action kept him from taking off running to find Alice. Work needed to be done first.

Finally, the *Mary B* was in her home dock in Sewaren. He paid his crew and started running through the chores he needed to do on board before he could go look for Alice.

"Go," Smitty said to him. "I'll take care of stuff here. You look like you're going to jump out of your skin. Go see the girl." He slapped him on the back. "But maybe shower first."

Not a bad idea. He nearly ran down Cliff Road to his parents' house. "Oh, Hank, you're home!" Mother called from the sitting room. "I wasn't expecting you for another day or so."

He put the brakes on in order to politely greet his mother. "We had a good run. How's Doug?"

"Doing fine. Spending all his time with that delightful young lady, Marty." His mother gave him a speculative look.

"I'm going to shower and see if I can have the same kind of luck with her sister."

His mother beamed. "By all means, don't let me

keep you!"

He showered and shaved, splashed some Aqua Velva on his face, slicked back his hair with brilliantine. He put on a fresh pressed shirt and gray flannel pants. He could take her out to dinner. He could take her to Perth Amboy. Heck, he could really splurge and take her to New York City. But first he had to see her. And she had to want to see him.

He fastened his gold cuff links and buffed his black shoes before putting them on.

Downstairs, his mother looked him over approvingly.

"You'll knock her off her feet." She gave him a peck on the cheek.

"Think I could borrow Douglas's car?"

"Sure," Douglas said, coming into the room, leaning on a cane. "I can't drive it yet." He patted him on the shoulder. "Good luck."

He hoped he wouldn't need luck.

The car, just to be contrary, didn't start the first couple of times he cranked it, but finally he got the motor running, only to have to stop at the railway crossing as a train lumbered past. He rested his head on the steering wheel. This just wasn't his day.

He knew Alice often complained about being stuck in the office typing up reports, so as soon as the train cleared the crossing, he headed to the police station. He parked on Main Street and tried not to run into the building. He opened the door to see that the woman typing up reports was not Alice but Irene Nagy.

She looked up and smiled when she saw him.

"Hank! I am working woman now! I type up reports for police."

Where was Alice? He wanted to see Alice.

"That's wonderful, Irene. Good for you!" He couldn't keep the question in any longer. "Where is Alice?"

Chief Murphy came out of his office, holding a cup of coffee.

"You're looking quite dapper, Mr. Chapman. Do you need the services of the police department?"

He was toying with him, Hank knew he was.

"I was hoping to find Alice Grady here."

Murphy grinned, apparently deciding not to tease him anymore. "She'll be back shortly. She is out on patrol."

"So she got her wish." Hank felt inordinately proud of her.

"She did." The chief seemed proud as well. "You're welcome to wait for her."

He didn't think he could sit here quietly and wait for her to show up. "Where does she usually patrol? Maybe I could find her?"

"Interrupting my officer on duty?" Murphy tried to sound stern, but Hank had the feeling he didn't object too much.

"Just to say hello, of course."

"She can usually be found somewhere between Main Street, New Street, and Second Street." Hank was already heading out the door and the chief called after him, "She gets off duty in an hour. I don't want to hear of a crime spree because my officer was otherwise occupied."

"Yes, sir," Hank said, barely paying attention to what was said. He could drive up and down the streets looking for her, but that seemed awkward. Instead he walked down Main Street, a spring in his step. He spotted her almost at once, coming out of Christensen's. She didn't see him and turned to walk in the other direction.

He hurried to catch up with her. Finally, when it felt he was within shouting distance, he called her name.

She turned, and her whole face lit up when she saw him. She ran toward him, and he ran toward her, and they met in front of the post office. He swept her up in his arms.

"I'm back."

"I missed you."

He kissed her, and she kissed back, but then they both came to their senses and realized they were standing in the middle of Main Street and she was still on duty and in uniform.

"I get off work in an hour," she said, trying to maintain some bit of decorum.

"I'll wait for you. I'll drive you home."

"That's hardly necessary." She smiled. "It's only a couple of blocks."

"Let me take you to dinner." All this waiting and he had to wait even more. It was more than he could bear.

"I'd like that. Come by the house around seven?"

He didn't know if he could hold out until then. He wanted to be spending all his time with her. He wanted her in his arms.

"I want to bathe and get dressed. I can't go out with you looking better and smelling better than me." She touched his hand. "We need to talk."

Those words felt like a punch in the gut. But there

was no reason it had to be bad that she wanted to talk to him. After all, he wanted to talk to her too. He forced a smile.

"I'll see you at seven."

He went home for the next couple of hours, where Douglas and his mother managed to keep him occupied until it was time to meet Alice.

At precisely seven he stood on the wraparound porch on the house on Green Street. He let the door knocker fall twice and then waited. It only took a moment before Marty answered the door.

"She'll be down in a minute. I've never seen her so concerned with how she looks. You're good for her."

Immediately Hank felt himself relax. Things were going to be okay. He looked up to see Alice at the top of the stairs. Everything about her looked absolutely perfect, from her dark red sleeveless dress to her shiny curled bob.

"You look...stunning."

"Thank you."

She descended the stairs, and he wanted to take her in his arms at once, but Marty and their mother were standing there, so he decorously took her arm. "I've made reservations at Caldwell's in Perth Amboy. Is that acceptable?"

"Lovely," she answered.

He helped her to his car. There were a million things he wanted to say to her, but he couldn't seem to start. They drove in awkward silence. When they parked by the waterfront, Hank helped her out of the car.

"The reservation is for eight. We have a little time. Would you care to walk with me?" He had to salvage this somehow. They had to find their way back to one another.

"That sounds nice," she answered.

They walked for quite some time before either of them spoke. Finally, Hank broke the silence.

"I was a rum runner."

"I know," Alice answered.

She knew? Of course, she knew. She'd brought down Jiggy; naturally she knew he was one of his suppliers. That was it. She wouldn't want anything more to do with him. It had all been a lovely dream.

"And it doesn't matter to me. I…" She broke off, as if unsure how to continue.

"It matters to me." He reached out and took her hand. "After what happened to Tomas, I decided it's not a good career choice for a family man."

"A family man?"

"Alice," he started again with renewed vigor. "I didn't think I could ever let anyone share my life. I was too messed up. But now I can't imagine going forward in life without you."

She leaned against him and his heart beat faster.

"I was wondering…" His voice cracked embarrassingly. "If maybe…you would give me a chance?"

She stopped walking and turned to face him.

"Hank, I'll give you all the chances in the world if you promise to never leave my side."

"As long as you want me with you, I'll be there." He took her in his arms. He felt whole and complete. Finally, he understood what it meant to really be in love with someone.

The details of their life going forward would have

to be worked out, but for now it was enough to know they would go forward together.

A word about the author...

Christine Marciniak has been writing ever since she can remember because she loves to tell stories.

She lives in New Jersey with her husband and two children.

christinemarciniak.com

www.ingramcontent.com/pod-product-compliance
Lightning Source LLC
Chambersburg PA
CBHW051530260626
47170CB00003B/870